THE
DEAD
LIE

THE
DEAD
LIE

A BLUE WATER MYSTERY

Ivanka Fear

LEVEL
BEST BOOKS

First published by Level Best Books 2023

Author Photo Credit: Amanda Belec

Instagram @thirteen13designsnphotography

First edition

ISBN: 978-1-68512-315-4

Cover art by Level Best Designs

This book was professionally typeset on Reedsy.
Find out more at reedsy.com

For my husband, Brian, without whom nothing would be possible
You are my light.
And
In loving memory of Mom, my inspiration to write again
I miss you and the stories of your life. Every single day.

Chapter One

There's no way I'm going to tell Jim about this.

My husband's face, contorted in anguish, flashed into my mind as I lay on the tracks, the subway train bearing down on me. We'd never had a major argument until last week when I told him I wanted to return to our hometown. Jim insisted it was too dangerous. For the first time in our relationship, he put his foot down, and forbade me to go. So, of course, I packed my bags, kissed Jim and the kids goodbye, and embarked on the seven-hour drive to the city of Hamilton, promising to be back in a week.

"Summer's over. The kids are in school; they can do without me for a few days. I want to sleep in my old room once again, walk around the neighborhood, pretend everything is normal," I had declared. More than that, I needed to know, needed to see for myself, whether there was a bounty on my head. I had lived in limbo for too long. "It's been 11 years. If it's not safe now, then when?"

If Jim found out what happened on the subway, I'd have to acknowledge that he was right and I was… Well, I had no intention of admitting *that*.

My next door neighbor and best friend from childhood, Haley, had suggested we celebrate my return with a trip to Toronto to attend the Janet Jackson concert. She recalled how I idolized The Jacksons, particularly Michael, during my teenage years.

1

I hadn't been to Toronto since university, and with the thrill of being back, I let down my guard. The morning after the concert, we had plans to shop at the Eaton Center, then sightsee.

It happened so quickly, I didn't see it coming. Haley and I stood well away from the edge of the tracks, peering down the tunnel, waiting for the train.

Haley glanced up at the arrival sign. "It should be here in a few minutes." She flicked her long, wavy, blonde hair away from her flawless face. Her familiarity with the underground system contrasted sharply with the small-town life I had experienced the last eleven years. My first time back on the Toronto subway, at the age of nearly 30, came close to being my last time doing anything.

"I hear it!" I stepped closer to the warning strip on the platform. People spilled across the tiles, pushing forward, feeding my claustrophobia. We had waited till after ten o'clock to leave the Royal York Hotel in order to avoid rush hour, but even this level of crowding smothered me.

"Lana! Don't get too close!" Haley shouted. It took a few seconds before I realized she was addressing *me*.

My name is Cheryl. Although, that's not entirely true. I go by Cheryl now, but my real name is Lana. Svjetlana, actually. It's Croatian, a name my parents chose because it means 'light,' and that's what I brought to them when I was born. Until the day I ran away, they doted on me to the point of ridiculousness and seemed convinced that if they took their eyes off me, I'd vanish from the face of the earth. I led a sheltered life—until the day that changed everything—with my parents being more than somewhat overprotective. Perhaps that was the curse of being an only child.

Haley's warning came moments before someone shoved me closer to the edge. I wobbled back and forth on high heels, scrambling to regain my balance before toppling over onto the tracks. Unlike a cat, I didn't quite land on my feet. I lay on my side, stunned and motionless, pain shooting through my hip and arm. People screamed above the rumble of the train, Haley loudest, as she frantically gestured for me to get up. *They* say your life flashes before your eyes when you're about to die. The only thing I saw flashing was the oncoming train and Jim's face. I struggled to get to my feet and...

Strong arms yanked me out of the trench and set me on the platform, away from the edge. All 5'6" and 130 pounds of me. The scale says 137 pounds, sometimes 140, but I swear we need a new scale.

"You are okay?" asked the tall, dark-haired man. "That was close call." He spoke with an accent much like that of my parents, only thicker, and he looked a bit younger.

They also say there are defining moments in your life. Facing a train head-on could well be one of them. As it screeched to a halt minutes after he hauled me up, passengers spilled onto the platform, oblivious to the fact that they nearly ran me down. Those who witnessed my fall applauded the man's rescue, then boarded the train and went about their business as usual. I supposed I wasn't the first person to fall off a subway platform. Either that, or people in the big city simply took accidents in their stride.

Haley rushed to my side, putting her arm around me. We were the same height, but the similarity ended there. Haley was slimmer, prettier, and likable.

"Thank you," she said, turning to the man who saved me. "You're a real-life superhero."

"It is no problem. I am happy I can help. You are sure you are okay?" Concern showed in the stranger's face, his brow crinkled over brown eyes.

I managed to bob my head up and down as Haley reiterated her thanks, steered my battered body toward a bench, and lowered me into it. "Thank goodness you're okay. Some guy jostled you and took off. He must have been in a real hurry."

"It was my fault. I should have been more careful." My voice trembled once I finally found it.

"Do you want to go back to the hotel and rest? We can shop tomorrow."

"No, no, I don't want to ruin our day." I stood and brushed myself off. "I'm okay, really."

My sore body, chipped red fingernails, bruised ego, and shaky voice told a different story. But the last thing I wanted to do was admit that Jim was right—I should have stayed home. Hamilton was a dangerous place.

Especially for me.

But this is Toronto, not Hamilton. It's just a freak accident.

Shopping took my mind off the subway fall. I picked up a few games and books for the kids, along with a "License to Sell" novelty t-shirt for Jim. I told Haley my husband worked in real estate. She remembered him being an avid James Bond fan.

"Oh, that's cool," Haley exclaimed. "He'll love it!"

The CN Tower was not the best place to go after my mishap, but I didn't want to spoil Haley's trip. Disembarking at Union Station, we dropped off our purchases in the hotel room. I took a long, hot shower to ease the pain in my muscles, then we ambled down Front Street. My fear of heights and enclosed spaces kicked in as the enclosure crawling up the side of the enormous edifice came into view.

"I don't know about this," I said as we stared toward the sky, our eyes following the elevator. "I'm not sure I'm up for it."

"Oh, I'm so sorry, Lana. I completely forgot your phobias."

I flinched at the mention of my weaknesses. You can change your name. You can change your address. You can change your looks. But when it comes down to it, you can't change who you are.

"If you want to skip it, that's okay." Haley placed her hand on my shoulder. "Especially after the subway. That guy should have got a medal, risking his life to save a stranger. You were really lucky."

That was one way to look at it. I'd been thinking I was *unlucky* to be thrown in front of a subway train. Perspective changes everything. I decided to go with a positive attitude for the rest of the day.

"At least I'll always remember my first experience back on the Toronto subway. The time I almost got run over by a train." A nervous chuckle escaped me. "I'll be fine. I *want* to see the view."

Besides, what could possibly happen? The cables break? The elevator get stuck? Someone shove me off the tower?

Eyes closed during the elevator ride, I counted to 40 (my magic number) almost twice. I opened wide once people began to spill out. As I stood on the glass viewing floor, heart in throat, the city more than 1000 feet below,

I congratulated myself on my bravery. From the platform, I scanned Lake Ontario as a plane landed on the island airport, the expanse of blue water stretching against the lighter blue horizon.

The view *was* amazing. And so, I told myself, was I. When it came down to it, I could do anything, no matter how much it scared the life out of me. No one ever really knows what they're capable of until after the fact.

The next day, sightseeing along the harbor and strolling the island trails provided plenty more views of the city skyline splayed against the vast blueness of Lake Ontario. Haley and I were two tourists having a great time in T.O. Completely carefree.

And I almost forgot about the subway incident—until the umbrella incident the day after my return to Hamilton.

Chapter Two

Coincidences happen all the time. I rationalized the events of that evening by telling myself I simply ended up in the wrong place at the wrong time.

The three of us finished our supper of chicken *rižoto* and garden salad on the back patio of the older red brick two-story home in the lower inner city of Hamilton, where we'd lived since I was four. It was the only home I remembered prior to running off with Jim before my nineteenth birthday.

Nothing had changed. Including my childhood bedroom, where I was about to spend my fourth night in over a decade. My parents accepted my return as though I'd been on an overnight stay next door rather than on an 11-year hiatus from my real life.

The memory of my departure years ago remained clear and ever-present in my mind. Mom and Dad were at work when I packed my belongings and left town without warning. I had notified them right away to let them know I was okay so they wouldn't call The Emergency Response Team to report me missing, but even so, my leaving broke their hearts.

"We're getting married. I know you don't approve, but I love him," I had explained on the phone. "We're going to start a new life up north."

"Come home. Now." Dad's stern voice quavered. "We'll talk about it."

"No. I won't be coming back, Dad."

Mom's wailing across the phone line almost made me change my mind. "Lana, please. Please come home. You can get married here, live with us."

But I couldn't return home, nor could I tell them why I had left so abruptly. "I'm sorry, Mom. I'm so sorry." Through my tears, I stuck to my decision.

"It's… I love you both. But it's complicated. I need a fresh start, away from… just away. It's not about you. Please try to understand. Something's happened, and I can't…I can't explain, but I won't be coming home. Not for a while, anyway."

The ensuing silence made me wonder whether Dad had hung up on me, too angry to continue the conversation. But then he answered with one word. "Okay."

Okay? That was so unlike Dad, I didn't know how to respond. I had expected him to hunt me down and ship me off to a nunnery. Or, demand a police search, then ground me for life. His quiet acquiescence frightened me more than the alternatives.

Even Mom settled down and ended our call with a plea to stay safe and remain in touch. No guilt trip about not loving her. No threats to end her life if I didn't return. A simple declaration of unconditional love no matter what I chose to do with my future.

The painful memory of leaving, mixed with joy at being home with my parents, no questions asked, caused a tear to swell in the corner of one eye. I excused myself from the table and carried my dishes inside. Mom followed.

"I'd like to go for a walk around the neighborhood," I said. As a teenager, I used to tour the surrounding area on a daily basis, my head in the clouds.

Mom said she would do the dishes, and I should head out if I wanted to beat the rain. Following her advice, I grabbed an umbrella in case of a downpour.

My solitary walks used to give me an opportunity to reflect and think of ideas for writing, a hobby that I'd enjoyed since the fifth grade. I hadn't had time for creative writing in the last decade; looking after our home and the kids was my priority. The only writing I did now was as a part-time reporter for the local paper, and an occasional diary entry.

Our immediate neighborhood consisted of stately older homes for middle-class families. Mature maple trees lined concrete sidewalks, few vehicles traveled the streets, and foot traffic consisted mainly of people from the area.

I passed the small community park and playground and continued toward the Escarpment Trail. The pedestrian signal at the intersection of Limeridge and Cobalt flashed green. I looked both ways and stepped off the curb onto the street. Out of nowhere, a vehicle made a left turn, directly into my path. I saw it out of the corner of my eye, fortunately, and stumbled backwards, heels regaining their footing on the asphalt. Tires squealed as the vehicle sped down the street.

Shaken, but unharmed, I strolled to my destination. I used to walk a couple of alternate courses every other day, with some deviation. Main Street was one of my usual haunts, with its traffic, office buildings, small stores, and restaurants. The quieter trail along the bottom of the escarpment held more appeal most days. At one point, a row of high-rise buildings lined the road opposite the wilderness.

Fifteen minutes later, I stood in front of one of the condominiums, gazing up to the tenth-floor balcony, remembering the times I had spent there, and imagining what my life would have been like now if things were different.

I often used to stand and stare when I passed this area. But something other than the vision of lives high in the sky nearly struck me as I looked up. An object flew through the air, heading directly toward me. In my stupor, I couldn't move, which was just as well since it landed with a thud a short distance away from me. A large patio umbrella obstructed the sidewalk ahead, its green canopy fluttering in the wind gusts, under a darkening sky.

Enough walking for one day. Hurrying home, I stayed alert at intersections, not allowing myself to daydream or compose poetry in my head, as I used to do.

When I walked through the door, I said nothing about the near miss with the vehicle. I hadn't told my parents about the subway mishap either, as I didn't need a lecture about paying attention. But, I did tell Mom and Dad about the umbrella. That, clearly an accident, presented no threat to me and my family.

The fact that it fell from Jesse's building—pure coincidence.

Chapter Three

The defining moment of my life, if I had to narrow it down to one, was when Jesse Jovanovich walked into my Grade Ten Math class. He stopped just inside the doorway, scanned the room, his eyes meeting mine, then strode toward the seat next to me, his mouth slightly upturned as he sat down. He turned to me and said, "Hi."

Once I realized I had been staring at him the whole time with my mouth gaping open, I lowered my head, mumbled an indecipherable 'hello,' and opened my Math textbook, pretending to be mesmerized by algebraic equations. Never having had a boyfriend, in fact, never having been on a date, I was socially awkward. Even though people commented that I was pretty, all I saw in the mirror was a bland-looking girl with long wavy brown hair and brown eyes. I didn't wear makeup and had no eye for fashion. As far as I was concerned, what I lacked in looks, I didn't make up for in personality or brilliant conversation. And it didn't help that I had a name no one could remember or pronounce—Svjetlana. Shortening it to Lana (Lawna) helped, and gave me an illusion of glamor.

I confided only in Haley, obsessing over my Jesse crush and swearing her to secrecy, too shy to let on that I thought of him as anything other than a classmate. When she started dating Garrett, Jesse's best friend, later that fall, I encountered Jesse in the hall and cafeteria as well as Math class.

Garrett was not only a perfect match to Haley physically, with dirty blond hair, piercing blue eyes, and perfect features, but he, like her, came from a respected, well-to-do family. A person could hate them based on their looks and financial status alone, but their geniality not only earned them a place

9

with the popular crowd, it made it impossible to dislike them. Why they let someone like me hang around, I didn't know. In any case, my association with Garrett put me in closer contact with Jesse and we began to hang out, the four of us, away from school.

Even so, it took me half the school year to work up the courage to sustain a complete conversation with Jesse. Once I did, I realized he was more than just a cute guy with black hair curling over his forehead, drawing attention to dreamy brown eyes, and an angular jawline. Jesse put me at ease with his sense of humor and gentle disposition. When he began holding my hand, the firmness with which he grasped it made me feel safe, and the way he ran his thumb along my palm sent tingles throughout my body.

The last day of school, he asked if I wanted to come to his place sometime during the summer to watch a video. Although he gave directions to his condo, I already knew where he lived. I had walked by his place every other day for the last year, since I locked eyes with him in Math, hoping to casually run into him, fearing I actually *would* run into him and he would think I was a stalker or something. And I was nothing of the sort—I simply had an inclination to observe things that interested me. Sometimes I saw him from a distance, but he didn't notice me, or if he did, he never mentioned it. My excuse for being there was going to be that I liked going for a walk along the Escarpment Trail, and the condos just happened to be on my way.

He finally called, to my surprise, ten days later. I knew the exact number of days because I bemoaned his absence in my daily diary entries.

Jesse met me in the lobby of his building, and we took the elevator to the tenth floor. "I'm glad you came. I wasn't sure you would." He opened the door to his home. "My parents are at work. We've got the place to ourselves."

Not entirely to ourselves. A gorgeous black cat met us in the entryway, weaving in and out between Jesse's legs, its purr like a motor. "Hey, Lucky. Meet Lana."

"Hi, Lucky. My cat's named Chloe."

I bent down to pet Lucky when he surveyed me with his big green eyes. "What a pretty kitty you are." Sniffing me, Lucky picked up Chloe's scent and rubbed his head against my leg, claiming me as *his* property now.

The condo seemed small compared to my house, but the furnishings and decor made it cozy. Jesse had set out a couple of DVDs, along with a pitcher of lemonade and a plate of cookies that looked homemade. He popped *Pirates of the Caribbean* into the player, and we settled on the couch.

Our conversation revolved around the movie. When it was over, Jesse asked what I'd been up to for the last week.

I didn't want to say that I was waiting for his call. "Nothing much. Reading, sitting in the back yard. I love summer."

"Me too. No school."

Jesse excelled at school, especially Math. If I were smart, I would have asked him to tutor me at the start of the school year. "What have you been doing?"

"Just hanging out with friends."

All year I'd been waiting to spend time alone with him, and finally, being in that position, I didn't know what to say.

After a few minutes of uncomfortable silence, Jesse said, "There's something I wanted to tell you."

"What?" Probably that he had a girlfriend I didn't know about, and he wanted me to stop bothering him.

"I've been wanting to ask you out for a while, like on a real date, but I was afraid you'd say no."

That certainly wasn't what I expected to hear. "Really? Why did you think that?" I would have jumped at the chance to go out with Jesse. Why did he wait so long to ask? I'd been mooning over him the entire year.

"You seemed kind of uninterested whenever I tried to talk to you."

"Oh. I'm sorry, I'm just shy, not uninterested."

Stupid, stupid. stupid!

I never for a moment thought he'd want to date *me*. There were so many other girls drooling over him. "Of course I would have said yes."

We spent the rest of the afternoon chatting. I had wasted an entire year because I was too shy to speak to him, and suddenly, I couldn't shut up.

When his mom came home, she invited me to stay for supper.

"Oh, thank you, but I really should be going." My parents thought I was at

Haley's, not alone on a couch with some boy I'd been lusting after.

Jesse insisted on seeing me home, even though I said it wasn't necessary. When the elevator doors closed, we began our descent normally, but came to an abrupt stop. The elevator shuddered. The lights went out.

"What's wrong?" Panic set in instantly. "What's happening?"

"It's okay. Sometimes this happens if the power flicks on and off."

"So we're stuck here?" I couldn't handle being stuck in an elevator, even if it was with Jesse Jovanovich.

"It's okay. There's an emergency button if it doesn't...." The elevator resumed its descent before he finished his sentence. Then it stopped again and lurched up and down several times, causing us to lose our balance and fall. I screamed. Jesse reached up and pushed the red button, telling me to stay down. "This hasn't happened before, but I'm sure someone will come soon...."

Just my luck...

As though there had been no problem, the elevator continued moving once again, stopping at the lobby. The doors opened, and I ran out. We'd been in there a few minutes, but it seemed like hours.

"I'm not going in there again," I said.

Ever. Or in any other elevator.

He assured me that this sort of thing rarely happens. "It must have been a fluke of some sort."

Holding my hand as we walked, Jesse expounded on the technology and safety of elevators. In front of my house, he said, "I'd like you to come over again. If that's okay with you."

"Yes, that's definitely okay." No point in being coy. That had wasted one whole year. "I'd like that. But no elevators."

"Well, there are stairs." Jesse bent down, and his lips brushed mine, sweeter than any chocolate that had ever melted in my mouth. I had the feeling we were being watched, but didn't see anyone. So I put my arms around his neck and kissed him back. I wanted to make sure he didn't think I was uninterested.

As he walked away, Jesse turned to smile and wave as I stood, gawking after him. Inside the front door, Mom waited, arms crossed and a stern expression on her face.

"Who is that boy you were kissing? You need to be careful you don't get pregnant."

Oh, Mom. Really?

My parents were old world and old school. We spoke mainly Croatian at home, interspersed with some English. We attended the Croatian Catholic church most Sundays, catered at the Croatian Hall for weddings and other parties on Saturday nights. In the summer, there were weekend picnics at the Croatian park. I hung around the Croatian daughters of my parents' friends at these events. My parents hoped I would find a 'nice Croatian boy' so they would someday have Croatian grandchildren.

"That's Jesse Jovanovich. He's a nice boy, Mama."

"Jovanovich? Where's he from?"

"He's from my Math class."

"He's not Serbian, is he?" She narrowed her eyes.

My parents never considered themselves discriminatory, but I supposed most people didn't.

My parents' food business occasionally catered to 'English' people, but most of their customers were Croatian, Slovenian, Serbian, or other European nationalities. Oddly enough, though, they made it clear that I should stay away from Serbians. Apparently, there was a history of bad blood between us. I didn't understand what the past had to do with the present, but being introverted, there wasn't much chance I'd befriend anyone outside my immediate circle, much less a Serbian.

"No, he's… I don't know what he is. He's a nice boy. And it was just a little kiss, that's all."

"That's the way it starts," Mom said with a sigh.

Chapter Four

My daily call home to Jim didn't go well.

"I'm going to stay a while longer," I said. "It's Haley's 30th birthday today. She invited me out for dinner with her and Garrett. And she wants me to go with them to the high school's twenty-fifth anniversary celebration next weekend. So, I won't be home for another week."

"Cheryl, come home," Jim said. "Don't push your luck."

I assured him I was perfectly safe and nothing was going to happen to me. "It's been over a decade. The whole thing's long forgotten. The police have plenty of other shootings to investigate. And if Stefan wanted to hurt me, he would have made a move by now. Everything's fine."

"The kids need you. *I* need you," Jim pleaded. "Please... if anything happens, I'll never forgive myself for letting you go."

I gulped down the knot in my throat, letting it lodge uncomfortably mid-chest. Without Jim and the kids, my world would cease to exist. With an open mouth, I exhaled a wheeze, ready to set aside my selfishness and tell him I'd leave for home immediately.

Our neighbor's sudden death had been the catalyst for the trip home to Hamilton. I recalled my words when I heard the news. "Harry was forty-eight and healthy. And he's gone, just like that, from a heart attack. I want to go home while I can, before something happens to *my* dad." Too late, I had shut my mouth, seeing in Jim's eyes the hurt he tried to disguise. If my husband could make do with an occasional phone call and a once-a-year visit from his parents, having sworn them to secrecy about our new identities,

14

then why couldn't I do the same? Jim had given up his life because of my mistakes. Never once did he place the blame where it belonged—on me.

But I wasn't about to let Jim guilt trip me into coming home. I missed the kids enough without being reminded this was my first time away from them for any length of time. Just listening to their voices over the phone made me wish I hadn't left. But this was something I had to do. For myself. And the kids seemed to be taking it in their stride, which hurt a little, knowing they could manage without me glued to their side.

"I'll be careful. I promise. You know how much I love you and the kids." I ended the call knowing I'd left Jim feeling, not for the first time, that he came in second to my own needs.

As I had done every night since returning to my childhood home, I tossed and turned. The next day, lack of sleep showed in the bags under my eyes, the mirror reflecting now familiar shoulder-length black curls, hollow brown eyes staring back. My new look for the past 11 years included tight and trendy jeans and skirts, heels, and layers of expertly applied makeup. But, the last few days, extra concealer and eye makeup failed to hide my recent troubled sleep patterns.

Haley chose to celebrate her birthday at d'Italiano's. The restaurant had been around forever, but I'd never been. When your parents own a catering business, there's no shortage of delicious food at home.

We started with the house salad and bruschetta. Although I downed a couple of glasses of red wine rather quickly, and they may have gone to my head, inattention was to blame. Ironically, as a reporter, I noticed everything and everyone. Except things that concerned *me*.

I had ordered linguine as the main course. The waiter set down the steaming dishes, and we thanked him, then carried on our conversation. Haley remarked she was looking forward to the movie, *Mama Mia*, while I twirled noodles around the fork and brought them to my mouth.

"Stop!" Haley cried out. "That's not chicken!"

I took a good look at my linguine. Sure enough, the 'chicken pieces' curled suspiciously.

"Are you okay? You didn't eat any, did you?" Garrett asked.

"No. Almost." With my seafood allergy, I could have broken out into hives, or worst case scenario, had difficulty breathing.

The waiter apologized and exchanged the shrimp linguine for free chicken linguine, and no harm was done. People make mistakes. I didn't want to cause a scene.

After dinner, we drove to the mall. On the escalator heading down to the cinema, Garrett and Haley stood behind me when my next mishap occurred. Someone shoved their way past, knocking me off the step. A scream erupted from my throat as I stumbled forward, propelled toward the bottom, sharp metal edges advancing.

"Whoa!" A man up ahead blocked my fall with his body, hands holding onto my waist to steady me. "I got you. You again?" His face, familiar as the accent, took me by surprise. "You get in a lot of trouble, little girl."

The term 'little girl' didn't really fit me, being the mother of a ten-year-old boy. When you look younger than your age, people often underestimate you, but as I grew older, no doubt I'd be grateful for my youthful appearance. I accepted it as a compliment, as I did a few years ago when a little old lady asked what grade I was in.

We reached the bottom of the escalator, and I thanked the man who saved me for the second time in one week, noting his attractiveness, thick black hair swept back, a hint of gray at the temples, and a five o'clock shadow.

"You are lucky I am in right place, right time," he said.

"Yes, I guess I *am* lucky," I conceded. "Thank you again. I didn't thank you properly at the subway."

Haley raised her brow. "You're the man from the subway. That's quite a coincidence, you being here in Hamilton."

"I am here to visit family in Hamilton and Toronto. I come on plane to Toronto is a few weeks now," he explained in broken English. "I come from Croatia. You know where is Croatia?"

"Yes, my parents come from there," I exclaimed. Haley tilted her head and stared as though she didn't believe it could be the same man from Toronto.

"Where they are from in Croatia?" he asked.

"It's just a small village. You wouldn't know it."

16

"I am from small village. What it is called?' When I told him, his face lit up. "I am from close to there."

"It's a small world," Garrett commented. "Good thing you were here to save Lana."

"Thank you again. We'd better get going," Haley said.

As we walked away, Haley whispered, "That's strange, him showing up again."

"What are your parents' name?" he shouted.

I turned around. "Janez and Marica Babic."

"No!" He brought his hands to the top of his head in astonishment. "I know them from back home when we were just young. And now I meet you here in Canada. Sure is small world! You tell them Matija say hi and I am happy you are okay."

He waved goodbye and was lost in the crowd before I could think to ask, "Matija who?"

Chapter Five

The weekend I disappeared off the face of the earth, or at least off the radar map in the greater Hamilton area, I had returned home from my cramped room in residence at U of T to visit Mom and Dad, as I did most weekends. Although we had a perfectly good university in Hamilton, they succumbed to my pleas to let me spread my wings and be on my own.

A fresh start to my second year of university, with me focusing on journalism studies, was the plan. But plans go awry. A couple of months earlier, I had brought home two new school friends, and we went out on the town to party. Little did I realize that night would change my life. Not knowing any other drinking holes, I took them to the seedy Serbian bar where Jesse worked part-time while attending university in town at McMaster. Although we broke up part way through the first year of university, then were on and off again in the summer, Jesse and I remained good friends. With so few life experiences under my belt, I had decided I wasn't ready to be permanently tied down.

Mom and Dad didn't outright dislike Jesse; that would have been impossible for anyone to do. For some reason, though, they weren't keen on our relationship. Maybe they had a hard time accepting that their little girl was becoming an adult. When we first hooked up, at 16, I wasn't a child. That didn't change the fact that I lived under their roof, by their rules. As much as I wanted to bring Jesse home and confirm my parents' suspicions that we were 'together', I didn't dare. Surely, I thought, I could tell my mom, and she would understand. Mom was young once, and she had a boyfriend—my dad. From what she'd told me, he was her only boyfriend, and it was love at first sight.

But, after that first date, when Mom saw us kissing on the sidewalk, she didn't seem pleased, so I didn't discuss our relationship with her. I told Jesse my Mom wondered whether he was Serbian, because of his last name.

"My grandparents were from Serbia and moved to the States," he said. "My dad was born in Montana, and they moved to Hamilton when he was little. Mom's from here. Why?"

Because my parents were prejudiced and thought people should stick with their own kind, and their definition of their own kind was extremely narrow. Instead, I said, "Because it's kind of neat that we're both from Yugoslavia. Not us, but our parents. It's our heritage."

"Yeah, I don't really think about it much. I'm just Canadian."

I thought it must be nice to be certain of your identity. I wasn't so sure of mine. Yes, I thought of myself as Canadian. But my home life was definitely Croatian.

I didn't hide from my parents the fact that I was seeing Jesse throughout high school, but I also said nothing about him becoming my steady boyfriend. I told them he was a friend from school, a friend of Haley's boyfriend. Sometimes we hung out together, that was all. Mom narrowed her eyes and gave me her 'I know you're lying' look, but didn't say anything to contradict me. We both were of the opinion that what Dad didn't know wouldn't hurt him.

So years later, having come to the decision that honesty was the best policy and I should tell my parents about the man on the escalator during Haley's 30th birthday celebration, on the off chance that he might meet up with them somehow and tell them he knew me, I, of course, kept part of the truth to myself.

"A funny thing happened yesterday. I've been kind of accident-prone lately, and I took a bit of a tumble on the escalator last night on our way to the cinema," I said nonchalantly at the supper table, a forkful of goulash halfway to my mouth.

"Accident?" Mom stopped eating. "Are you okay?"

"Yes, I'm fine. It's just like the umbrella that blew off the balcony. Bad luck." I shrugged, then told them about the near miss with the vehicle, and the linguine mix-up. Mom gasped, and for a moment, appeared to be having a heart attack at the thought of what might have happened. "But I guess I must have good luck, too. A nice man helped me on the escalator. We got talking, and he said he knew you in Croatia, when you were young." Nothing about the near death on the subway.

They stared at me like I was speaking a foreign language. I was. Mostly Croatian, with some English mixed in, along with some words that were half Croatian and half English.

"What man? Did he say who he was?" Dad creased his forehead.

"Matija."

One word changed everything. We were having a nice, normal family meal, and then my parents dropped their forks and stared at me with their mouths open.

"Matija? What else did he say?"

"He said he was happy I was okay."

"It can't be…." A gray pallor crept over Mom's face. Dad shushed her before she got any further.

Afraid to say anything more about Matija, I remained quiet, hoping they'd forget I was still there. No such luck. Dad asked me over and over to tell him exactly what happened and what Matija looked like.

"If you ever see him again, you tell me right away," Dad demanded, then picked up his fork, a signal that we were all to resume life as normal.

Later, as I helped Mom with the dishes, I said, "He seemed nice. He said he knew you from your village. I thought he was one of your Croatian friends from back home."

"He's not one of our friends. And he's not from Croatia. He's Serbian."

For a second, my eyelids fluttered as I considered the implications of that. Was Matija connected to the reason for my sudden departure from Hamilton 11 years ago? "How did you know him, then?"

"That's not important. It was a long time ago. You need to worry about your future and your kids, not something that happened before you were born." A shadow crossed over Mom's face.

"What happened before I was born? Why doesn't Dad like him?"

"Don't go opening a Pandora's box of the past. Move on with your life."

I had no idea what that meant. But it brought the conversation to an end.

The end of my life almost came a few days later, when I drove to the lake, my favorite part of the city. A ten-minute drive or an hour walk would bring me to the edge of Lake Ontario. I should have walked.

As I steered my Toyota through the residential streets, away from the escarpment and toward the water, something felt off. At first, I blamed the roads for their roughness, muttering to myself that my parents' tax dollars should have been more than adequate to smooth the cracks and repair potholes in the pavement, not to mention the uneven manholes all over the road. As I continued to bump and clunk along, it occurred to me that my vehicle could be at fault. The difficulty with which it handled made me consider pulling over, but I'd reached the more traveled main street, and it seemed best to keep moving with traffic. By the time I approached the bayfront area, several people had honked at me as I slowed down, gripping the wheel, my Toyota behaving erratically, pulling me off to one side, then the other.

I attempted to steer my car into the harbor parking lot, but missed the turn and kept wobbling toward the wide pedestrian pier. As the edge of the concrete walkway drew nearer, my heart pounded at the sight of waves lapping up along the flat surface, coming in my direction, ready to drag me into the deep blue water. Brakes slammed on, hands braced on the wheel, struggling to gain control. I screamed as I envisioned myself plowing down walkers and joggers enjoying the first days of fall along the lakefront before my vehicle plummeted off the edge.

With a jolt, I stopped, front wheels teetering over the side of the pier, the car's nose pointing down into the depths of Lake Ontario.

I didn't dare move.

Thanks to several good Samaritans who extricated me from the death trap, I found myself standing at a safe distance as someone called for a tow truck and the police.

"No police. I'm fine, everything's good. I just miscalculated the distance. Not used to city driving." I laughed off the fact that my car nearly took a plunge. "No harm done. No need to bother the police. They're busy with more important things." Definitely, no police.

"Who put your tires on?" A middle-aged gentleman gestured to the twisted back wheels, half off their hubs. "Didn't do much of a job."

People gathered and pointed while I searched for a way to escape without garnering further attention. My call to Dad resulted in him hightailing it to the waterfront in record time.

"What happened?" Dad demanded, scrambling out of the catering van to wrap his arms around me. When I told him, he inspected the car. "The tires are almost off!" he exclaimed. "The lug nuts are loose! You shouldn't have driven off before I had a chance to torque them. What did I tell you?" He wagged his finger at me, pretending he and I were responsible.

The spectators, used to vehicles getting pulled out of the Hamilton harbor—most often with bodies weighted down inside—and minding their own business about it, began to lose interest and disperse once he explained the reason for the faulty tires was simple neglect.

But once I sat next to Dad in the van, he asked, "Did you see anyone near the car, messing around with it?"

"No, it was in the driveway and in the school parking lot."

Haley and I had stopped in to register for activities to celebrate the twenty-fifth anniversary of Central High's opening. I couldn't have watched my car the whole time, but surely it would have been safe enough sitting outside the school doors.

"Get inside the house," Dad ordered as he pulled into the driveway.

Mom and I watched through the window as the tow crew delivered my Toyota from the pier and set it securely behind the van. Tears escaped Mom's eyes as she said, "You could have been...."

"I'll get the torque wrench and fix this," Dad said, clambering down the basement stairs to get his tools.

Once Dad fixed my tires, he ordered me to take a time out as though I were still five. "Go to your room. Mama and I have something private to discuss." The tone of his voice told me there was no chance for discussion on the topic.

Opening and slamming the door to my room to indicate I was following orders, much as I used to do, I crept back down the hall and listened to my parents' conversation from the top of the stairs. I had the right to know what they were talking about because I was pretty sure it involved me.

"Someone loosened the lug nuts intentionally," Dad said.

"You don't think...?"

"I think we're going to have to...."

They continued their conversation in whispers, and I couldn't hear the rest, so I quietly opened my door and sat on the bed, waiting, like a child, to be summoned downstairs.

"How long am I grounded for?" I asked Dad, rolling my eyes, when he came to my door to apologize for treating me like a toddler.

Dad put his arm around me and quietly said, "Sunce." His term of affection meant 'Sunshine'. "We're just worried about you and think it would be best if you go back home to your family. All those accidents you've been having lately...."

"I've just had some bad luck, that's all."

I enjoyed the time I had spent with my parents the past week, but I agreed with Dad. Homecoming needed to come to an end. But first, I had an event to attend—our high school twenty-fifth anniversary celebration, as promised to Haley—and I'd be back to being Cheryl MacGregor of Lake Kipling, far from Hamilton and the past I had managed to escape years ago.

Not mentioning the subway incident and how Matija saved my life had been a wise decision. As was not disclosing the truth about why I left Hamilton a decade ago. Honesty is overrated. If Mom and Dad found out the truth, they would probably lock me away for life and throw away the key. Anything to keep me safe.

Chapter Six

October 11

"Svjetlana Babic, please report to Mr. Cruikshank's office."

The announcement over the school loudspeaker jarred me as I sat in my old Math class, picturing Jesse at the door, wishing I could go back in time. Life is full of sorrow, a fact that had slipped my mind when I joined Haley and Garrett on a journey to our past. I had signed up for the high school reunion with my given name, keeping my new identity under wraps to protect Jim and the kids, but even so, hearing my real name sent a chill through me. I could only hope that Stefan wouldn't get wind of the fact that I was back in town.

The high school's 25th anniversary weekend was designed to take former students back to their so-called glory days of high school—two full days of pretending we could relive our teenage years—including attending classes, sports events, drama presentations, orchestra recitals, suffering through the cafeteria lunch, being shushed in the library, and smoking in the student parking lot.

"Come on, Lana. This could be our only chance to be teenagers again," Haley had coaxed, four months pregnant with their first child. Her husband, Garrett, eager to be on the football team once more, insisted he needed me cheering from the bleachers.

The summons to the office cut short our carefree teen fantasy.

I had no idea what I'd done to deserve a special invitation to the office.

24

During all my years of high school, there had been few occasions when I'd been asked to honor the administration with my presence. I'd always been a good student, not quite straight A's, but a good solid A-. Well, okay, B+. Apart from participating in an odd moral protest now and then, I was quiet, and no one took notice of me. Hearing my name announced over the speakers more than a decade later, I nearly jumped out of my seat. Haley caught my eye, raising her eyebrows as I shrugged my shoulders.

I excused myself from class, all eyes on me, wondering what I'd done to get myself hauled down to see Mr. Cruikshank (still here after all these years) during a throwback to Math class. I couldn't for the life of me recall any infraction, large or small, of which I might have inadvertently been guilty that day or at any point during which I attended Central High.

I walked past putrid yellow lockers, my eyes on the beige linoleum tiles, avoiding the gaze of any stray hall lurkers who hadn't yet figured out what part of high school they wanted to relive.

I had a bad feeling as I descended the stairs, holding the railing as though I expected it to support me through whatever ordeal awaited me in the office. I'd always believed I possessed a sixth sense—although it seemed to be taking a holiday recently, with my inability to avoid accidents—that made me more intuitive than most people. Maybe it was because I read too much and read between the lines—including too many mysteries, too many thrillers, too many horror novels. But I wasn't prepared for the horror that greeted me in the institutional box of a room referred to as The Hub.

The long wooden counter served to keep students on one side and staff on the other. A row of chairs along the wall, the holding area for miscreants, sat empty of the usual law-breaking citizens of Central High as only alumni walked the halls on this Saturday. Behind the counter, the school secretary hovered, playing her role, acting as interim warden until the principal or vice-principal took over. The color scheme was so bland it defied description. Windows overlooked the front of the school, while the adjacent floor-to-ceiling glass wall offered a view of the goings-on in the hall. Mr. Cruikshank's office door stood open. I remembered all those details later for some reason, as though I knew once I left the neutrality of the main

25

office and entered the principal's den, nothing would ever be the same.

"Just go right in, dear," the secretary said. The glistening in her eyes warned me to brace myself. Something was very wrong. Little did I know the world as I knew it was about to implode as I walked through that door.

Both the principal and vice-principal sat at the desk. At the sight of the two uniformed officers standing beside them, a wave of dread washed through me. They had come to arrest me. Eleven years was not enough of a cushion between me and my sins. Miss Pritchard (I recalled her being the guidance counselor) stepped away from the corner, took hold of my hand, and told me to have a seat. I didn't want to sit. If I sat, I would acknowledge that I was about to receive a shock. And one thing I knew for certain was that I couldn't handle whatever they had to say.

"I'm afraid we have some bad news," Miss Pritchard began as I remained standing. She looked uncomfortable, as though this role had been foisted on her without consent. "There's been an accident."

My mind went automatically to Jim and the kids. But how would they even know about them? Svjetlana Babic was a single woman.

My parents?

I stared dumbly for what seemed a long time as I waited for her to tell me everything was okay. It would be like the other accidents that happened to me recently. Everything would turn out fine. When she didn't reassure me, I turned to Mr. Cruikshank, who stood next to the officers.

"I'm so sorry, Svjetlana," he said in a quiet voice. "It's your parents. They were in a car accident."

The confirmation that something horrific had happened slapped me in the face, and I sank into the chair that had been offered moments ago. "Are they okay?" I asked. The question hung in the air as though there was no answer. Just like in English class when the teacher had asked who the hollow men are in T. S. Eliot's poem.

Miss Pritchard moved her hand to my shoulder in an attempt to shield me from what was coming. "I'm sorry. It was a bad accident." She hesitated before adding, "They didn't make it."

The next words I heard were an anguished, repetitive, "No! Oh no, oh no, oh no…" The sound seemed distant, remote, as though it came from another room. But then I realized I was hearing my own voice, hollow, like Eliot's stuffed men. My arms wrapped around myself, I rocked back and forth in the chair, willing to be transported to some other time and place.

* * *

April is not the cruelest month, Mr. Eliot. October is. With the promise of death foreshadowed in the crisp night air and darkness descending too early. Lilacs preparing for temporary dormancy, their 100-year lifespan a taunting reminder of the permanence of our own demise.

I used to write as much as I read. I kept a diary to record my thoughts, my feelings, my boring life. I wrote poems to express myself. I told stories on paper. Lately, I told true stories—those I wrote for the *Lake Kipling Gazette*. I was born with the ability to create my own reality. When Miss Pritchard uttered the words, 'they didn't make it', I retreated to some fantasy world where my parents suddenly woke from the dead and told me it was all a mistake, they were perfectly fine. But when I opened my eyes, Miss Pritchard's face brought me back to the present, where my parents no longer existed.

How could that possibly be? My parents, barely fifty, had immigrated to Canada over thirty years ago and never returned to their homeland. At least that's what they told me. They told me a lot of stories about the old country, stories I didn't pay attention to, stories I'd long forgotten, stories I wasn't sure I believed. But I would never again have those stories go in one ear and out the other, or listen to them with half an ear, or question their veracity and accuracy. My parents were gone.

And yet, it hadn't really hit me. I expected them to walk through the door. To tell me there was no accident. But that wasn't going to happen. Because there *was* an accident. They wouldn't have lied to me about something like that. The thing was… I didn't believe them.

The police fed my disbelief when they told me their bodies were unrecognizable. Something didn't seem right.

"I…I…want to…see them," I sobbed as Miss Pritchard stood close, looking down at me with pity, and something more. Empathy, I thought. Although surely no one could understand what I felt at that moment.

One of the officers said, "I'm afraid that won't be possible. There was a fire."

"I don't…." I lifted my head, almost expecting to be told they had made a mistake. "You said they were in a car accident."

"Your parents' vehicle went off the escarpment on the mountain road. It burst into flames. Two bodies were found in the front seat, but…." The officer stopped abruptly, seeing my reaction to the word 'bodies.'

"So, you're not sure it's them?" I looked from one officer to the other. "Is that what you're saying?" A surge of hope coursed through me, but it was false hope. I knew that immediately. They were both so solemn.

"The bodies were too badly burned to be recognizable. But it's your parents' delivery van. We've verified they were on their way from the kitchen to cater a luncheon for a funeral," the second officer explained. It was the last word he uttered that brought home the irony of the situation I refused to acknowledge. Now *I* would be planning a funeral—for two.

Miss Pritchard asked if she could call someone for me. I stared at her, uncomprehending. "Do you have a family member we can notify?"

"No. There's no one." Cheryl had a family; Svjetlana was alone. Apart from telling Haley and Garrett about Jim and the kids, I wanted to keep the existence of my family private.

"An aunt or uncle? Grandparents? Cousins, maybe?" She seemed to be grasping at straws as I shook my head. "How about a friend, or a neighbor? A co-worker of your parents?"

"Zora. Yes, Zora."

"Zora?"

"Zora is my mom's friend. She works at the catering business with my parents." Mom's best friend. They grew up together, raised in the same small Croatian village. She was the closest person to both me and my parents that I could think of.

"Why don't we give her a call, then? And let her know what's happened,"

Miss Pritchard suggested, as though we were about to have a little chat to catch up on the latest news.

It took me a while to recall the phone number for the commercial kitchen of Marez Caters, my parents' business. Miss Pritchard took control of the situation with a sense of purpose once she found something concrete she could do. After making the call, she ushered me to the staff washroom to pat my face with water and put a warm compress on the back of my neck, then had me lie on the sofa in the teacher's lounge. She remained by my side, holding my hand until Zora's arrival.

As Mr. Cruikshank escorted her through the door, the look of anguish on Zora's face confirmed that she just lost her best friend. But there was something more there, something I couldn't put my finger on. Guilt? It was almost as though she thought she was somehow to blame for what happened to Mom and Dad. But, of course, she wasn't.

Because the only person to blame was me.

"Oh, Svjetlana, I'm so sorry," she cried as she joined me on the sofa. We hugged each other, sharing our grief. "I'm so sorry, Sunce." I winced, hearing Zora call me Sunshine, the same term of affection my parents used.

Why did people say they were sorry whenever something terrible happened? What were they sorry about? Had they done something wrong?

Zora had no children of her own. She had never married. Somewhere around 45, she was a spinster, although she retained her youthful looks, quite striking, with her tall, willowy body, long flowing wavy brown hair, and high cheekbones set in a heart-shaped face. None of her relationships seemed to be serious enough for her to commit. Mom told me Zora lost her one true love tragically when she was 15. When I asked what happened, Mom simply said he died.

As she hugged me and rubbed my back, Zora said, "What's done is done. What's important now is to keep you safe."

I didn't know what she meant at the time, but later I wondered—how could she possibly know I was in danger?

My reckless behavior had destroyed so many lives. And now, my hubris at thinking I could make the mistakes of my past disappear simply by willing them to do so had cost me my parents. You can't go back to the past. You can't undo what you've done. I killed my parents. Although a bullet didn't pierce their hearts, I shot them down just the same. It had to be Stefan's doing, taking my parents in retaliation for his son's death 11 years ago—a loss he attributed to me.

Chapter Seven

Zora insisted I stay at her place for the night until Jim could make arrangements to get there, but I told her I wanted to be in my own house, close to my parents. Even if it meant being alone.

"I'll be fine. And I haven't told Jim yet."

Zora brought a hand to her mouth. "Oh, Svjetlana. You need to call him."

"I will. I just don't know how to tell him and the kids." Besides Mom and Dad and Jim's parents, Zora was the only other person entrusted with my new identity as Cheryl MacGregor.

"Well, I'm not going to leave you by yourself. You should be with people who care about you." Zora said she was going home to pack a few things and would be back shortly.

I'd never felt so alone in all my thirty years. I took my parents for granted, even as an adult. For some reason, I thought they'd always be there when I needed them, even though they had been nothing more than a background fixture in my life the past decade. I thought they were invincible. They weren't.

Not long after Zora left, Haley rang. She was a true friend from way back when. Although we lived next door to each other, our paths hadn't crossed until we started school. My parents stuck to their own crowd, only waving politely and saying hello to our 'English' neighbors. In kindergarten, our teacher arranged a play date for us, and we just meshed. Both of us were shy and having difficulty socializing with the other kids. Over the course of our school years, Haley made new friends and became part of the popular crowd, but I had remained socially aloof and just tagged along with her. But

Haley stuck with me. And, even though I had abandoned our friendship years ago, with no contact for 11 years, Haley still hadn't given up on me.

"I just heard what happened. Miss Pritchard called me to the office after you went home. My parents were the ones who told the police where to find you. I'm so sorry, Lana."

Someone else who was sorry, as though she were to blame. Besides Garrett and the baby on the way, Haley had two sisters and two living parents. Not to mention a huge extended family. She would never be alone in the world. I wished I had a brother or sister to share my grief and try to make some sense out of my parents' sudden deaths. Or an aunt or uncle to talk about the good old days when Mom and Dad were young. I wished I knew what it was like to be spoiled by grandparents.

"I'll come and stay over," she offered.

"No, it's okay, you don't need to do that. Zora's staying with me."

"We're still best friends, Lana. Of course I need to come. I'll be there in a while." She hung up, not allowing me the opportunity to discourage her.

I wandered through the house, looking for some clue as to why it had happened. Everything appeared normal, but things would never be that way again. I thought back to the last time I saw them.

It was only hours ago, but it seemed like a lifetime. We grabbed a quick breakfast and got ready for the day. Never in my wildest dreams did I imagine my parents would be dead before noon.

When I thought back to that morning, I struggled to remember whether there was anything out of the ordinary. Memory is a funny thing. The more times you think about something, the more chances there are that you might unintentionally change the memory. I think I read that somewhere.

Why did Mom hug me a little longer and tighter than usual that morning?

"Goodbye, my sweet Sunce. I love you. Always," she said as they left for their industrial kitchen.

And Dad? He kissed me on the forehead and told me he was proud of me, becoming a journalist and such a good mother. Where did that come from?

Zora and Haley arrived almost simultaneously, as though they had planned a concentrated intervention. Setting their bags in the hallway, they sat down on either side of me on the sofa. This resulted in a fresh round of sobbing, reminding me why they were there.

"It's okay," Haley said softly. "Let it all out." She put her arm around me and tried to console me, though we both knew she couldn't. But I was glad she was there, in spite of the fact that I had said I wanted to be on my own.

"The pain is fresh now." Zora shared my suffering. "And the next few days will be even harder. But things will get better, trust me. It won't always be like this. And I'm here for you. Haley's here. A lot of people cared about your parents, and people care about you. You just need to reach out to them to help you through this."

The phone rang as if to confirm her words.

"I just heard. From Garrett, of all people. I don't even know how he got our number. Why didn't you call me, Cheryl? I'm so sorry, honey. I'll make arrangements for the kids to stay with Julia and get the first flight out....." Jim began, but I stopped him. If Stefan caused my parents' accident, I wanted Jim and the kids as far from Hamilton as possible.

"No, don't. I'm okay. I've got Haley and Zora. It's all the support I need for now. Just take care of the kids. I need to know they're safe. Please… watch out for them. I love you." I hung up and turned off my phone before he could argue.

The three of us spent the evening alternating between silence and sharing memories of good times with my parents. Haley took it upon herself to force me to eat something, although I wasn't in the least bit hungry for the first time in my life. While Haley fussed in the kitchen preparing soup, pasta, and salad, Zora said something I had a hard time processing.

"Mama and Tata wouldn't want you to be sad. I know this is hard, Sunce, but you're going to have to move on with your life and keep living it to the fullest. It's what they want." Zora's use of the Croatian words for Mom and Dad and Sunshine reminded me of how I'd felt I didn't quite fit in anywhere growing up. Being a first-generation Canadian, I was caught between my Croatian heritage and the 'English' country where I was raised.

"What they *want*?"

"What they *would* want, Sunce, even though they're gone. You need to give your parents a proper burial, settle their affairs, then go back to your family. They would want you to go on with your life and your dreams. To be happy."

Haley announced dinner was ready. As we made our way into the kitchen, the aroma of Mom's homemade chicken *juha* filled the air. She had made soup for supper last night and put what was left in the fridge. It would be the last time I ate my Mom's cooking. She had tried to show me how to cook the traditional Croatian recipes she served, but I never took much interest. I always thought there'd be another time, like maybe next year, during one of their visits.

"I wish I had paid more attention when Mom was cooking. I'll never be able to make the kind of food she did." It seemed ridiculous to worry that I'd never learn how to cook traditional Croatian cuisine when I had just lost my parents. Food was the least important thing to think about. It was strange where my mind took me in its grief.

"I can teach you," Zora offered.

"It's not just the food. I wish I knew more about my past, my parents' past, where I came from. All those things Mom and Dad talked about and I wasn't interested in—I wish I had listened better and asked more questions." I always assumed they'd be there with stories of their childhood and courtship, their lives before coming to Canada. I found myself grieving for more than my parents' deaths. I mourned the loss of eleven years we could have spent together, with them as grandparents to my children, all because of a series of stupid mistakes I had made. And being reminded of what I had done just before my nineteenth birthday triggered another thought. I did *not* want to live to mourn my husband and children. As hard as it was to lose my parents, I couldn't deal with the possibility of losing Jim and our kids. I would do whatever was necessary to keep them out of danger.

Even if it meant leaving them.

"You can always talk to me. But focus on the future, Svjetlana. The past is over. Mama and Tata wanted only the best for you. You know that. They loved you so much. Just remember that and know they would want you to be happy."

34

After supper, we sat together a while longer. Haley tuned the television to a program Mom and Dad liked to watch.

"You'd better try to get some sleep," Zora said just before midnight. "Tomorrow's going to be a hard day."

Tomorrow is going to be a hard day? So today wasn't?

Chapter Eight

Somehow Zora knew. The next day did prove to be harder than the day before. Upon awakening, I suffered a moment of delusion that nothing had changed. I expected to run downstairs to join my parents for breakfast, head back to my life with Jim and the kids, and see Mom and Dad in the summer when they came up north for their yearly visit. When the realization that they were gone hit, it was worse, in a way, than when Miss Pritchard told me they didn't make it. Because I knew beyond all doubt that it was true.

The door to their bedroom stood open, but no visible sign of them materialized there or in the bathroom. Voices drifted up the stairs, but they were foreign in the early morning.

"Did you get some sleep?" Zora greeted me as I entered the kitchen.

"A little. I must have slept a while because I just woke up. For a minute, I thought Mama and Tata were here."

"It'll be like that for a while. You'll expect to see them, expect them to be where they usually were."

"You mean like ghosts?" Zora wasn't aware, but I had lived with a ghost the past eleven years. Or perhaps, the ghost lived *inside* me.

"In a way. They'll always be with you, in spirit."

Haley asked if I wanted her to stay for the day, and I surprised myself by saying yes. Yesterday, I thought I needed to be alone. When Zora and Haley insisted on staying, I realized I couldn't face my darkest moments alone. As John Donne long ago stated: No man is an island.

"You're going to have to deal with the arrangements today," Zora said.

"The funeral home, the church. I'll make some calls and notify friends and co-workers."

"What about Grandma?" I had only one living relative left, apart from Jim and the kids. My mom's mom.

"I'll take care of it."

"Will she come?" I had never met my grandmother. Mom talked about her and kept in contact with letters and the occasional phone call. But we had never visited, nor had she made the journey to Canada.

"No, I don't think so."

I didn't ask why. I assumed the trip would be too hard for her. Zora suggested I eat breakfast and get dressed while she called the funeral home to make an appointment. Once again, the reality of my parents' deaths hit me full force.

"Do you have any preference for the funeral home?"

I shook my head. What did it matter?

"Let me take care of it then. And I'll call some of your parents' friends, let them spread the word. I've already called Father Malkovich. He'll stop by this morning."

Relief washed over me, having someone else take over the difficult job of preparing my parents' final goodbye. Haley kept me company while I forced down tea and toast, then retreated upstairs to dress and prepare to face our family priest.

Father Malkovich arrived shortly after Sunday service. I remembered him from my teenage years. I'd always thought of him as a rather unconventional priest. Maybe it was his relative youth or his good looks, so different from old by-the-book Father Vlasich, who retired a couple of years before I ran off. His easy-going manner, which was especially evident at events other than the traditional Sunday church service, made him easy to like.

Compassion emanated from him when he greeted me and took my hand. "I know this is hard for you, Svjetlana, but be assured that Mama and Tata will be in a better place."

Not in a frame of mind to hear his spiel about the kingdom of heaven, I listened politely nonetheless as he tried in vain to comfort me. Inwardly, I cursed a God who would allow this to happen. Mama's voice interrupted my hateful thoughts, telling me to be a good girl, and I apologized to God for my waywardness. The four of us prayed for the immortal souls of my parents, Haley included, even though she wasn't Catholic. Zora asked Father Malkovich to bless the house to help me heal from the pain of my loss. Somehow I got through the discussion about the funeral service, although I barely remembered what they decided at the end of it all.

"I just want Mama and Tata back," I managed to say as Father Malkovich rose to leave. With his hand on my shoulder, he stood silent for a moment.

"I understand." When he finally spoke, I could tell he was there for me on a personal level, not just as my priest. "But you're going to be okay. You're not alone."

That turned out to be true. When I reflected on it, the rest of the week passed in a blur, with very few moments spent in solitary. My parents had friends who demonstrated kindness during the visitation and funeral, sending cards and flowers, hugging me, telling me to stay strong and that I wasn't alone.

But when faced with the task of picking caskets for my parents, I felt absolutely alone. Even with Zora and Haley by my side, I found myself wanting to ask Mom what she thought would be best. Thankfully, the director knew exactly what to do and led me through the process of making the necessary decisions with Zora's input.

Not having bodies to physically mourn made accepting their deaths that much more difficult. Perhaps for that reason, I determined that either they were still alive, or their unexpected demise was the result of a deliberate act. Even as I received more confirmation that my parents were permanently gone, part of me believed I would eventually wake up from my nightmare, and things would go back to normal.

When Zora, Haley, and I entered the hospital, where their burned bodies lay in the morgue, I asked again if I could see my parents, as though they were in a hospital room in an induced coma waiting to come out of it. I would have happily ridden the elevator to the top floor, if that were the case. The hospital staff, under the recommendation of the coroner and the hospital chaplain, denied my request. Zora agreed that it was for the best.

What right did she have to speak for me?

"Were there any personal effects?" Zora asked.

A nurse handed me a baggie. I recognized the scroll-engraved two-tone wedding rings immediately. Mom's diamond ring glared at me, the one Dad bought on their tenth wedding anniversary when he could finally afford one he deemed worthy of gracing her finger. The rings and their death certificates were the only things with which I left the hospital. The coroner would release the bodies to the funeral home later in the day.

"I want to go to the police station," I said. "To find out what happened."

"Svjetlana, you already know what happened. It was an accident. There's not always a reason. It is what it is. But you're right. You should be able to ask questions," she acquiesced with a sigh.

As we entered the red brick Central Station and approached the counter, my mind wove a fantasy where the officer would tell me they had located my real parents, tied up out back by the dumpsters behind their commercial kitchen, having been robbed. Someone had taken their cash and stolen their catering van, then drove it off the escarpment in their haste to get away.

Zora took charge and found the right person to talk to. An officer led us to a private room. "I'm sorry for your loss," he said. "I understand you have some questions about your parents' accident."

"Yes. How did it happen? Was there something wrong with the van?" That seemed like a logical reason for the accident. "A few days ago, my car's tires were loose. Was it something like that?"

"We're going to look at all possibilities, of course, but that will take time—an examination of the vehicle, the coroner's report, along with an examination of the scene, interviews with your parents' employees. No one else was involved in the accident, and no witnesses have come forward so far. I can have someone take you there if you want to see where it happened. Sometimes people set up roadside memorials. It's a bad stretch of road, I'm afraid. There could be any number of reasons why your father lost control of the vehicle."

Why did he lose control? He's an excellent driver. Was. Although he did have a heavy foot.

I wanted to see the accident scene, but at the same time, I didn't. I fingered the gold rings through the baggie in the inside pocket of my purse. All that remained of them. That and the burned bodies they wouldn't let me see.

"I think that would be a good idea, don't you, Svjetlana? We could lay some flowers there," Zora suggested. Haley agreed we should do that.

I nodded. It was the last place they were alive. Maybe there would be some part of them still there. An officer accompanied us to the site. When I eased myself out of the back of the police car, I shivered, despite the unseasonable warmth of October. The speed limit sign on the curved stretch of two-lane road read 30 mph. Orange pylons and yellow police tape cordoned off the broken black guard rail. Beyond that, vegetation and trees spread along the steep ravine, tire tracks visible on the dirt-covered slope. From what I could gather, the van stopped three-quarters of the way down, quite a distance, slamming a tree and bursting into flames.

Zora tried to shield me from the horror down the slope, but I needed proof with my own eyes. I'm not sure what I expected, but no sign of my parents greeted me. Only a blackened spot where the inferno had erupted. A tree, singed but still standing, as though it refused to accept responsibility. The van had been towed away, the bodies unrecognizable.

"We'll bring flowers tomorrow," Zora said as I blinked back my tears, and Haley patted my back.

We returned to the house, exhaustion overtaking me. I'd never been so tired. Zora removed pre-cooked schnitzels from the freezer and peeled potatoes for supper, while Haley kept me company. I lay curled up on the sofa, and my heavy lids fell, the accident site burned into my eyeballs.

My body jerked with the shrill ring of the home phone. Haley answered. Jim had ignored my request to stay away.

"His flight just landed. He'll be here within the hour," Haley said.

"I'll take out another schnitzel," Zora called from the kitchen.

I protested, though I couldn't stop him from coming. When Jim appeared on the front doorstep, and Haley ushered him in, I cried out, not from pain, but with gratitude. Jim knew exactly what to do. Sitting down, his arms around me, he didn't say anything. Jim held me for a long time, stroking my head. Haley excused herself to help Zora in the kitchen.

"You shouldn't have come. You shouldn't have left the kids." I wanted to be angry, but I was so relieved to have him by my side, my voice came out whiny, not aggravated.

"The kids are fine. They're safe. I left them in West Kipling, with Julia. She and her neighbor, Mavis, are looking after them. No one's going to find them there."

"You were right. It's too dangerous. I should have listened to you. It's all my fault," I admitted, tears stinging my eyes.

"Shh… just relax, get some rest." Jim smoothed back the curls from my face, and his lips skimmed my forehead, my closed eyes, my nose, my lips. "Whatever happens next, we'll face it together." He repeated the same words he had said 11 years ago when he gave up his life for me.

As Jim held me, I fell asleep. I dreamed about Mom and Dad preparing food for their own funeral. The sound of Mom calling out that supper was done woke me. Except it wasn't Mom. Zora, wearing Mom's apron, greeted me in the kitchen.

Chapter Nine

The next few days evaporated from my life as though they'd never existed, with me in a trance. My support system of Zora, Haley, and Jim kept me on track, doing what was expected and providing what I needed. If not for Jim and the kids, I might have driven my Rav4 up the mountain road and followed the path my parents' van took, down the escarpment, into the tree, leaving some unrecognizable form of me in the morgue.

As I prepared for the funeral visitation, the image in the bathroom mirror stared vacantly, unrecognizable. Medium-length black curls lay limp, permanent bags took up residence under dead brown eyes, and an ashen tinge coated my gaunt face. Haley had taken me shopping to find something suitable in black. My jeans and t-shirts weren't going to work, nor were the skirts and blouses, and the one dress I'd brought with me was a bright fuchsia, definitely not right for the occasion.

Thanksgiving Day. A day to give thanks. The day my parents lay in their closed caskets for their viewing.

During the visitation, Jim, who I introduced as my friend, and Zora stood by me as people offered condolences. We had scheduled an afternoon and evening viewing at the funeral home, with the church funeral scheduled the next day, followed by a simple reception in the basement.

The quiet in the funeral chapel tempted me to scream. A line formed down the aisle, waiting to stop by the caskets to pay last respects to my parents and to dole out pity.

"Sorry for your loss." People I knew, and didn't know, sidled up to me as

I stood guarding the closed caskets. Everyone was sorry, but no one was able to do anything about it. People sat on wooden benches, waiting for Father Malkovich to lead prayers. Jim's parents were there, as were Haley and Garrett, and Haley's parents. The staff of Marez Caters, who my parents considered friends rather than employees, came with their families. So did people from our neighborhood. I recognized the faces of girls I used to hang around with at the Croatian Hall and their parents. Some of the people I'd gone to school with had shown up. A couple of my old teachers, the ones I'd met up with again during the 25th anniversary, along with the administrative staff, were there. Miss Pritchard sat with her hands folded, an encouraging nod in my direction every now and then. My parents also had a lot of acquaintances from their catering business, so there were plenty of strangers. Still, I was surprised the chapel was packed, the line forming out the open door seemingly endless. Maybe it was because Mom and Dad had died under tragic circumstances.

When Matija walked through the door near the end of the evening, I blinked several times, not believing my eyes. What was *he* doing there? Matija scanned the room before joining the line. I turned to Zora to ask if she knew him, but someone placed a hand on my shoulder, steering me in the opposite direction.

"You poor girl. Such a tragic accident. You're going to miss your Mom and Dad. They were wonderful people, both of them. They loved you so much." The woman who grasped my arm looked to be fortyish, with medium-length brown hair, and spoke with an accent. I'd never seen her before. "They would want you to be strong, Svjetlana. I know it's hard, but they wouldn't want you to be sad." She gazed into my eyes, her tight grip unwilling to release its hold.

"Were you a customer of Mom and Dad's?" I wanted to place this woman who thought she knew what my parents would want.

"No, I knew them from back home, a long time ago. But we've stayed in touch. My name is Draga. Take care of yourself, Svjetlana." Letting go of my hand, she hugged me and whispered, "Be strong. Take care."

She moved on to Zora, and they stood with their backs to everyone, chatting about the flower arrangements, then walked off to the other side of the room, away from where the line formed. People continued to take my hand, tell me how sorry they were, and say nice things about my parents. Jim stood quietly by, patting my back once in a while, shaking hands with people, most of whom he didn't know. I myself wasn't sure if half these people had ever met my parents.

By the time Matija approached the front of the line, I wondered where on earth Zora had gone. I wanted to ask her about Matija. Was she in the bathroom? Still chatting with Draga? I asked Jim if he would check on her.

"So sorry, Lana," Matija said as I stood alone with my parents' caskets. "Too young they were. But you never know what can happen. You be strong. You will be okay."

"Thank you for coming. I wanted to ask how you knew my...."

Matija moved away, and someone took his place before I could finish my question. He didn't stay for prayers. I sat in the front row, waiting for Zora and Jim.

Jim returned just in time and put his arm around my shoulder. "I saw Zora walk out the door with some woman. I waited for her, but she didn't come back."

As Father Malkovich led prayers, I wondered what happened to Zora. When the visitation ended, I asked Haley and Garrett if they had seen her.

"Not since she left your side," Haley said.

"I don't know what to do. She came here with us, and now I can't find her. She went outside with some woman who knew my parents. It's so strange. She said her name was Draga. I've never seen her before."

Jim and I looked throughout the funeral home after everyone had gone. When the director assured us no one remained in the building, we went outside and searched the grounds.

Zora was gone.

"She must have left with someone else," Jim said.

That made no sense, but she obviously wasn't at the funeral home anymore. My car was the only vehicle left in the guest lot.

Shortly after we arrived home, the phone rang.

"Svjetlana," Zora apologized. "I'm so sorry I left like that. I was talking to Draga, an old friend of your parents, and I suddenly fell ill. She helped me to the washroom, and once I was well enough, she sent me home in a taxi."

"Oh, no! Are you all right?"

"To tell the truth, I'm not the best. I must have caught some sort of bug or something. I'll see you tomorrow. I hope you're okay."

"Yes, I'm fine. Just worry about getting yourself well."

Jim caught the gist of the conversation. "I hope she's well enough for the funeral tomorrow. You should try to get some rest yourself."

"I am tired," I agreed. "But I'd like to lie on the couch with you for a while with the T.V. on. I don't think I'll be able to sleep."

Jim turned on the television and heated milk on the stove while I grabbed a couple of pillows and a blanket out of my bedroom, and changed into pajamas. The two of us drank milk and ate cookies, watching some stupid show until the news came on. I curled up beside Jim, my head on his lap.

The clock on the wall chimed twelve times, waking me. I nudged Jim. He looked uncomfortable with his head flopped down on his shoulder. I didn't want him to get a crick in his neck. "Let's go to bed."

Early in the morning, Zora rang as Jim zipped me into the black funeral dress.

"I'm so sorry, Sunce. I'm not going to make it to the church. I wish I could be there for you, but I'm afraid my stomach hasn't settled down, and I'm too dizzy to stand up."

I told her it was fine. She should rest and take care of herself.

How dare *she get sick the day of my parents' funeral!*

Chapter Ten

In the end, I attended my parents' funeral with Jim and his parents, the four of us occupying the center front bench, like sitting ducks. I was the sole blood family member on a lonely pew in a church filled to capacity. A sudden awareness hit me. Whatever the cause of my parents' deaths, their demise put me, Svjetlana Babic, front and center in the local news. And with that understanding came the knowledge that although I wore the bullseye on my back, those around me were within target range.

As Father Malkovich droned on, I imagined my parents' spirits overlooking the service. I jumped as though a shot had rung out when one of the flower arrangements fell over, silence filling the church for a second or two after. I imagined my parents had knocked it down, furious their lives had been unjustly taken.

At the cemetery, I stood gazing down at their graves as Jim and I placed roses on their caskets, a final goodbye. Rain pelted the assembled crowd. Black umbrellas shielded those who cared about Mom and Dad enough to brave the weather. They stood in line on the soggy grass, rose bushes bordering row upon row of black, gray, and brown tombstones adorned with candles, fading annuals fronting many of them. Once everyone added a rose onto the caskets in the hole in the ground, they dispersed. Father Malkovich set his hand on my shoulder, made the sign of the cross once more, turned around, and left, leaving me with Jim. I felt utterly alone as I cried for I don't know how long above my parents' graves, and I might have thrown myself down on their caskets if Jim hadn't been holding me tightly by the waist. Mom and Dad's deaths had been ruled accidental, but in the pit of my stomach, I knew better.

I was a murderer.

A desire to die washed over me like a tidal wave, then my head jerked up as I sensed a presence. The cemetery gave off an ominous aura, as though the dead begrudged my wanting to throw away the life I possessed. Seemingly out of nowhere, a fog rolled in amongst the tombstones and through the trees that had begun to change to autumn colors, frightening me out of my morbid thoughts.

"I want to go home now," I said, pulling away from Jim and walking briskly toward my car.

The Toyota crept toward the cemetery gates, and I envisioned dead souls buried under the tombstones rising up and following. It would have made the perfect setting for a horror novel. As I imagined all manner of ghosts and ghouls wandering through the mist, my mind snapped.

From behind the mausoleum, situated several hundred feet from the fresh graves, a shadow moved. That was disconcerting enough, but I recognized the familiar silhouette. I could have sworn on my life that Dad watched as we drove out of the cemetery. I remembered what Zora had said.

You'll keep seeing them where you expect them to be. They'll always be with you in spirit.

Maybe it was completely normal for Dad's ghost to skulk around the cemetery, watching me. Or... maybe I was going crazy. "Did you see that man? Over by the mausoleum?"

But Jim's eyes focused on the road, wipers swishing across the windshield.

Only one more ordeal awaited me, and the funeral would be over—the reception. In the basement of the church, people congregated with food and drinks, chatting. Jim stopped to talk to Garrett and Haley. I wandered alone over to people lined up at tables laden with sandwiches, salads, and baked goods, and overheard some of their conversation.

"I heard he'd been drinking before they left to cater the funeral."

"Isn't that ironic—heading to a funeral?"

"What was he thinking, drinking?"

The talking stopped when they noticed me. "Dad wouldn't drink and drive," I said in his defense.

"Of course he wouldn't," someone agreed. "Some people like to start nasty rumors, and other people believe them. I'm sure that's all it is."

I didn't know who 'some' people were, but it made me wonder how the rumor started. Who would say such a thing about Dad? He did drink too much sometimes, but he let Mom drive if he'd had too many. So if he was drinking, why was he driving? And at work, early in the day?

"How you are holding up?" I recognized the voice even though many people in the room spoke with accents. I turned around as Matija filled his plate.

"Okay, I guess."

"Don't worry what people say. People like to talk. Maybe road was slippery."

"No, I don't think so. I think maybe there was a problem with the van."

"What the police are saying?

"They're investigating."

Matija nodded. "Could be car trouble, then?"

"He liked to drive fast," someone interjected.

"Isn't the speed limit just 30 mph on that road? How did he lose control at that speed?" someone else added.

I confirmed Matija's suggestion that car trouble might have been the cause. It was much more likely than drunk driving and involved less culpability than speeding.

"You never did say how you knew my parents," I said to Matija.

Jim came to rescue me from an awkward conversation with a man I barely knew and some 'friends' of my parents I could hardly recall. "Excuse me, I need to get Lana to eat something." He placed a plate in my hand, took one for himself, and swept me along the length of the table, plopping more food on my dish than I could possibly eat even if I had an appetite, then led me to a table where his parents, Haley, Garrett, and Father Malkovich sat. I was only too happy to have him take charge and whisk me away from people who implied my father had somehow caused the accident.

"I hope Zora will get well quickly," Father Malkovich said. "It's too bad she couldn't be here, but I'm sure she's with you in spirit. She loved your parents."

"You don't think it's contagious, do you?" Haley turned to me. "The last thing you need is to get sick yourself."

"I'm okay," I assured her, although I wasn't. I didn't feel ill, not like Zora, but I did feel sick to my stomach. The overwhelming nausea made me want to throw up, not just the contents of my stomach, but my stomach along with them. I was sick with grief, and no medicine could cure me.

"You should take a few days to rest, get things in order, then return to your life," Father Malkovich advised. "That's the best thing for you now—go home and get back into your routine and keep busy. Be with your friends."

"I'll take good care of her," Jim promised, stroking my upper arm as he pulled me closer.

Something struck me as rather odd as we engaged in our quiet conversation. Glancing around the room, I realized what it was. Laughter. People engaged in talking, some loudly, and smiling, nodding their heads, and eating and drinking. If I didn't know better, I would have thought it was a party. For the umpteenth time, I considered that maybe my parents weren't really dead—this was all some sort of trick or mistake. They'd show up anytime, through the church basement door, and tell a whopper of a story about what really happened to them.

But, as people dropped by our table to say goodbye, and my parents didn't appear, I knew I had to accept reality. The funeral ended, my parents lay in the cold ground, everyone went home. Tomorrow they would go back to their lives and carry on as normal. I had no idea what tomorrow held for me. I only knew I had to face it alone.

"You need to get home to the kids," I said as Jim drove to the house. "Give me a couple of weeks to settle Mom and Dad's affairs, go through their things."

"No. I'll help you. I'm not leaving you alone."

"I won't be alone. I have Zora and Haley. And I don't want the kids left with strangers, neither of us there for them," I insisted. "They come first."

"They're fine where they are. My place is with you, wherever that is." His hands gripped the steering wheel as his jaw tightened in the dim light of the car.

"I don't want to argue. I *need* you to go home to the kids. Please try to understand. It's what I want." I didn't add that if my suspicions were correct, the kids could be in danger.

Neither Jim nor I had voiced the possibility that Stefan was responsible for the accident, but it *had* to have crossed his mind. "I just can't deal with worrying about the kids on top of this. I just can't." I sobbed without restraint.

We drove the rest of the way with no further conversation.

As we undressed out of our funeral gear, Jim finally spoke. "If you're sure. If it's what you want." His brown eyes filled with sorrow and hurt as he cupped my face in his hands. "You know I'd do anything for you, honey."

"Thank you. I'll be home before you know it. I promise. But this is something I need to do on my own. I love you. So much."

I kissed him, and he lay me down on the bed and made love to me, gently, treating me like a fine china doll as though it were our first time, then with a passionate intensity, as though it were our last time.

Jim made arrangements to catch a flight back to Lake Kipling the next afternoon, and we fell asleep, wrapped up in each other, exhausted from the ordeal of burying Mom and Dad.

I awoke a short while later to use the bathroom, and on my way back to Jim, I entered my parents' room and lay on the bed. I stared at the ceiling for a while, then fell asleep again, so worn out from the worst day of my life. Or the second worst day. The first was when I heard my parents had been killed in a car accident. I wasn't sure which was worse. Every day since the crash counted as the worst day of my life.

I woke around the time dusk settled, and my eyes scanned the room. Enough light came through the window to illuminate the disturbed scene. A couple of dresser drawers gaped slightly open. The closet offered a glimpse of Mom's shoes, some knocked over.

I didn't recall it being that way before we left for the funeral.

Chapter Eleven

The next morning, Jim kissed me goodbye and took a taxi to the airport. I lay wallowing in sorrow, alone in bed in an empty house, when my parents' lawyer called. I'd met him before when Dad had me drop off paperwork for the business. He asked if I could come to the office that afternoon to go over my parents' wills.

A large lock box sat bolted onto the floor of my parents' bedroom closet. I took the key taped to the bottom of Mom's jewelry chest yesterday morning and placed it on my keyring. Dad had told me it opened the metal container, which held important papers and emergency cash. He also instructed me not to poke my nose inside unless something happened to them.

Copies of their wills lay on top. I read Dad's first. A lot of jargon I didn't understand jumped out from the pages, but I skimmed to the part that stated Dad bequeathed all his possessions to Mom. I read on. In the event that Mom's death preceded his, I was the sole beneficiary. Mom's will contained the same wording as Dad's. I had already assumed their property would become mine, so nothing surprising there. I locked up the box and dropped the keyring into my purse.

Jim called to say he had landed safely and was at Julia's picking up the kids. He passed the phone to Brent, and then to Jamie. They said they were sorry my Mom and Dad had died. Those words coming from their innocent voices brought fresh tears even though I had already emptied several tissue boxes.

"Mommy has to stay here… a while longer, but you be good for Daddy. I love you… so much."

"Love you more." Their three voices, joining in chorus, were the last words I heard before ending the call and succumbing to another round of uncontrollable blubbering.

Feeling the need to connect to my parents in some way, I called Grandma, my only other living blood relative. Mom had written her number in a personal address book. Although Mom seldom called, save for holidays or special occasions, I recognized Grandma's voice. Mom had always made me say hello when she talked to her. Our conversation usually consisted of the same few words. She would ask how I was doing and what was new. Since I didn't really know Grandma, I didn't share details of my life with her.

"Baba?" I greeted her with the Croatian word for Grandma when she answered, fearing she had forgotten me over the past decade. She had no idea I was married and had children. "It's Svjetlana. How are you doing?"

Upon hearing my voice, she began to cry. "My poor little Svjetlana. My baby girl. Your Mama's gone."

Her sobbing was contagious. I tried to control myself so she could understand me despite the blubbering and my English accent. I wouldn't say I spoke fluent Croatian, but I could get by. Grandma didn't speak English. "I miss them so much, Baba. But I'm okay. Zora's been a good help with the funeral, and I have my friends. I can't believe they're gone."

We spent the next several minutes trying to console each other. There wasn't much else to say. Zora had already told her about the accident. As I said goodbye, Grandma added a bit of grandmotherly advice. "Be happy, Svjetlana. It's what your Mama would have wanted for you. Don't be sad. Go on with your life and remember the good times with your parents."

Maybe. Maybe I could have done that if I had known for certain their deaths were accidental and not the result of my actions.

As it was, I now had three ghosts buried inside me. And my grip on sanity was slipping as their voices accused me of murder.

When I arrived at Mr. Novak's office, he greeted me personally. Younger than my parents, he spoke with no accent, although he was of Croatian background. "Svjetlana, I'm so sorry to hear about your parents' accident. Zora Ljubovic called me a couple of days ago."

Good old Zora. Taking charge. I would have thought to look for their wills and call the lawyer sooner or later, to pay bills or put the house on the market. Jim and I were in no position to pay for funerals, much less take care of any other expenses.

"Did she? She's been helping me cope since I got the news about Mom and Dad. I brought copies of their wills with me."

"Okay, good. The first thing I want to do is check that they correspond to the signed copies on file."

He looked back and forth between my papers and the originals and nodded, affirming everything correlated. "Your parents have left you well off. There are no debts. They have enough savings and investments to take care of the funeral, as well as any house and business expenses for quite some time. The house is mortgage free, so you can move in or sell it."

He stopped talking and watched my expression, then pulled some other documents from a file. "They also have personal life insurance policies. The two policies combined will pay out a million dollars."

My mouth flew open. One million dollars? "I didn't know. I knew they had some life insurance, but I didn't realize it was that much."

"You'll also be the new owner of the business. Since they rented the facilities, there are few capital assets, but the business *is* profitable. Insurance will replace the delivery van. So it's up to you whether you want to run the catering business or sell. Your parents' accountant should be able to help with details." He handed over a business card with the accountant's contact information.

"Oh, okay. I don't know what I'm going to do. I'll talk to Zora and the other employees about that."

"It will take a while to get things settled. Bring me the funeral bills, and I'll take care of that. I'll have the bank release enough funds to cover everyday house expenses and to ensure the business continues to run smoothly. Let me know if you need anything else in the meantime. I'm sure the bank manager will be accommodating since you're the only beneficiary, and there's no one to contest the will. With the money coming to you from life insurance, they're going to want your business, going forward."

As I left Mr. Novak's office, I couldn't help but wonder why my parents had such a huge life insurance policy. I was going to be a millionaire, but at what expense? I would have given it all away to charity if it meant I could have my parents back.

When I arrived home, the front door was unlocked. That was odd. I could have sworn I had locked it. Zora rang as I stepped into the entry hall. When I asked about her health, she started to say she was fine, then added, "Still a bit under the weather, but definitely on the mend. I'm really sorry I wasn't there for you."

"It's okay, you've done lots for me. I appreciate it."

"Have you given any thought to the business? Everyone's been wondering whether they'll still have a job." By everyone, she meant the six other employees at Marez Caters. They'd been managing themselves since the accident.

"No, not really."

Zora suggested I drive over to the kitchen and check in with the staff.

She met me at my parents'…well, *my* business establishment. The strip mall also housed a plumbing supply store, a flooring store, and a restaurant supply warehouse, among other businesses. When we entered the mainly stainless steel and white professional kitchen, all six employees were scurrying around, organizing and preparing for two parties that evening. They stopped when I entered.

"Svjetlana, how are you doing?" someone asked.

"Are you managing okay?" another added.

Everyone was concerned about me. I told them I was fine, which was a lie. "I wanted to check in, though, to make sure everything is okay here."

"It's all good, we're doing the best we can," one of the women said, and several others nodded to show things were going as smoothly as possible in my parents' absence.

"We are wondering…, and I know you have a lot to think about right now, but we've been wondering whether you were planning on continuing with the business," someone else said.

"Should we be looking for new jobs?" another asked.

I made my first big independent decision as a business owner. "No, there's no need for that. Keep on as usual. Zora is going to be managing things on a daily basis from now on. She'll be in charge."

Zora gasped. "Oh, I don't think I can... I mean, I'd love to help, but I'm not sure I'm up to managing the business."

I assured her I trusted her to look after my interests. "Just keep things running. I'll let the accountant know that you're managing the everyday part of the business. He'll take care of all the paperwork." I surprised myself with the ease with which I took control and made decisions that involved the lives of other people. I left them knowing they had job security and their families wouldn't suffer from loss of income.

Zora offered to take me out for an early supper at a nearby restaurant to thank me for the promotion. I asked about her stomach.

"Oh, it's fine now. Must have been a forty-eight hour bug or something."

I was glad to hear she was feeling better. As I lifted a piece of chicken to my mouth, Zora picked up a slice of toast and asked how I was really doing.

"I'm managing, thanks."

"Are you?" Zora knew me well. She searched my face, waiting for me to elaborate.

I swallowed and set down my fork. "No. I'm so mad. Why did this happen? Why wasn't Dad careful? How could he drive the car over a cliff? Was he drinking? Speeding? That's what some people are saying." I couldn't look her in the eyes and speak the truth – that I may have put their lives in danger.

Zora stared at her bowl, swirling the spoon through her soup. "I don't have any answers for you, Sunce. Sometimes things just happen."

We finished our meal, and Zora asked if I wanted company for the rest of the evening.

"Thanks, but I'll probably call it an early night."

"I could come by tomorrow and help you go through your parents' things, if you want. Maybe you could give their clothes to the Thrift Shop."

"I appreciate the offer, but I think it's something I need to do on my own." I didn't mean to be insensitive to Zora; she was Mom's best friend and wanted to be there for me. "I'll let you know if I need help."

She hugged me before we drove off separately to our empty houses.

Needing a distraction from my sorrow, I spent the evening wandering the neighborhood. That night, I fell into a fitful sleep, haunted by a recurring nightmare.

Lana looked down at the black asphalt in the poorly lit back alleyway, dark liquid forming a puddle at her feet. Cold drizzle pelted Lana's face as she moved big brown eyes to meet the dark eyes of the young man she had loved. They were fixed on her, still holding her captive, as she stood frozen in disbelief.

Backing into the shadows, Lana watched as Stefan burst through the back door of the bar and fell to his knees, his unearthly wail piercing the night air. Two drunken, laughing patrons followed, stumbling on the wooden steps. The blood on the blacktop, mixing with rain, the bar's owner splayed across his son's body, in the dim spotlight as though they were on a stage, abruptly sobered them as the anguished cries of rage rang through Lana's ears.

At 3:14, I awoke to shuffling in my parents' bedroom.

Someone is in the house.

I listened carefully as the sound of someone moving around traveled through the thin wall. I didn't dare turn on the lamp, and I was too afraid to get up and confront whoever was in their room. Then a thought occurred: If I was right and Stefan had killed my parents, he would send someone after me, too. It could be him roaming through my house. That prompted me into action. I crept out of bed, stuffed pillows under the covers to make it look like I was still there.

The closet bifold door made a scraping sound as it opened, and I buried myself amongst the clothing, assuming the intruder wouldn't hear if he was busy rummaging around. The doors remained open a crack so I would hear if he entered my room. Sitting in a cramped position at the back of a dark closet for any length of time wasn't the most comfortable way to hide from a potential assailant, but I did my best to keep quiet.

The door to my room creaked, followed by the sensation of footsteps across the carpet. A shadow loomed in front of the closet, and I placed a hand over my mouth to stifle a scream. Whoever was in my room unzipped my purse, which I'd plopped on the floor in front of the closet, and rifled through it. It didn't hold much money, but my parents' wedding bands and the diamond ring were still in there. I refused to allow anyone to steal them.

"Nooooo…" I shoved open the bifold door, knocking the thief off balance and into the night table. The lamp crashed onto his back, eliciting a groan, but he scrambled to his feet and stumbled out of my room before I could get a good look at his face. Down the stairs I rushed after him, missing the bottom step. Out the front door into the night, I hobbled, and caught a glimpse of his silhouette under the streetlight.

Dad? It can't be. He's dead and buried.

"Dad! Dad! Come back!"

In the last two days, since I had buried my father, he had appeared to me twice. At the cemetery, Jim hadn't seen anything. And I wondered if seeing ghosts was a normal part of the grieving process. But, this man was flesh and blood. No question.

He disappeared into the night as though he'd never been there. I closed the door, coming to my senses.

A simple trick of the light. That's all.

Meanwhile, my confusion had allowed the thief time to escape. I needed to call the police. I grabbed my phone and pressed 91…

No, no police.

I returned to my parents' room and turned on the overhead light fixture. More drawers were ajar, and the contents examined. Mom's jewelry box sat open on the dresser. Everything seemed to be there, as far as I could tell. A few gold pieces – necklace, bracelet, small hoops – , her birthstone pendant and earrings, a string of pearls and matching earrings, and a diamond bracelet. All gifts Dad had given her over the last few years, since the business had taken off. The rest of it was costume jewelry she had bought herself. The intruder wasn't interested in jewelry.

I turned to the lock box on the floor in their open closet.

Chapter Twelve

I took the small key from my keychain, unlocked the box, and found what I expected the thief had been searching for. A brown envelope at the bottom held $10,000 in large bills.

Someone must have known about the money and had searched for the key. Who knew my parents kept cash in that box? Was it a random guess? Maybe. But why leave the jewelry? They could have easily sold it.

How did people justify taking advantage of others in their time of grief and robbing them when they were most vulnerable?

I locked up the money, returned to bed, and slept until almost noon with the keychain tucked under my sheets. After I awoke and got ready to face the day, which meant organizing and cleaning, I procrastinated and looked in the lockbox again.

As I rummaged, I found bank statements and wondered exactly how rich I was going to be at the expense of my parents' lives. Besides the money, statements, and their wills, the box held insurance papers, business documents, the family bible, our passports, birth certificates, and Mom and Dad's marriage certificate.

I looked at my certificate first.

Svjetlana Babic, November 30, 1978, Hamilton. Mother - Marica Babic, Father - Janez Babic.

I hadn't actually seen Mom and Dad's birth certificates before, but I knew when and where they were born.

When I glanced at Mom's birth certificate, I knew immediately that it contained an error. I picked it up and examined it closely. Her birth date was listed as May 19 when it should have been May 29, 1957. That was odd.

I dropped the certificate on the floor and stared at it as if it were an alien being. The year read 1961. As I scanned it again to make sure I hadn't misread the numbers, I noticed something else. Her name wasn't listed as Marica. It was Mimica. Mimica Babic, who would have been Forty-seven years old this past May. Forty-seven years old when she died, not fifty-one. It also dawned on me that my last name was the same as Mom's maiden name.

How could the birth certificate be wrong? Then I remembered what they had told me about records in the old country. They weren't always accurate. I'd heard Mom and Dad tell stories of people's birth dates being recorded incorrectly back in the old days. So it was obviously just one of those things. But, very strange. There were a lot of mistakes.

Picking up Dad's birth certificate to see if it contained errors, I threw it down as though it had caught on fire.

It wasn't even *his*. Not his birth certificate.

Retrieving it with trembling fingers, I read the information that belonged to some man named Luka Nikolov, born on July 6, 1959, in some town in Croatia I had never heard of. I had been told Dad was born on July 22, 1955, in the same village as Mom.

Who was this man, Luka Nikolov? Why was his birth certificate in Mom and Dad's lockbox? And where was Dad's birth certificate?

None of it made sense. As I shoved the birth certificates back into the large brown envelope where they had been stored, they slipped and slid, refusing to go back in. My hands fumbled until the papers were secured, and I calmed myself enough to stand.

If anyone could explain this, it would be Zora. Taking several deep breaths, I grabbed my purse and headed to the car. Nausea overtook me as I slid the key into the ignition, and I counted to forty several times before backing out of the driveway.

Five minutes later, I pounded on the door of her small bungalow. She answered, an anxious look on her face. "What's the matter, Svjetlana? Has something happened?"

Not waiting to be invited in, I pushed my way into her living room. "This… this is what's the matter." I showed her the birth certificates.

The color drained from her face. "What is this?"

"These are the birth certificates I found in Mama and Tata's lockbox. Why is Mom's wrong? And who is this man? Where is Dad's birth certificate?"

"Sit down, Sunce. Let's try to figure this out."

"You grew up in the same village. Mama said you were good friends, although she was a bit older than you. How much older was she?"

"A few years," Zora answered vaguely.

"How many?"

"What does it matter how many years? She was like an older sister to me."

"Why is her birth certificate wrong?"

"I don't know. Sometimes they made mistakes in the old country."

I wasn't buying that. Mom always looked young for her age. Finally, I understood why. "What about Mama's name?"

"Her real name was Mimica. She liked to go by Marica. It's kind of a nickname. It's like Mary in English—it can also be Maria or Marie."

"And she never married?"

"Of course she married. She married your Tata."

"Her maiden name is the same as her married name. That can't be right. Unless… he was her cousin?"

"No, not unless he was a very distant cousin from way back. Lots of people have the same last name, especially in the small villages back home."

Zora seemed to have a reasonable explanation, but it was odd there could be that many discrepancies on Mom's birth certificate.

"Who is Luka Nikolov?"

Zora said she didn't know.

She was lying to me. I could tell by her pallor. I demanded answers. "Why is Luka Nikolov's birth certificate in the lockbox? And why isn't Dad's?"

"I don't have an answer for that. But your mom and dad's driver's licenses, don't they have the right dates and names? Credit cards? Social Security cards? Have you checked all those other pieces of identification? There was an obvious mix-up in the birth certificates from Croatia. Maybe your dad got someone else's by mistake, some sort of switch in the records office. I don't know." She shrugged to indicate she had no explanation.

I had seen their IDs before. They corresponded to what I'd been told. "So you think it's just some mistake?" How could they make such blatant errors? It wasn't like Croatia was a third-world country, and it wasn't the Middle Ages.

"I think you should trust what your parents told you. There was obviously an issue with the paperwork. Opening that lockbox has made you question what you've believed all your life. Put those papers away and concentrate on moving forward," Zora insisted, her eyes pleading with me to forget all about it. What was Zora hiding?

"But I don't understand any of this."

"If it was important, or something your parents thought you should have known, they would have told you. It can't be anything other than a mistake of some sort. Don't make more of it than there is. Why don't you get some rest and come back for supper? You look exhausted." Zora abruptly changed the subject and started discussing the menu. She wasn't willing, or able, to provide answers to my questions.

"Yes, I will come back." I'd hit a brick wall with her and would need to try again later.

When I got home, I looked at the documents again. I considered that all three of us had Mom's last name, and maybe she *did* marry her cousin. I recalled stories Mom had told me of how people in the village rarely married outside their circle, and a lot of families in the area had the same last name. Maybe it wasn't so unusual that my parents were both born with the name Babic.

I pulled out their marriage certificate and found my parents had lied to me.

On July 24, 1978, Marica Babic and Janez Babic were married in Hamilton, Ontario at the Croatian church. Zora Ljubovic witnessed the nuptials. The other witness was someone I didn't know. My parents *did* have the same last name before they married. What shocked me was that they were married four months before I was born. I had been told they were married in Croatia a few years before I was born in Hamilton. Why did my parents lie to me?

Are Marica and Janez really my parents? Were they?

Later that day, I headed back to Zora's house to confront her with the marriage certificate. There was no way she could lie about that. She had attended their wedding.

"So now you know the truth," she said.

"Do I? What is the truth? I have no idea what to believe."

"Your parents didn't want you to know they were already expecting you when they got married. They had a very small ceremony and kept quiet about the pregnancy, with your Mama wearing loose clothing."

"But they could have told me that. Why wouldn't they?"

"I can't say."

I wasn't sure what that meant. Was it because Zora didn't know or because she didn't think she should tell me? "Is there anything else they were hiding?"

"Like what?"

I asked again about the discrepancies in the birth certificates. And once again, she claimed it must have been a clerical error of some sort. "All their other IDs are correct, so it's a mistake, that's the only possible explanation." I didn't get any more information out of Zora, and she busied herself in the kitchen, leaving me with the T.V. in the living room.

We ate supper in silence, with me chewing and swallowing the ham, pan-roasted potatoes, carrots, and salad, without tasting them. Zora had made dessert—potica, a type of walnut roll—and she insisted I eat my fill, then packed a couple of large containers with leftovers.

"Thank you," I said as I took the bag of food. "For the food. And the company." I tried to catch her eye, but Zora turned and headed for the front door, opening it.

She hugged me and told me to take care of myself. "Anytime you need company, just give me a call. At home or at work. It doesn't matter. I'm always here for you."

When I arrived home, a huge white wicker basket covered in plastic awaited me on the covered front porch. Pink (my favorite color) tissue paper surrounded the contents. I lugged the basket into the house and set it on the living room floor.

An unsigned card read 'Take care of yourself'. The basket contained my favorite things: a package of assorted herbal teas, hot chocolate, flavored popcorn in a tin, a wrapped box of Laura Secord chocolates, a Mary Higgins Clark novel, a Michael Jackson CD, a shiny gold-covered notebook and pen, a lilac scented candle, lavender bubble bath, a bouquet of fresh cut flowers, and a soft, white, stuffed cat (like Chloe, who passed away a few years ago) with a heart-shaped gold locket wound around its neck. The items had obviously been personally selected by someone who knew me well.

Jim.

I called immediately to thank him.

"Cheryl. I didn't send it. I wish I'd thought of it, but it wasn't me."

After a brief conversation in which I asked about the kids, and he begged me to hurry home, I called Zora to thank her for the basket. She said it was a lovely thought on someone's part, but not hers.

Haley? Of course. But when I called, she didn't know anything about it. The employees at Marez Caters also hadn't sent it. I didn't know who else to thank. Could it have been from the school? Maybe the neighbors got together? Perhaps people knew more about me than I knew about them. I decided not to dwell on it. Whoever sent it obviously wanted to remain anonymous. It was most likely Jim and the kids, or Zora, Haley, and Garrett, being nice without taking credit.

I removed the gold chain from the cat and opened the locket. A photo of my very young parents, Mom in her wedding gown, adorned the inside. Definitely Zora. But why did she lie? I opened the clasp and put it around my neck, where I planned to keep it forever.

I needed to make some decisions about my parents' belongings so I could get back to my family, but I couldn't bring myself to do that just yet, so I went to my room to sort through my own mess. Going through the bookshelf, I ran across Wuthering Heights, one of my favorite love stories, and I considered my own parents' relationship. They weren't particularly demonstrative in public, or in front of me, for that matter, but they loved each other. It was obvious to anyone who saw them together—the way they gazed at one another and brushed against each other accidentally, even in the way they bickered over nothing and then compromised to keep the peace. I wondered what they were like when they were young and newly in love. Mom told me they met at a dance and fell in love immediately.

I picked up the novel, struggling to keep my mind off the accident. After a couple of chapters, I realized I had read the words, but they may as well have been in another language for all I got out of them.

Another book caught my eyes. A photo book about Niagara Falls. During our many family trips to the Niagara region, I had examined the historic plaques recounting the local battles of the War of 1812. Dad was a real history buff. He enjoyed reading books about Canada, although his English made it tough going. Sometimes I helped him with vocabulary and pronunciation. In turn, he taught me about Croatia, which was one of six republics in the communist country of Yugoslavia when they were growing up, and how the 1980 death of President Tito brought about big changes, not good, according to him. My parents and Zora had been deeply affected by news of the civil war in the 1990s.

As my thoughts wandered to the recently war-torn country that had been my parents' home in their youth, it helped me focus on something other than their deaths. I wondered what it had been like for them, growing up in Croatia. I wanted to see for myself the homeland they had always talked about. Maybe someday Jim and I would take the kids on a family vacation to Europe.

Too many memories filled my room. I moved on to the main bathroom to begin sorting, packing, labeling, and garbaging the remnants of my parents' lives, trying to make sense of it all. I collapsed on my bed, exhausted by grief.

When the phone rang in the middle of the night, I expected it to be more bad news. "Hello?"

No answer. Only static. Then my name crackled through the line, the voice uttering it as familiar as the nose on my face. "Svjetlana." More static. "danger... go home."

A click told me the call ended; we must have been disconnected. My eyes went to the caller ID, and didn't recognize the number. But the country calling code jumped out at me.

Dad? In Croatia?

Chapter Thirteen

M y repeated calls to the number went unanswered. In frustration, I made a decision Jim would never support.

I checked out my parents' lock box, looking for a passport. Inside, I found three of them. One for Svjetlana Babic, expired three years ago.

Just great.

Tucked inside were my old driver's license, healthcare card, and Social Security card. Unsure of the logistics of legally reclaiming my old identity, I called a contact up north who excelled at churning out fake IDs quicker than gossip could spread in a small town.

"I need it all by yesterday," I said, impressing upon him the urgency of the situation as I sent copies of my expired IDs his way.

Mom and Dad's passports listed their names and birthdates as I knew them to be. However, they entered Canada on June 14, 1978, just months before I was born.

Before leaving the house that morning, I called one of the locksmiths listed in the phone book to secure the house. I spent the rest of the day setting things in motion.

Zora's advice to leave the past behind and move forward sounded like a good plan. Unfortunately, in the end, it wasn't the one I went with. Upon discovering my parents' birth certificates, I had considered for the first time whether the car accident had nothing at all to do with Stefan or my past. Maybe it was simply an accident. Or maybe... there was a lot more to it than I knew.

I checked in with my lawyer and accountant to let them know how they could reach me, then stopped at the travel agency. Having never traveled out of the country, I had no idea how to book a trip overseas. The travel agent led me through the whole process, taking care of the details, asking whether my passport was current.

"Um, yes. It's all good." Not a complete lie. I held a valid passport under the name of Cheryl MacGregor. What I needed, though, was an up-to-date passport for Svjetlana Babic. Fingers crossed, it would be ready in time.

At the mall, I popped into one of those 'No appointment needed' expensive beauty salons for a makeover that would better match Svjetlana's ID photos, and did a quick shop for new fall clothing. After stopping at the bank to deposit the $10000 from the safety deposit box to cover the check I had written for my ticket to Croatia, and to take out some traveler's cheques, and convert Canadian cash to Croatian kuna, I returned home to find a security van parked on the road, reminding me that I was supposed to be home to have the locks changed.

"Hope it's okay we've already started," the man with the drill said as I walked up to the front door. I let him continue with his work while I packed for my trip.

My curiosity had gotten the better of me. I wanted to know about my parents' pasts. Mom had gotten pregnant in Croatia. I was going to Croatia to learn more about my mom and dad. And to find out about the mystery man whose birth certificate they kept hidden in their lockbox.

Luka Nikolov.

Chapter Fourteen

One jam-packed large suitcase and a carry-on, which were in my parents' closet, and the large duffel bag I brought with me to Hamilton. Just waiting for my up-to-date passport and ID, hopefully in time for my flight, then I'd be on my way.

Not wanting Zora to know I was leaving, I checked in at the caterers, but kept our conversation to the immediate business of food. "So you're okay with running things?"

She flitted from one workstation to another, overseeing the staff. "Yes, no problem. Thank you for giving me the opportunity. I think I'm going to enjoy it."

Confident my business would be in capable hands, I purchased a map of Croatia and a travel guide at the bookstore, to affirm my decision to leave the country. A late lunch consisted of McDonald's takeout on the living room couch, flipping through the book, and deciding which sites I wanted to visit.

When Jim called and asked why I hadn't answered his calls, I told him I was busy running a few errands.

"I can come back and give you a hand," he said. "For a few days. I'll get a flight…."

"No, no. Don't do that. Thanks, but… this is something I need to do myself. It won't be much longer, I promise."

I hated lying to Jim. But if he knew what I planned on doing, he'd stop me before I could set foot in the airport and haul me back to Lake Kipling, kicking and screaming. How could I explain that I needed to go back to the past to unravel my parents' secrets and understand the reasons for their unexpected deaths before moving forward with my own life?

"Let me say hello to the kids," I said, tears tickling my cheeks. "I love you."

The overnight courier rang my bell not long after, presenting me with the package I'd been anxiously awaiting. Svjetlana Babic and all her official documents, verifying she still existed, stared back at me.

The locks had all been changed, the lawyer and accountant were taking care of the bills in my absence, the business would continue without me, and I'd be ready to return to my life when I got back. Hopefully, with all my questions answered.

That evening, I found my parents' Canon camera. Even if they themselves had never returned to Croatia, I'd have photos of their homeland to treasure. I made sure Grandma's phone number and address were in my purse so I'd be sure to get to my destination. Feeling my parents' rings inside, I glanced at the simple gold band I'd switched to my right hand since my arrival in Hamilton, to keep the existence of my family from being common knowledge, and a pang of guilt shot through me. I was lying to my husband. Shutting him and the kids out of my life. I may as well have been cheating on Jim—something I would never in a million years do—keeping secrets and not inviting him to come with me. With a few twists, I removed my wedding ring and placed it, along with my parents' bands, into their lock box.

Whatever I encountered in Croatia, I would face it as Svjetlana Babic. Whether or not Stefan was involved in what happened to my parents, I had no idea what dangers awaited me there. Although I hadn't run into Stefan in Hamilton, he may well have assigned someone to follow me. I couldn't risk him finding out my new identity. Until I could be certain my parents' accident was simply that, I refused to put my family at risk along with myself. Once I had answers, I would bury Svjetlana Babic permanently and return to my happily ever after as Cheryl MacGregor.

I called Haley to let her know where I would be, in case of an emergency, and to give her a house key and the alarm code so she could check on things. After the taxi dropped me off in front of the airport, I called Jim.

"I'm leaving today for Croatia for a week or two to visit my grandma. I want to see where my parents were born, where they grew up."

A few seconds of silence followed. I waited for the explosion.

"You're what? Cheryl? Why on earth would you do that? Why now?" His voice rose in volume, then he asked, subdued, "And why didn't you tell me?"

"I'm telling you now. It was a spur-of-the-moment decision. I was afraid people would try to talk me out of going." Jim, in particular. And Zora. "But I've decided I need to go back to the past, my parents' past, before I can move forward with my life. I need to make sense of what happened to them. I'm positive it has nothing to do with Stefan. Please don't worry about me."

Silence again.

"I *will* be back," I assured him. "But, I want to visit their birthplace, to feel closer to them. Please try to understand. And give the kids a big hug from me." I couldn't bear to say goodbye to them myself.

Jim remained quiet, no doubt considering how to stop me. But he knew, better than anyone, how stubborn I could be. Arguing would only result in me digging my heels in deeper. "I'm going to miss you. And the kids… Cheryl… think about them. Don't stay away much longer."

I gave him Grandma's phone number and address. "I'll let you know when I'm coming back."

"I'll be waiting for you. I love you."

When I walked through the glass doors of Toronto International Airport, I nearly turned around, ready to abandon my plans. I'd never been to the airport before. The vast space, the escalators, and people, the counters, the signs—it made me dizzy. Where did one even begin to figure out where to go? "Now what?' I asked out loud to no one. If I couldn't figure this out in my own country, what was I going to do in a foreign one?

"Just follow the signs," a man said, noticing my distress and pointing to Departures.

The flight was scheduled to leave at 8:15 pm. Luggage checked in and boarding pass in hand, I bought a coffee and chocolate chip muffin before going through security. I couldn't believe the size of the airport. As I walked past stores, restaurants, and lounges, it struck me that it was a city in its own right.

I'll be okay. People fly all the time.

The thought of the enclosed space and of being above the clouds was starting to affect me. I'd brought several paperbacks with me. Immersing myself in a fictional world always helped when I felt stressed.

A while later, heading down the jetway, I patted myself on the back, proud of what I was doing. I'd made a big decision to forge ahead with my future. There I was, on my own, getting on a plane, going to a different country. I hummed a song about leaving on a jet plane.

My confidence took off once I boarded, found my seat, and buckled in. Even though I had chosen to be in the middle row of seats, the walls of the plane felt constrictive. People boarding pressed in on all sides of me. I whipped my head around, searching for an escape hatch, and when I realized it wouldn't do me any good once we were thousands of feet in the air, a full-blown panic attack washed over me. I unbuckled my seatbelt and scrambled to get off the plane.

"Excuse me, I need to leave," I said to the person sliding into the seat next to me.

"Svjetlana!" she exclaimed. "What a coincidence! Oh, I like what you've done with your hair, and…." She gestured up and down, indicating my makeover.

Stopping to take a good look at her, I realized I knew her. Sort of. It was Draga, the woman who spoke to me at the funeral, then led Zora away. What was she doing on my plane?

Curiosity overpowered anxiety, and I settled into my seat. "I wasn't expecting to see anyone I know on the plane," I said. What were the odds of meeting someone who went to your parents' funeral on a plane headed to Europe a week later?

"I'm going back home," she explained in her accented English. "I was visiting family in Hamilton for the last few weeks. When I heard what happened to your parents, I couldn't believe it. Such a terrible thing."

The plane filled with passengers, and I realized that if I was going to back out of this trip, it was going to have to be right away. How to go about excusing myself and walking off the plane, I wasn't sure, but I didn't imagine anyone would try to stop me.

"Where are you going?" At first, I thought Draga was referring to the fact that I was about to bolt off the plane, or at least strongly thinking of it. "Do you have family to visit in Croatia, maybe?"

"Yes, my grandma still lives there."

"Oh, that's nice. I'm sure she'll be glad to see you. Where exactly does she live?"

I told her it was a tiny village she wouldn't have heard of. "What about you?"

Draga said she was from a small town, but now lived in the nearby city of Orakia, on the Danube River. When she said this, I was surprised, but then I remembered she was a friend of my parents from back home. So, of course, she would be from a town close to Molono. "How did you meet my parents?"

"At somebody's house. There wasn't much for young people to do. We'd have a party every Saturday night. People went from one village to another. You got to meet a lot of people."

When I asked how well she knew my parents, she told me it was a long time ago, and her memory wasn't all that clear. "We saw each other here and there. When they moved to Canada, they sent an odd letter now and then. It's good to reach out to old friends, but everyone goes on with their own life and loses touch sooner or later."

Our conversation ceased as the announcement came over the speakers.

Ladies and gentlemen, welcome aboard Lufthansa Flight 243 from Toronto to Munich...

In my surprise at seeing Draga and curiosity about her relationship with my parents, I didn't realize the plane had taxied down the runway, ready for takeoff. The engine roared, and the rumble underneath my feet scared the life out of me as the plane prepared to take off. It was too late to back out.

The plane tilted upwards, and the change in pressure plugged my ears as we ascended skyward. Holding tightly onto the armrests on either side of me, I closed my eyes and imagined myself lying on a beach, gazing up at the clouds. Draga asked if I was afraid of flying.

"It's my first time," I admitted, the words strange, as though coming from somewhere other than me. "So yes, I'm a little nervous." That was an understatement. Any bravado I'd felt before boarding the plane had long deserted me.

Draga assured me everything would be fine. "They'll be coming around with headphones soon so you can watch a movie, if you like. I usually read when I fly. The good thing about flying overnight is you sleep most of the time."

She removed a book from her bag and opened it. I followed suit to get my mind off the fact that I was in a heavy metal vehicle somehow slicing through the air thousands of feet above ground, heading toward the Atlantic Ocean. Although I had learned about the principles of flight in Science class, I didn't understand *why* they worked.

I had brought along the paperback from the care package on my doorstep — *Where Are You Now?* Draga seemed absorbed in whatever she was reading. I asked if it was a good book.

"Oh yes, very good. It's a thriller. I read slow, my English is not so good."

Her English was a lot better than my Croatian. "I like thrillers, too. This is the one someone just gave me." I showed her the cover and told her about the enormous gift basket someone left at my door.

"Isn't that nice? People can be so thoughtful." She showed me the cover of her book—*Pandora's Daughter*.

Sometime later, after the attendants served our meals, and we each had a couple glasses of wine, Draga fell asleep with the book closed on her lap. As much as I would have liked to join her, my nerves were wound tight. Darkness cocooned me, with some light from the screen, and I tried to focus on what was happening in the movie, when the plane jolted. Then again. People around me didn't seem terribly concerned. When the plane rattled the water glass on my tray, the pilot announced we were experiencing turbulence. The plane shook enough to wake Draga. Holding onto my glass with one hand and grabbing the arm rest with the other, I tried to hold myself in place, steeling myself for whatever was coming.

"Are we going to crash?" I panicked, heart thumping, but Draga remained calm.

"It's just turbulence. It's okay. This happens sometimes. Don't..."

The plane's sudden drop cut short her words. Some people screamed, me the loudest. My body jolted this way and that; if not for the restraining belt, I would have flown out of my seat. Draga assured me it would be over soon.

Wouldn't it be ironic if I died while going back to my parents' birthplace to investigate if their lies had something to do with their deaths? I wouldn't even be buried properly for my family to mourn at my grave if my body sank to the bottom of the deep blue ocean, never to be found. My glass of water had long since flown out of my hand, and rolled down the aisle. Whatever lights had been on, flickered.

Then it all stopped. The plane leveled off, and the jostling ended. "See, it's all fine." Draga held onto my arm to reassure me. "Turbulence is perfectly normal. Sometimes it is worse than other times, though. Are you okay?"

"Thank you."

"For what?"

"For being here. I don't think I could handle this on my own." My body shook as tears flowed, even though the plane had righted itself.

"Yes, you could. You can handle anything. You're a strong young woman." She patted my arm, and told me to try to get some sleep. That was easier said than done. I worried that if I fell asleep I wouldn't wake again.

Getting up to go to the bathroom, I wobbled toward the back of the plane and the WC signs. Everyone settled back into what they had been doing — sleeping, watching a movie, reading. On my way back down the aisle, someone called my name.

"Lana?"

It must be some other Lana.

"Lana! Over here!" I turned to my right, and Matija waved from the middle row, an elderly woman seated to his left. "Come sit." He indicated the vacant seat to his right.

"What a surprise! What are you doing here?" I wondered whether everyone I knew had followed me onto the plane. Who else might I meet if

74

I continued to walk up and down the aisles?

"I am going back home," he stated, then raised his eyebrows. "You look different. Nice change. And you? Where you are going?"

I explained I was going to visit my grandma. When I asked Matija where he was from, he said, "Not far from your village. Is a small country."

I knew it wasn't *that* small. The Eastern Croatian village my parents were from had a population of 237, and these two strangers I had just recently met knew my mom and dad. A lot of my parents' friends in Canada came from Croatia, but didn't know them from the old country. Except for Zora, who came from the same village.

"Did you know my parents well?" I had been wanting to ask him that since he showed up at their funeral.

"No, not well. We were... how do you say... not friends, just... we met at dance, we talk... And then I meet their daughter in Canada. Like they say, is small world, no?"

"No, yes, I guess it is. Well, I'd better get back to my seat."

I considered the odds of him being on the same flight with me, and with Draga. My guardian angels, maybe. I had thought I could do this alone, but I was grateful to have Draga sitting next to me. And seeing Matija, the man who had rescued me twice, a familiar face, was comforting. Nonetheless, I wondered why my parents had been shocked when I mentioned him.

Sounds and smells awoke me sometime later. I must have been able to doze off, secure in the knowledge that I wasn't alone on the plane. Familiar faces had a way of making one feel at home. Eating breakfast with Draga, I remembered the breakfasts Mom and Dad, and I had shared, talking about the day ahead. There wouldn't be any more meals together, but the memories remained.

As the pilot told us to prepare for landing, I smiled. More memories awaited me on this trip. Mom's mom was there; my parents' homeland held an allure. I didn't even flinch when the plane landed, bouncing up and down a couple of times before rolling down the runway to Munich airport. I was on a new continent, on my way to the homeland where I had been conceived.

Chapter Fifteen

"Well, here we are, Svjetlana," Draga said as we unbuckled our seatbelts. "Why don't we stick together on the flight from here to Belgrade?"

That sounded like a plan. Draga was familiar with the whole process of disembarking and heading to the connecting flight. The vastness of the airport struck me, just as it had done in Toronto. All the space, the people, the confusion. Draga maneuvered us through to the departure gate for Belgrade, with a bathroom stop in between.

As we waited to board, Draga told me to prepare for this plane to be a lot smaller. "The good thing is we'll only be on it for about an hour."

By the time we landed in Belgrade and navigated our way through the airport, I considered myself an experienced traveler. We picked up our luggage at the carousel.

"I have someone picking me up. Can we give you a lift?" Draga asked.

"No, thanks. I'm renting a car." Although I'd neglected this small detail, I assumed I could take care of it at the airport.

"Okay, if you're sure."

Pointing out the sign indicating car rentals, Draga kissed both my cheeks and left. "Maybe we'll meet again."

Exhaustion and excitement hit me at once. I'd done it. Survived my first flight. Soon I would be home. The home where my parents grew up. The home where they fell in love.

I dragged my luggage along to the car rental area, getting in line. A tap on my shoulder startled me.

"You look lost, mala." The corners of his mouth turned up. Did he just call me babe? The translation was unclear. "Poor little girl all alone in a strange country. You never know what could happen." Matija spoke using a mixture of English and his native language.

"I'm fine, thanks. Just need to book a rental."

"Okay. Maybe I see you again sometime." He left me at the counter.

The woman behind the desk shook her head. "No, sorry. No cars left." I asked her to check again. She shrugged and indicated I could use the taxi service.

An hour and a half in a taxi? There had to be another way. I tried another car rental booth only to be told the same thing. As I moved to a third booth, I noticed Matija watching me, an amused expression on his face.

"You should book ahead," he said as he approached me. "Cars are very popular. I can give you a lift, if you like."

"Yes, thank you," I said, grateful to have a way out of the airport. "I'd appreciate it. We seem to be bumping into each other a lot."

"Must be fate. Lucky for you, I'm going your way." Matija's smile widened.

In the rental, heading to our destination, I asked where exactly he was from.

"It is a small town in Serbia, sharing the border with Croatia. Just across the Danube River."

Serbia. That's right. Mom told me he's Serbian. Like Stefan.

"Are you a friend of Stefan's?" I thought a direct approach might be best. "Do you work for him?"

Matija kept his eyes on the road. "Stefan? Stefan who?"

When I mentioned Stefan's last name, Matija shook his head. "Sorry, no. He is a friend of yours?"

"No. Just an acquaintance." I left it at that. "And tell me again, just how well, exactly, did you know my parents?"

"Like I said. Not that well. Acquaintances, as you say. We met at a dance at somebody's house. It was in your village, in Molono. I went with my brother one night. He knew a lot of people, liked to party, liked the girls. You know." He turned to me for a second and winked, adding, "Girls can get you into a lot of trouble."

So can guys.

I settled in for the long drive, rock music on the radio, hoping I hadn't misjudged Matija.

Not every Serbian knows Stefan.

Not every Serbian is a member of the Mafia. Not every Serbian is like Stefan. Jesse wasn't.

In the silence that followed, my thoughts wandered, taking me back to the seedy bar where Jesse worked part-time, the place where I met and fell for Darko, the bar owner's son. My first encounter with Stefan, his dad, was the day I told Darko I was pregnant.

"You're better off without him," Jesse had said after Darko broke up with me. "He's bad news."

"What do you mean? He seemed really nice," I justified my relationship with Darko, although he dumped me after I slept with him. I was sure Jesse was jealous because I'd fallen for another guy. "He always treated me well. He said he loved me. I don't understand why he doesn't want me anymore."

Jesse scanned the alleyway and turned to check the back exit of the bar where he worked to help pay for his university education. "I tried to warn you to stay away from Darko and that gang of his. His dad, Stefan, heads up the Serbian Mafia in town, and he's grooming Darko to take over his operations someday."

"That's ridiculous. I don't believe that."

"What do you know about his family?" continued Jesse. "What has he told you?"

"Nothing. I mean, nothing that ludicrous. His dad owns the bar and quite a few other businesses."

Jesse put his arm around me and said he was sorry I was hurting, but it was all for the best. "You need to forget about Darko." He kissed me on the forehead, and I was tempted to do just that.

But there was more to my relationship with Darko than Jesse knew.

That afternoon, I drove up the circular driveway to Darko's grand two-story home to tell him what I hoped was good news, I thought his home was rather ostentatious, even for a businessman such as his dad. Darko met me at the door.

"What are you doing here?" he said as he ran a hand through his thick head of hair. "It's not a good time. My dad's here." He turned around and glanced down the hallway.

"Well, what is a good time, then? I've been calling you and leaving messages. You don't seem to want to see me anymore at all!"

"Calm down. You're hysterical."

As I pushed my way past him into the entrance hallway, I shouted, "I'm hysterical, am I? I'll show you hysterical." My hormones were getting the best of me, but I couldn't seem to stop. "I'm not going to let you push me aside like some toy you've gotten tired of. I love you! I want us to be together, to be a family. When were you planning to introduce me to your dad? After our child is born?"

Darko's mouth flew open. "What are you talking about?" he asked, stunned.

"I'm pregnant! What are you going to do about it?"

"What? How do I know it's even mine?" he asked, trying to escort me back outside.

"Of course it's yours! I haven't been with anyone else. You're going to be a dad. We're going to be a family."

At that point, a door near the entry hall opened, and Darko's father emerged. A tall, dark, handsome, solemn-looking man in his early fifties, he barked, "Darko! In the kitchen, now!"

Darko obeyed and followed him to the back of the house, leaving me behind in the entrance. Their loud voices carried, a mixture of English and Serbian. I caught snippets of the conversation—"shame our family name", "gold digger", "bastard child"—were a few of the phrases his dad used.

When I heard Darko's response, my blood ran cold. "Get rid of her", "deal with her", and "gone" were words I hadn't expected to hear him say.

I pushed the memories aside and concentrated on the good things my life. Jim, the kids. When we arrived in Molono, about three hours out of Belgrade airport, Matija asked if he could call me while I was in the country. "I can show you some of the sights."

He stopped in front of Grandma's house, and I gave him my number, assuming he was being polite and I would never hear from him again. Matija donned sunglasses before exiting his vehicle and dragging out my luggage. I thanked him for the ride, and he hit the gas as I knocked on the front door.

"Baba?" I asked the woman who answered. She looked to be around 70, with gray hair and a pleasantly plump figure. Her face still retained enough youth that traces of Mom were visible in it. "It's me, Svjetlana."

Her hand flew to her chest as if she were about to drop to the ground. She hugged me tight, sobbing and crying out, "Moje dijete, moja mala! My child, my baby!" We cried for the longest time, standing in the doorway, in an embrace that was our first ever.

Grandma held me at arm's length and looked me over, top to bottom, then ushered me into her cozy one-story stucco and stone home to the kitchen area, where we sat at the table. Grandma had lived on her own since the death of my grandfather many years ago. "Why didn't you tell me you were coming?"

"I didn't plan ahead. After the funeral, I decided I wanted to see where Mama and Tata were born and raised. I thought it would help me feel closer to them if I knew more about where they came from." Grandma watched me intently with a smile on her face as I spoke in my not-so-perfect Croatian. I could tell she was searching my face for some part of Mom in me. "I hope it's okay if I stay here for a while."

"Okay? I'm so glad you came. So glad. You poor thing, all alone now." Grandma jumped out of her chair as though she'd just remembered something. "What am I thinking? You must be starving!" She milled about the kitchen in an efficient manner, talking the whole time, telling me she would show me around the village tomorrow after I'd had a chance to rest. "There's not much to see, but it's where your Mama grew up; it's all she knew when she was young."

"And Tata?" I had no idea where his parents lived. I wasn't even sure they were still alive. Dad never talked about them. "Can you show me the house where he grew up?"

Grandma stopped what she was doing for a fraction of a second, then continued placing food on plates. "We'll see." Minutes later, the hand embroidery on the tablecloth disappeared under plates and bowls filled with bread, prosciutto, sausage, cheese, pickles, grapes, and a tossed lettuce and tomato salad, along with a platter of homemade apple strudel. At the sight of food, hunger pangs overtook my fatigue. Grandma brought a flask of homemade wine to the table and poured two glasses. "Eat, eat. You must be hungry. If I had known you were coming, I would have made a decent meal."

Once she satiated my stomach, Grandma showed me the spare bedroom where I deposited my luggage. "This was your Mama's room. Why don't you lie down and rest?"

The small, sparsely furnished room held a twin bed that took up one wall, a wardrobe, and a chest of drawers along another. A hand-sewn quilt covered the bed, with embroidered pillowcases; a cloth doll sat in front of the two pillows. Handmade curtains hung from the window. A hairbrush and a handheld mirror, along with a framed photo of Mom as a young woman adorned the dresser. I could see some similarities between her and myself. She had the same long, wavy brown hair and brown eyes, but not the same facial features. Mom was beautiful, but I'd never thought of myself as such.

I called Jim to let him know I was safely tucked into Mom's childhood bed.

"Okay, good." He let out a sigh of relief, or maybe it was a yawn. "I didn't sleep last night, thinking about you on the plane."

"I didn't sleep much, either. I'm going to turn in early." I hugged Mom's doll to my chest. "Give the kids my love."

I stared at the ceiling as my mom must have done so many times, and felt at peace for the first time since I'd heard about the accident. My eyelids grew heavy, and the room faded as I drifted off. Around midnight, voices from the living area startled me into consciousness as I looked around the unfamiliar room. Opening the door a crack, I stood and listened.

"You know she can't stay," a male voice whispered. "You have to send her back where she belongs."

"I know that. But I want to spend some time with her first." Grandma's voice held an air of authority, as though she expected to have the last say.

"What if she starts to ask questions?"

"We'll worry about that if it happens."

"I'll let everyone know to keep their mouths shut." The door opened and closed quietly as the man left.

Who was he? What did he mean about asking questions and people keeping their mouths shut?

Slipping back into bed, I tried unsuccessfully to go back to sleep. My curiosity piqued, I couldn't wait till tomorrow when I would meet some of the locals. Maybe someone would remember my parents.

Chapter Sixteen

"How about we go for a drive and see some of the beautiful scenery in the area? My neighbor said she'll take us out today," Grandma suggested. During breakfast, I commented that I wanted to walk around the village and feel what it was like for Mom and Dad when they lived there, but Grandma had other ideas. "There's lots of time to take the five-minute walk around this one-horse town another time. It's a beautiful day to go sightseeing."

The sun peeked above an orange and pink background, far too early for anyone to be up, in my opinion, especially with jet lag, but I wanted to witness the dawn as my parents did years ago.

"We'll go to Paruka," she continued, the itinerary already decided. "It's a couple of hours away. You like nature, don't you, Svjetlana? It's a beautiful place."

I could hardly refuse. If Grandma wanted to show me the sights, I'd indulge her. She probably didn't get out much herself.

I might as well get a feel for the country as a whole—the country and culture that is my heritage.

Grandma packed a cooler with food and drinks, told me to wear a sweater and running shoes, and bring along a light jacket. "It can get cool in the mountains, next to the water and all the trees."

I wondered how she managed without a car, living alone in a small village, without the amenities of a larger center.

"Oh, it's never a problem," she explained. "People here help each other. I get a ride into town with neighbors for groceries every week. Whenever I need something, there's always someone more than happy to lend a hand. I try to do what I can for them, of course, even though I'm a helpless old woman."

She looked far from helpless. In fact, she looked perfectly capable of doing whatever needed to be done. Her culinary and domestic skills certainly weren't lacking. Nor was her gardening expertise, I discovered as she took me on a tour of the yard after breakfast.

Grandma's neighbor, Kata, picked us up at eight o'clock. She seemed a bit younger than Grandma.

"Kata's a widow. Her children are grown, and her son and his family live with her," Grandma said, opening the door for me as I lugged out the picnic cooler.

With traffic sparse on the two-lane highway, flat farmland on either side of us, fields of corn, wheat, and vineyards, there wasn't much to sightsee. Once in a while, we drove through the outskirts of a town or village. Eventually, some larger towns materialized, with more traffic and four lanes. Grandma sat in front with Kata, chatting about who was doing what in town. The monotony of the scenery, and the steady drone of the women's voices, along with jetlag, caused me to doze off and on.

"Almost there," Grandma announced, turning around. When I opened my eyes, trees, shrubs, and tall grasses along a narrow lane had replaced farmland. Ahead lay the great expanse of colorful tree-covered mountains in Paruka National Park. "Mount Paruka is the highest spot in the area." From the valley, Grandma pointed to a peak in the distance. I hoped we weren't going to climb it. I didn't know how Grandma and Kata would manage, but I certainly wasn't eager for a trek up the mountain.

Kata parked at the Welcome Center, and we strolled along the path encircling the small lake, then set off through the forest, following the footpath.

"We're not climbing to the top, are we?" I snapped away in all directions with my parents' Canon camera.

With a chuckle, Grandma assured me we were going for a short hike, not mountain climbing. "Stick to the trail," she admonished as I ran ahead of them. "This forest goes on for hundreds of miles."

The chatter of birds and burbling of water accompanied us as we walked, peaceful and calming. The sun, framed against a blue sky with few clouds, warmed the air to perfect hiking temperature. On our left, water flowed over rocks in the winding stream. More rocks, along with trees lined the incline to the right.

"If you watch closely, you'll see many varieties of birds. Maybe even a deer," Kata said. "There's all kinds of wildlife out here."

As we walked across the small wooden bridges that traversed the rivulets and trickling waterfalls, I asked Grandma whether Mom had ever been there.

"No, we didn't travel far from home when your Mama was young. Just the nearby towns for shopping or sometimes to the river for a walk and a picnic."

To our left, the area opened to a small pond populated with ducks and geese nestled amongst reeds and tall grass, and waddling through fallen leaves. Mom, a nature lover like me, would have enjoyed it. To the right, alongside waterfalls that cascaded down the rocky treed slope and crashed to moss-covered rocks below, wooden steps carried us away from the valley floor. Doing my best to slow down and wait for the two older women, I took the opportunity to stop and enjoy the scenery. We met a few people now and then, but mostly we seemed to be alone in the middle of the Croatian forest. I imagined Mom and Dad with me, walking side by side, holding hands.

"Wow, that's cool!" A voice from up ahead drifted down. As I met the teenager and his parents on the steps, I sped up, excited to see what he was talking about. At the next landing, on the side of the rocky cliff, an opening gaped wide. I dared to venture into the mouth of the cave, aware there might be bats or snakes, and explored for a few minutes. Not really my idea of 'cool.' Backing up onto the wooden landing, I waited for Grandma and Kata. When they didn't show up, I wondered what happened to them.

"Baba!" I peered over the railing, down the stairs. Not seeing anyone, I shouted louder. "Kata! Where are you?" I tried not to panic. Grandma told me to stay on the path. As long as I did that, I couldn't possibly get lost. Worst case scenario? If I retraced my steps, I would end up back at the parking lot.

"Svjetlana! Up here!" Grandma's voice came from above. My eyes moved up the side of the cliff and found them on the next landing. I jogged up to join them. "How on earth did you end up behind us?"

After a couple hours of hiking, we circled back to the Welcome Center. "I bet you're hungry," Grandma said. "I've certainly worked up an appetite." She and Kata took the cooler out of the car and spread a tablecloth on a picnic table overlooking the lake, its gentle ripples reflecting autumn colors. While I slept last evening or this morning, Grandma had managed to prepare a lunch of potato salad, bean salad, coleslaw, assorted rolls, salami, baked ham, tomatoes, pickles, and a variety of sweets, along with flavored water. "Kata and I packed a bit of food." There was enough for a small family to join us.

"What do you think, Svjetlana? You like it here in Croatia?" Kata asked. "Maybe you want to stay?"

"Yes, I like it very much." And for the first time since my parents died, I felt something besides grief. Being in the midst of all this beauty, close to where my parents were born, instilled a sense of contentment. "Maybe I would like to stay longer." I noticed Grandma flinch and wondered what that was about.

"I'd love to have you stay, of course. But you have a life back home, the life your parents built for you in Canada. I'm sure you're going to want to get back as soon as possible. How long did you plan to stay, by the way?" Grandma asked.

"I'm not sure." That all depended on how long it took me to find out why my parents had lied to me all my life.

"We'll go for a drive," Kata said after we ate. "Through the mountains."

It hit me fresh, a blow across the chest, as the vision of my parents' accident scene flashed through my mind. I wanted to say I wasn't keen on driving through the mountains, but I held my tongue. Not wanting to be rude, and knowing I needed to face my fear of heights at some point, including mountain cliffs, I kept quiet.

"You should see Ravina," Kata continued. "Do you like castles?"

Who doesn't like castles? But, in the middle of a vast forest?

"Is there a castle here?"

"There are a lot of castles here. They go back to the Middle Ages. It's in ruins, so it's not like you'll see it in its glory. But you might find it interesting."

The narrow, winding road through the mountain wasn't quite what I expected. Trees, shrubs, and rocks covered both sides of the road, so there wasn't much to see. Not until Kata stopped the car and we stepped out did I get a good view of the valley below. Absolutely breathtaking. Wilderness enveloped us—lakes, rivers, waterfalls, trees, rolling valleys, and peaks. A sea of green and autumnal colors against a blue background.

"What's that?" I pointed to a massive stone edifice perched on a peak in the distance, in the midst of the rolling mountains of Paruka forest.

"That is Ravina," Kata answered. "The castle in Paruka. It dates back to the thirteenth century."

The beauty of the stone structure set deep in the woods called to me, although the sense of isolation was overwhelming. I asked if we'd be able to get close to it.

"Oh, yes. You can go right in. It's a little hard to get to, but if you don't mind the climb, it's very nice. A piece of our history."

It was somehow *my* history. That of my ancestors, who likely lived as peasants in some medieval village centuries ago, right here in Croatia. It never occurred to me that I'd be digging that far back when I returned to their homeland to search for my parents' bygone youth. How much of their own history did they know? What did Grandma know?

"Can we go?" The romance of that ancient structure sitting in the midst of all those miles of forest wasn't lost on me. "I'd like to see it."

Grandma and Kata agreed we would stop there.

As the road wound down to the valley, Kata said, "There's a lovely lake at Ravina, at the bottom of the mountain, very popular in summer for swimming. And an old town with lots of history—tourists visit for the heritage, the culture. But you'll have to do some climbing if you want to go inside the castle. We can only drive so far up the mountain it sits on."

We traveled downward, then upward again through mountains and valleys, past villages, trees, lakes, and rivers, ending up on a narrow gravel road. After passing some old homes and a church, we came to a dead end. Kata parked on the side of the road.

"Now we walk. Uphill," Kata announced.

Looking at the steep dirt incline with no railing, I wasn't sure Grandma would make it, but I desperately wanted to visit the castle.

"Will you be okay to climb there?" Doubt came through in my voice.

Grandma shook her head and said she didn't think her old legs could carry her. "It's okay, I've been there before, a few years ago when I was younger. But you go, with Kata."

Kata suggested the two of them stay below and walk through the village shops. "We can meet back at the car."

"Just be careful to stick to the path," Grandma reminded me. "Don't get lost in the forest. And come straight to the car when you're done."

Kata gave me her second car key in case I made it back before they did.

The first part of the climb wasn't bad, but soon my legs ached, and I strained to move upwards. Not many people trekked alongside me. A couple chatted ahead. Another couple greeted me on their way down. The path wound around, making it longer, but also less steep. The surrounding vegetation closed in, feeding my claustrophobia, pushing me forward. Every once in a while, I stopped to rest and catch my breath, gazing up at Ravina.

The castle beckoned me. In one of the doorways, a figure passed, indicating I wouldn't be the solitary visitor; curiosity and desire to enter the stone ruins didn't entirely overpower my fear of being alone with the ghosts of Ravina, but I kept climbing. The ascent took about twenty minutes, including rest time.

Disappointment set in. The 'castle' was a mere shell of its former self, what was left of the moss-covered stone walls standing as a reminder that nothing remains unchanged. It had been battered by time, by nature, probably by man. Shrubs and trees grew throughout the interior, on the floor, rising through the open doorways, threatening to swallow what was left of it.

Yet, it stood as a testament to its history, proof that the past endures. I imagined the ghosts of those who once inhabited it still lingered in the open-air rooms. Did they leave some part of themselves behind when they left this world? No doubt I was not the first person who wondered what the walls would say if they could talk. The plaques erected for tourists were of little help, being difficult to read, weathered, and in need of replacement.

I trod among the vegetation, through the former halls and rooms, up the stone stairs that led nowhere, preserving its beauty on film with one click after another The maze-like layout seemed sinister, leading me from one enclosed space to another. What if I got trapped within the ancient walls? The enormity of the structure blew my mind, even as the stone walls pressed in. I didn't run into anyone, and I wondered what happened to the couple who had been ahead of me, and the person I had seen in the doorway when I looked up earlier. I envisioned the nobility that once walked on the ground where I now stepped with caution. Dad would have loved all this history. It occurred to me that maybe I should have left a trail of breadcrumbs, like Hansel and Gretel. I entered rooms and corridors with no second exit. My sense of direction failed me.

As I searched for a way out, a rustling stopped me in my tracks. Someone else occupied the castle, moving in my direction. Relief flowed over me, knowing I wasn't alone, swallowed up in some ancient ruins with a history no one truly knew.

"Hello?" I called. No answer. I tried again. "Hello? Is someone there?" They must have wandered farther away and couldn't hear.

Continuing along the wall, an open doorway led outside, and I walked away from the structure to look over the town. The view took my breath away. I stood and watched, then turned to gaze back at the ruins, at the arched windows and doorways, set against overgrown bushes.

And I saw him.

Only for a fraction of a second, then he vanished. In one of the windows, he watched, then disappeared before I could be sure of what I had seen. My mind had to be playing tricks on me. No one inhabited the castle. Only me. Only Ravina's ghosts. Only my ghosts.

Yet, I had seen Dad peering down at me from the stone ruins of Ravina castle.

Did the grieving process include seeing dead people or was I simply losing my mind? Why did I only see Dad and not Mom? Was it because his spirit had unfinished business, something to set right?

I stumbled back to the castle, the rocks, and vegetation impeding my progress. Once I tripped, set myself upright again, rubbing my bruised knee. I approached the nearest doorway, shouting, "Dad! Dad! Where are you? Dad!"

As I made my way through the passageways, a young couple appeared from around a corner and asked if I was lost.

"Have you seen a man, about fifty—my Dad?" I didn't mention he was a ghost. When Zora told me my parents' spirits would remain with me, it never occurred to me that she meant literally.

"No, we haven't run into anyone else," the guy said. "Just you. Do you need some help? We were about ready to leave."

"No, it's okay, I'll meet up with him sooner or later." I thanked them and continued my search of the ruins, looking for a sign, some clue, that would lead me to Dad. Nothing but emptiness greeted me, my own voice bouncing off the walls. I climbed the stone steps to the window where I had seen his shape appear, and stared out at the forest. He could be anywhere. He could be nowhere.

It took considerably less time to climb down the steep incline than it did to go up. When I reached the car where Kata and Grandma waited, I decided not to mention what I had seen.

"Well, what did you think? Was it worth it?" Grandma asked.

"Worth it?"

"The climb? Was it as good as you expected? Did you see what you wanted to see?"

"Oh, yes...yes, it was amazing." I saw exactly what I wanted to see. Unfortunately, it was all in my mind. My grip on reality threatened to slip away, leaving me not only orphaned, but mentally unhinged.

We stopped at a tavern on the way home to grab a bite to eat. As I got out of the car, the outline of mountains loomed in the distance. I wondered whether he remained there, roaming from room to room, searching for me.

When we arrived home, the kitchen phone was ringing. Grandma answered and passed it to me.

"Where were you? I've been going crazy thinking something happened. Your phone must be off." Jim sounded frantic, his tone not its usual calm.

In all the excitement, I got so caught up in finding out more about my past, I forgot my present. I should have let Jim know I was going away for the day. Not that I was one of those women who needed her husband's permission for everything. But given my situation, Jim's concern was justified.

"I'm so sorry. I didn't think. We left early to go on a sightseeing trip. We just got back."

"I'm just glad you're okay." After a moment's silence, Jim added, "Where did you go? Did you have a good time?"

After telling him about our excursion, I spoke with Brent for a minute and said hello to Jamie. "Mommy's having a nice trip, but she misses you. I'll see you soon. Love you."

I told Jim not to worry. "This feels right, being here with Grandma, in Mom's old room. I'll be home before you know it."

"I'm glad you're having a good visit. But make sure your phone's on so I can contact you. And Cheryl? Lana? Stay safe. I love you."

"Me, too. I love you, too."

I fell asleep soon after my head hit the pillow, dreaming of Ravina as it might have been in its glory, with me dressed as a princess, and Jim, my knight in shining armor, riding up to the castle on his white horse, to rescue me from myself.

Chapter Seventeen

During breakfast, Grandma wondered how I wanted to spend the day.

"Do you think you could show me around town today?" I asked. "I'd like to see where Dad lived."

Her expression changed from cheerful, her eyes shifting when I talked about Dad. "Okay, we'll go for a walk this morning, and you can meet some of the locals. But there's nothing exciting to see here."

"Which way is Dad's house?" We exited through the side door, and walked past the garden and fruit trees. A small barn sat at the back of the yard.

Grandma indicated we would be going to the left as we reached the sidewalk. "Your dad's family moved away. I don't know where, but I'll show you the old house. It's boarded up now."

No traffic passed, so we walked along the narrow asphalt roadway, past a variety of homes with red roofs, some of them newer two-story red brick homes, others older stone houses, but mostly white stucco buildings. Some of the houses stood close together, whereas scrubland adjoined others. Along the way, Grandma waved to people in their gardens or on their way to the fields. The surrounding farmland, the hills in back yards, the wilderness of forest, cradled the village. Farm machinery stood in front of homes or over to the side. Grandma explained that most people still farmed, and the fields were situated away from the residential area. We passed a small schoolhouse that looked newly built in contrast to most of the homes.

When Grandma said it was a five-minute walk around town, she downplayed the size of the town more than a little. It took twice that long to reach the highway. To the left, where the highway led out of town, a tunnel carved out of the rocky hillside accommodated vehicles. In the other direction lay the downtown, consisting of a small food store, a tavern, and a church, with more homes stretching out on the highway. At the church, we turned right, walked down the other main road in the village, then followed the curved road leading off to the left, passing several houses until we reached a dead end.

An old boarded-up story and a half-red brick house with weeds, brush, and trees growing all around had been abandoned to the hillside it backed against. Scrubland bordered one side, and the forest the other. Across from it, on the corner lot, more brush covered the ground. Houses were visible down the road that led away from the corner.

"This is where your father's family lived, but like I said, they're long gone." Grandma began to walk away, but I remained, staring as though I expected Dad to poke his head out from one of the boarded-up windows. I took a shot of the front of the house. Maybe his ghost would materialize in the photo. "There's nothing left here. Come."

I scurried to the door and pushed on it, but found it locked. I had no choice but to follow Grandma. We followed the road leading from the empty lot, which curved back toward Grandma's road.

"And there you have it—Molono." Grandma said this with a bit of a flourish and a wave of her arms. "So what do you think? Not as exciting as the city you're from, I'm sure."

I couldn't argue with that. Even my small town was a metropolis in comparison. But this village, although small and quiet, had its charm. It seemed to have been plopped down between the rocky hills that flanked it, and then forgotten by time. "Is there anything else here? Stores, parks? Restaurants?"

Grandma chuckled. "There are the woods. There are the fields. There's the river."

"What's on the other side of the river?"

Grandma stopped laughing. "Serbia. Stay away."

Having read about the history of Serbia and Croatia, I understood the animosity between the two nations hadn't been entirely smoothed over, as Serbs and Croats had clashed, not only during the War of Independence, but long before that. I didn't question Grandma's advice, but of course, what she didn't know wouldn't hurt her.

As we headed home, my phone buzzed. I answered immediately. "Hi, honey. How's everything?"

Silence for a moment.

"Matija. Sorry to disappoint you. You were expecting someone else?"

"Oh, no, I just thought...." I'd forgotten I'd given him my number. Why was he calling me? "It's nice to hear from you, Matija."

"I was wondering if you're not busy, could I take you around and show you some of the sights today?"

"I... no, I'm not busy."

"Good. We could have lunch, then sightsee for the afternoon. Can I pick you up in front of the tavern on the highway?"

"Yes, that would be fine. What time?"

Matija asked if I could be ready in 45 minutes. After explaining (my version of the truth) to Grandma that I was going to spend the day with a friend I met in Canada, who was visiting Croatia, I changed clothes, brushed my teeth and hair again, and touched up my makeup.

"Be careful, Svjetlana. People here are friendly, but you still have to watch out for strangers," Grandma warned.

I assured her I'd be fine and strode to the end of the road to meet my Serbian 'friend'. Acquaintance. Handsome older man who rescued me. Some guy I didn't know from Adam who seemed to have worried my parents.

I didn't need to wait. He leaned up against his car in front of the tavern, shades pulled over his eyes. When he saw me approach, he waved.

"I am glad you decided to come," he said, holding the passenger door for me.

When he turned the car around and headed in the opposite direction from what I expected, I panicked. Alone in a strange country, in a car with someone I didn't really know, I realized my mistake. No one knew where I was going. I had my cell phone with me, but what good would that do? I reminded myself that Matija had rescued me on more than one occasion, and he'd been to my parents' funeral, so he surely couldn't mean me harm.

"Where are we going?" I gripped the door handle as he drove through the tunnel and sped down the flat, straight stretch of highway, away from Molono.

"Serbia. I want to show you where I'm from."

Just great.

What was I thinking, going off with this stranger who my parents had told me was no friend of theirs? What if there was more to it than simple discrimination because of his heritage? Worse yet, what if he *did* work for Stefan, and he caused my parents' deaths? Had I unwittingly put myself into the path of danger?

Jim is going to kill me when he finds out how foolish I've been. If I live to tell him.

"I don't want to go far. Grandma might worry. For all I know, she'll get the police out after me if I'm gone too long." I hoped to convince him to turn the car around and take me back.

"It's not far. Just across the bridge, on the other side of the river. We'll stop for lunch, and we can talk about what you'd like to see. You'll be home before supper." Matija stole a glance at me, but I couldn't read his expression, with the sunglasses hiding his eyes. "It's okay. You're safe with me."

We passed through several small towns, the road becoming curvy now and then. When the river appeared to our left, I set aside my reservations, excited about my surroundings. "Is that the Danube?"

Matija confirmed it was. "Do you like to swim with the fishes?"

What did he mean by that? Did I misunderstand? "Not with fish, no."

He laughed and said there was a nice lake with a beach in the Danube area where we were heading, and it was also famous for its fish hatchery.

"It's too cold for the beach, isn't it?"

"Seventeen degrees Celsius, is nice for October, no?"

"I didn't bring a swimsuit."

Another chuckle escaped him. "That's too bad. It's not a nudist beach. I wouldn't want you to get arrested your first time in Serbia. But maybe you can dip your toes in the water and tell your friends you swam in the Danube."

As we drove through a bushy section of highway, my fear blossomed into a frozen terror. Would I become a victim, along with my parents, courtesy of Matija? What was to stop him from taking me down one of the side roads, and dumping my body in the bush? Throwing me into the Danube?

I tilted my head sideways just enough to steal another look at him without being obvious. His eyes held the asphalt as he maneuvered the winding road. He seemed harmless enough in his jeans and button-down navy shirt, sleeves rolled up. Nice to look at, with his thick wavy black hair and chiseled face.

"What do you do for a living, Matija?" I hoped to put my mind at ease by learning more about him.

"Family business."

"What kind of business?

"This and that. We have some properties we look after, nothing too exciting."

With all the twists and turns in the last twenty minutes, the Danube flowed directly in front of us instead of to the left. We crossed the bridge spanning the river, from Croatia to Serbia. I failed to understand how living on the other side of a bridge made people different. Why were my parents and grandma so adamant that I stay away from Serbians?

Why did people fight wars? Wasn't there a better way to solve disagreements?

Was I prejudiced like my parents, thinking Matija could be dangerous simply because of his ethnicity?

"Here we are." He parked the car in front of a restaurant on the Danube. "I hope you're hungry. The food here is great."

Matija and I had begun to speak a new language—a mixture of English and Croatian/Serbian. We seemed to have little trouble understanding each other in spite of that.

"It looks lovely," I replied. The location of the restaurant was enough for me, never mind the quality of food.

"There's a patio in the back, on the river, if you'd like to sit out."

"That'd be nice."

We were seated at an outside table with a gorgeous view. Matija went over the menu with me and helped select my meal. He said the seafood was excellent. When I explained my allergy, he suggested the stuffed veal cutlet and roasted potatoes, along with Serbian salad, while he himself substituted trout for veal. He also asked for a bottle of Sauvignon Blanc.

"How old are you, mala?" He teased me with a grin, using Serbian for 'baby' or 'little girl.' I still wasn't sure what he meant by it.

"A lot older than I look."

"Good enough for me." He winked as he filled my glass. "But seriously, when is your birthday?"

"November."

"November? What year?"

"1978."

He drew his brows together and studied my face. "Hmm… thirty years." He stared.

"How old are you?"

"Old." He snapped out of it and chuckled. "Forty-four."

We ate our meal while people walked, jogged, biked, and kayaked past. I imagined Jim across from me, the two of us enjoying a romantic luncheon as the Blue Danube flowed by.

"We'll go for a walk along the water after lunch, if you like," Matija said. "Do you enjoy boat rides? They have a river cruise from Belgrade. We could go tomorrow."

What would *I* do if Jim decided to take off and go sightseeing with a beautiful woman? I'd be heartbroken. Try to make him jealous in turn. Put my foot down. Get a divorce.

No, never that.

Maybe I'd kill her.

It felt like a betrayal, but I could hardly turn down a cruise on the Danube, so I said I would love to go. Just because Matija was an attractive male didn't mean we couldn't be friends.

I swallowed my guilt with another sip of wine and gazed across the water.

"And what about nature? There's a nice park here," he suggested.

"Sounds good." I'd had enough walking yesterday, but I didn't want to disappoint Matija. He seemed excited to show me around, and he put me at ease, my stomach full and the scenery calming. After the third glass of wine, though, I was a little wobbly on my feet as we exited the restaurant.

Matija steadied me. "You'll be okay. We'll walk it off."

Swans swam on the water and walked along the grassy area bordering it. It was magical, just like Ravina yesterday. "Shoot. I forgot my camera," I said. "I want to take a photo of the two of us with the swans."

"Come. I'll take one with my phone." Matija pulled me next to him and snapped a few pictures with the Danube in the background.

We strolled on the sandy part of the shore, and as Matija suggested earlier, I took off my running shoes and dipped my toes in the water. My feet sank in, then my ankles, and the next thing I knew, I was up to my knees with my jeans rolled up. Matija joined me and linked his arm with mine.

"Just so you don't fall," he said.

It must have been the wine. For the first time since my parents died, happiness swept through me, lifting the fog that had enshrouded me.

As we continued our walk, he removed his arm from mine. The path took us beside the river (thankfully, there was a railing for me to hold onto), through the woods, and to a marshy area. Others were out enjoying the day, both on the water and along the path.

True to his word, Matija had me home in time for supper. He dropped me off in front of the house. "I'll pick you up at eight o'clock tomorrow for the boat cruise."

"Sounds good. Thanks."

"Who's that man you were with? Where's he from?" Grandma asked, her arms crossed, as I came through the door. "I thought you had a boyfriend in Canada. Be careful you don't get into trouble."

It was like hearing my mother's voice again. Ghosts do exist. They don't always take the form you expect.

Chapter Eighteen

Matija waited in his car in front of the house the next morning. With the tinted windows, only his silhouette was visible. Grandma asked his name and how I knew him.

"Matt. I told you before, I met him in Canada." It wasn't an outright lie. When she asked what she should tell my 'boyfriend', Jim, if he happened to call the house, I added, "Just tell him I'm sightseeing. And that I'm perfectly fine."

I wanted to say, 'Tell him I love him and the kids. And I miss them.'

But as Svjetlana Babic, a single, recently orphaned woman, I had no husband and children. And until I could be 100 percent certain my parents weren't murdered, whether by Stefan, Matija, or someone from my parents' past, any thread connecting me to the MacGregors needed to be cut.

We drove an hour and a half to Belgrade, over flat terrain with fields on either side. Before long, the two-lane road stretched into a major four-lane highway. Once again, the sun-dappled trees decorated a beautiful fall day. Matija, sunglasses covering brown eyes, turned up the radio, tuned to a Serbian rock station.

"Do you have a girlfriend?" I wondered how he managed to be single at 44, with his good looks and charm.

"I have lots of girlfriends." A mischievous upturn in one corner of his mouth told me he was toying with me. "None are serious."

"So why are you spending time with me?"

"I like you, Lana. And I thought maybe you could use some fun after what happened. You seem so sad, like a lost little bird fallen from the nest, squawking for Mama."

"I miss my parents."

"I know you miss them, but you have to live your life. Don't you think they would want you to be happy?"

"Yes." I didn't try to explain that I was searching for them, that I felt them with me everywhere I went, but couldn't seem to quite grasp them. I didn't tell him that I'd come to Croatia hoping to find some part of them still there. I understood they were gone and buried in the cemetery in Hamilton, but I couldn't shake the feeling they were still alive somewhere. "I know they would want me to be happy. It's just hard."

"Of course, it's hard," Matija acknowledged. "They were your parents. You love them, and you miss them. But you're still alive. There's a whole world for you to discover and lots of people to meet. Life is for the living. You need to live it. What about you? You have a boyfriend?"

"Um... sort of."

"Sort of?" He took his eyes off the road long enough to flash me a cheeky grin. "Lucky guy, your 'sort-of' boyfriend."

As we approached the city, fields gave way to condos and commercial properties, more lanes, overpasses, and signs appeared, and it felt similar to being on the 403 back home. The world wasn't so different thousands of miles away from home, and neither were people when it came down to it.

"The cruise is later in the afternoon. We have about five and a half hours. There is lots to do here. Shopping, museums. We could visit an old church or palace. There are parks and gardens. A zoo. What do you like?" Matija asked as we neared Belgrade.

"I don't know. I'm sure I'd like any of those. I like animals and nature. I'd really like to see some of the history, too, the old buildings."

"Okay, there is a big park not far from the river cruise. There is a little bit of everything, if you don't mind a lot of walking. An old fortress and monuments, nice view, and the zoo."

Matija parked the car, and we strolled past war monuments, into the stone fortress. He explained the citadel dated back to the 3rd century BC and contained the city within its walls. Like Ravina castle, it impressed upon me the fact that the past stays with us. Matija recounted some of its history as we walked along cobblestones, through archways and tunnels, up stone steps, pointing out the significance of statues, while I snapped away, as I'd been doing the last three days, preserving every minute in photos. I would show my family once I got home, and tell my children this was the homeland of their grandparents, while reminding them we were MacGregors, and that was all that mattered going forward.

Although Matija presented a lot of information for me to take in, he held my attention. Not only did I receive a great history lesson, but the natural beauty of trees, grass, flowers, and birds surrounded us. Absolutely amazing views of the city and the river from the top of the cliff made it perfect.

"We'll get a light snack at the coffee shop, if that's okay, and have a nice dinner later," Matija suggested as we overlooked the Danube.

Out of the corner of my eye, someone familiar strolled on a lower level of the fortress. He vanished out of sight before I could register whether I'd actually seen Dad or someone who looked like him. Why was Dad following me?

"Lana?" Matija brought me back to reality. "Is that okay?"

"Yes, yes. It's good." I wasn't sure what I was agreeing to. Later, as we watched the big cats at the zoo, I almost forgot about Dad. Matija was right — I had a lot to live for, even in that very moment. The beauty of nature, the company of a new friend, the knowledge I had yet to accumulate. History was important, but it was what came out of it that mattered.

"We'd better head out," Matija said around 3:30. "I called ahead for our cruise tickets, but we need time to park and get to the boat."

We said goodbye to the giraffes and hurried to the car.

During the short drive to the river dock, Matija asked, "Did you enjoy it?"

I told him it was great, that I wished it could have lasted longer. "I can't wait for the boat tour. To actually be on the Danube. It's the dream of a lifetime. This has been a great day. Thank you."

"It's not over yet, Lana." Matija turned to me as he parked the car, placing his hand on mine. "There's so much more I'd like to show you."

Had I been leading him on?

We boarded the small tour boat, and Matija found a table, ordered himself a beer, and a glass of wine for me. Through the large windows, the fortress spread out on the cliffside. As the boat set off on the river, a view of the city skyline treated our eyes. The commentary, given in both Serbian and English, allowed both of us to understand it in its entirety.

Most people onboard watched the scenery. Except for one man. He watched *me*. I felt his stare before I glanced in his direction. In his forties, dark hair and brown eyes, no distinguishing features. And yet, I knew I had seen him before. Had he been following me? I remembered Grandma saying most people were friendly, but you still had to be careful. He looked away when he noticed me spying on him. I turned the other way, my cheeks flushed. No doubt he considered me rude, staring at him.

It occurred to me why he seemed familiar. He had probably been at the fortress, a tourist, like me. My paranoia had the best of me, causing 'ghosts' to appear and people to follow my movements.

"Do you want to go on the deck for a while?" Matija asked.

We grabbed our drinks and exited the cabin, stood on the bow gazing over the river, a bridge up ahead spanning the water. The man followed and stood a distance away, his eyes on the water. I didn't want to cause a scene, so I ignored him. He had as much right to be there as I did.

Matija put his arm protectively around me and told me to be careful as I leaned into the railing. "I don't want to have to fish you out of the river." He laughed as he said it, but I took a step back. With my track record, another accident wouldn't be out of the question.

"I think that man is watching us," I whispered, leaning in closer to Matija. "The one on the other side of the boat."

"What man? I don't see anyone."

When I looked again, no one stood in the spot the man had occupied moments earlier. Either my imagination worked in overdrive, and the men I'd been noticing had nothing to do with me (certainly I hadn't seen my dad), or someone was actually spying on me. I didn't know which possibility was more upsetting — that my mind deceived me or someone knew my every movement.

"He was about forty, just a normal-looking man."

"Maybe he was jealous to see I have such a beautiful young woman," Matija joked as he tightened his grip on me. "Don't worry, you're safe with me. I won't let you out of my sight."

"I have a boyfriend, remember?"

Matija released me, set his hands on the railing, and looked over the blue water as it lapped against the boat. "Sorry, Lana," he said after a moment. "If I offended you. My intentions are…how you say?… honorable?"

The red flush on my cheeks burned. "No, no offense. You've been nothing but kind."

Following the cruise, a delicious dinner on a patio, as the sun set on the Danube, ended a perfect day.

"Thank you," I said when he dropped me off at Grandma's. "It was great, all of it."

"You're welcome. I really enjoyed our time together, Lana. Here, I'll give you my number, and if you ever need anything, give me a call." He handed over a slip of paper and said goodbye.

As he drove off, I wondered whether I would see him again. Probably best if I didn't.

Chapter Nineteen

Enough sightseeing. Time to get down to business. My reasons for this trip across the ocean had nothing to do with wandering through ancient ruins or floating away on the Danube. I came to the land of my parents' youth to discover if their past was linked to their deaths. I needed closure. And beyond that, I needed to find myself. If my parents lied about who they were, then who was *I*? And who was the mystery man whose birth certificate they kept?

The answers lay buried in the small village of Molono. Somewhere in that small community lay the shovel that would uncover the secrets my parents kept from me for thirty years, along with the reason for their lies.

"I'm going for a walk," I informed Grandma the next morning. "To meet some of the locals."

"Let me come with you," she insisted. "I'll introduce you to the right people. They'll be friendlier if I explain who you are, that you're from here. Most of the people in Molono have lived here all their lives, and so have their parents and grandparents. Outsiders stand out."

After breakfast, we strolled to the right, where the road dead-ended at a walking path. The neighboring house was Kata's. We skipped it and the next house.

"An old lady lives there. I'm sure you won't have much in common with her. She's older than me," Grandma said as we continued walking past the next house as well.

"What about here?" I pointed to the third house.

"Just troublemakers. I wouldn't bother getting to know them."

She stopped at the fourth house. "A young unmarried woman lives here with her parents. She's in her twenties. Maybe you'd like to meet her. Tina." The door opened promptly when she knocked.

"Marija! How nice to see you." A woman in her late forties stood in the doorway. "And this must be the granddaughter I've heard about."

Grandma introduced me to Ana, who called her daughter to join us. As we sat around the kitchen table, Ana engaged me in a conversation about what I'd been doing since I arrived in town. Her daughter seemed quiet, introverted—something I could relate to. I hoped she would come out of her shell so we could strike up a friendship. No such luck. She jumped out of her chair, saying it was time to go to work, and disappeared out the door. Grandma and I left shortly after, with Ana telling me to drop by anytime to visit Tina.

At the next house, a woman bent over her garden plot picking vegetables. She called a greeting to Grandma, who waved back, but kept walking. "A busybody," Grandma explained.

The last house had clearly been abandoned some time ago. Next to it, the dirt path at the end of the road led to fields where villagers grew fruits and vegetables. Grandma herself tended a small field of corn, grapes, and other crops. That, and the garden outside her house, allowed Grandma to be rather self-sufficient.

We headed up the other side of the street, only scrubland growing out of the rocky hillside for several hundred feet. As we reached more houses, Grandma introduced me to a few neighbors, mainly older people. "Most of the young people moved away, for work," she said. "No one wants to live here." We passed several homes with boarded-up windows.

By the time we covered the twenty or so houses on the street, I met the inhabitants of about a dozen. "Maybe later, you'd like to visit Tina."

I accompanied Grandma to the small barn, where chickens roamed in a penned area. She collected some eggs to make *palačinke* for lunch. I loved crepes, especially the way Mom made them, with a raspberry jam filling.

Grandma's *palačinke* didn't disappoint, filled with homemade peach jam, topped with fresh peaches. We ate on the back patio, in full sunshine, enjoying one of the few days of decent weather left in October.

"I'm going for another walk," I said after lunch. "To get some exercise."

I jogged toward the highway, past the houses we covered that morning. From the highway, I turned down the other main street in Molono, then followed along to the run-down red brick building at the end, set apart from the others.

Dad's house.

With nothing but scrubland surrounding it, and the woods to the right, it seemed lonely, if a house could be that. This time, I stumbled all the way around, even though thistles, difficult to traverse, impeded my progress. A rocky, overgrown mess, with bushes next to it, comprised the side yard. The back yard, set into a hill that no longer allowed access with its overgrowth, barely allowed enough room to walk past the back of the house, with shrubs encroaching upon the back door. To the right, a bit of flat landscape would have provided a usable lawn, but no one had cut the grass and weeds in ages. Beyond the lawn, the ancient woods spooked me despite the daylight; dark gnarled trunks guarded the secrets beyond, branches loomed above, bombarding the dirt paths with their colorful leaves, warning me to stay out.

I tried the side door again, but it was locked up tight, as was the back door. Gazing up at the front windows, I imagined Dad peering down on the street as a child, but I couldn't feel any sign of him. Maybe it was too long ago. I wondered who he played with as a kid and who he hung out with as a teenager. Were any of his old friends still around?

Houses lined the street a short distance from where I stood. I doubled back the way I came and, starting at the first building, walked down the length of asphalt, knocking on every door, even the boarded-up ones. "Do you remember Janez Babic? From the old red brick house at the end of the road?"

No one had any recollection of Janez Babic living on their street. That was odd, considering some of the people who answered the door were about his age. "No, no Janez Babic." From what Grandma told me, new people didn't move into town, so they must have lived there when Dad was young. They would have been his neighbors. How did they not remember him?

At one house, I thought I might have gotten lucky. "Babic?" a woman asked. "I know the family."

Finally, someone who remembered Dad.

"Not here. The other main street in town. Marija Babic. But, no Janez."

Grandma.

I returned to Grandma's street and tried some of the properties Grandma had skipped that morning. On my third try, I found someone who knew something. "Janez Babic?" the man in his fifties asked.

"Yes, did you know him?"

"I think maybe you mean *Janko*. We went to school together. He moved away some time ago. Why are you asking?"

"He's my father." If this man went to school with Dad, maybe he could tell me about his childhood.

"Your father? I didn't know he had a daughter."

"Yes, he did. I'm Svjetlana."

The man stared at me as if he were trying to figure out a puzzle. "Do you live with your dad?"

"He died a couple weeks ago."

"What? I didn't hear that! I would have gone to his funeral."

He must have been a good friend of Dad's if he would have traveled to Canada to attend his funeral. Why didn't Grandma tell him he died? "Well, Canada *is* far away."

"Canada? Ah, that's where you're from—your accent. What was Janko doing in Canada? I just saw him last month."

I wondered if my lack of fluency in Croatian was causing a misunderstanding. "No, that can't be right. Dad hasn't been back here for a long time."

"Ah, I understand now. You are probably from another Babic family. Maybe from one of the villages close by."

"No, my family's from Molono. My grandmother lives just down the road. Marija Babic."

His brow wrinkled in confusion again. "Marija had three children - Janko,

Petar, and Mimica. Petar lives in Orakio, same as Janko. Mimica went missing years ago."

I tried to make sense of this new information. Were Mimica and Janko, brother and sister, my parents? Was that the big secret they were keeping from me? Did Dad somehow survive the accident and return to Croatia? Is that why I was seeing him everywhere? "Where in Orakia does Janko live? Do you have his address?"

"He visits Marija every couple of weeks. Why don't you ask her?" He gently closed the door as he bid me farewell.

I ran back to Grandma's house and found her in the garden. "Why didn't you tell me Mama has brothers? I have uncles I didn't know about. Why did everyone keep that from me?"

Grandma sat me down on a bench by the garden. "Janko and Petar are your Mama's older brothers. I don't know why she didn't tell you about them."

"Why didn't *you* say anything?"

"You never asked."

For some reason, my parents had lied to me. On top of that, they had kept family members from me. "I'm asking now. Can I go see Janko?" I wanted to be absolutely sure this wasn't the same man who I knew as my father, the 'ghost' I had been seeing. I needed to know why Mom and Grandma had kept Janko a secret.

Grandma hesitated, as though thinking of how to answer my question. "I will call him. See if he will come here to see you."

Chapter Twenty

J anko came for supper that evening. Definitely *not* Dad. And *not* the
ghost that haunted me. In his early fifties, he had some resemblance to
Mom; unlike Grandma, though, he didn't appear happy to see me. No
hugs, no terms of endearment.

"So you're Mimica's girl? I'm surprised you're here." I recognized his voice
as the one I overheard telling Grandma to send me home the night I arrived.

I told Janko I wanted to find out more about where my parents came from,
that I thought it would help bring me closure.

Janko said he was sorry about Mom, but didn't seem interested in getting
to know me. As Grandma flitted about the kitchen, with last-minute meal
preparations, I carried on a one-sided conversation about Hamilton, about
the catering business, about our home. He sat opposite and nodded once
in a while. Obviously a man of few words. I considered telling him and
Grandma about Jim and the kids to soften Janko's heart, but shot down that
idea before I could open my mouth. It would only take one person and a
slip of the tongue to put my family in danger. If Stefan found out I had
something precious to lose, he'd strip them from me like the insides of a
fish, leaving me gutted.

When I asked him to tell me about Mom when she was young, he said he
was a few years older, so he wasn't close to his little sister. "We didn't play
together. Petar and I are closer in age. Mimica liked to play with her doll
and hang around the kitchen with Mom."

That was all I got out of him. He changed the topic to the weather. "You're
lucky the weather is nice for your visit. You'll be going back home soon, I

suppose?"

"I'd like to stay for a little while." I asked how well he knew my father, Janez.

Confusion clouded his face, and Grandma answered for him. "Janko didn't really know Janez, Svjetlana. She didn't bring him home."

"Oh, Janez. Yes, your father. No, I didn't know him. I met him maybe once," he confirmed what Grandma said. "To be honest, I'd almost forgotten his name."

I asked when Mom and Dad left Croatia.

"She was just a young girl when she ran off with your father. I never heard from her again." When I asked what year she left, he glanced at Grandma, and she nodded for him to continue. "1978."

1978 was what their passports showed, the year I was born. But, why did they make me believe they had come to Canada already married, and that I was born a few years later?

Grandma set the food on the table and shifted the conversation away from me and my parents. She asked Janko how his wife and children were doing. His son, Niko, was expecting another child. "Only two more months to go," he said.

He told me about his other two boys, Marko and Mika, the twins, in their last year of high school. All this time, I had cousins I didn't know about. Despite the fact that we lived on different continents, it seemed strange my mom had never mentioned them. As we finished our roast chicken meal, Janko said he'd better get back to his family. The whole visit lasted less than two hours.

"Well, it was nice to meet you, Svjetlana. I hope you have a safe journey home," he said, shaking my hand before walking to his car.

It certainly wasn't the heartwarming welcome I had expected from my uncle. There was no exchange of phone numbers, so we could keep in touch. As I helped Grandma with the dishes, I tried to elicit more information, but got nowhere.

"Janko and your mom were five years apart. He teased her sometimes, like big brothers do, and he was fond of her, but they didn't share the same interests or friends."

I knew I'd hit a dead end with Janko. But there was one other person who might be able to tell me about my parents' youth. Petar, Mom's other brother, who was only three years older. A trip to Orakia, tomorrow, without Grandma, might provide answers.

Chapter Twenty-One

I called Tina, the young woman Grandma introduced me to yesterday. "Hey, Tina. It's Svjetlana. I wondered if you were free today. I was hoping to do some sightseeing in the city."

"Yes, I'm off today, actually. When would you like me to pick you up?"

Grandma thought it was a great idea, spending the day with Tina. "You need to have some fun with people your age, not just with your old Grandma."

Tina, who seemed quiet when I first met her, became more talkative on the road to Orakia. "I work here, in a store," Tina said as we passed the town of Vlasilo. "But I want to get a job in Orakia." She and her boyfriend were saving to get their own place in the city. "There are lots of stores and restaurants. And a nice park with gardens on the river. Much better than Molono. There's nothing to do there. No jobs, no fun. All the young people want to move."

When I said I needed to find someone in Orakia, she asked, "Who are you looking for?"

"My uncle, Petar. How can I find his address?"

"Did you ask your grandma?

"No. I'd rather she not know."

Tina tilted her head my way and raised her eyebrows. "I see. We could try looking online."

"I thought of that, but Grandma doesn't have internet."

"Nobody does in Molono. But I'll call one of my friends in the city. She can find out."

I hated using Tina this way, but I needed to see Petar, and I didn't know how to get to Orakia without asking Grandma and making her suspicious of my intentions.

Tina seemed to enjoy acting as a tour guide on the cobbled back streets, pointing out historic buildings, which I captured on film for the photobook I planned on putting together upon my return to Lake Kipling.

We passed through the university grounds and strolled along the river walkway. "I went to school here." Tina gestured to the series of red-tiled buildings surrounding a large three-story institutional structure.

"Did your parents know my mom?" I asked as we sat on one of the benches overlooking the river.

"I guess Dad knew her. He grew up in our house, so he would have been there when your mom was young. And everyone knows each other in Molono."

And yet no one remembered Janez Babic. Maybe he came from a different village. My parents lied about other things, so why not that?

But Grandma had shown me his family's home in Molono, unless *she* was lying...

"I'm having a hard time finding anyone who knows my dad," I confided. "Grandma showed me his old house, but said his family moved out."

"Lots of people have moved out over the years. People our parents' age and younger. It's mainly the old people left." Tina changed the topic. "I'm starving. Do you like pizza?"

"Doesn't everyone?" I laughed.

It turned out to be the best pizza I'd ever tasted. Different than Canadian. They served individual pizzas, on large plates, and I wondered how I'd be able to eat it all, but I managed.

"Svjetlana!" Someone called from across the restaurant. I turned my head.

Draga waved and walked toward us. "I just noticed you from where we were sitting. What a coincidence, seeing you again. What are you doing in Orakia?"

"Sightseeing." I wondered what *she* was doing there. Of all the places in Croatia, how did she happen to be at the same spot as me?

"Oh, that's nice. This is our favorite spot for pizza. We come every Friday night."

Oh, right. Draga told me she lived in Orakia.

Draga motioned to her male companion, still at their table. "That's my boyfriend, Rok." A good-looking tall guy with longish brown hair and an unshaven face looked in our direction and waved.

"This is Tina, a neighbor of my grandma's. She's giving me a tour of the city."

"Nice to meet you, Tina. So what else have you been doing during your visit to Croatia?"

I told her about my outing to Paruka with Grandma and Kata, and my cruise on the Danube with a friend.

"And how do you like Croatia so far?"

"Very nice. How long have you lived in Orakia?"

"Several years. So, how long do you plan to stay in Croatia?"

"I'm not sure. But, being where my parents grew up is nice." The tears stung my eyes.

Draga patted my shoulder, saying she understood. "You'll go back when you're ready. You have friends in Canada, and your home is there. But it's nice you could come to see your parents' homeland. I'm sure your grandma is happy to have you visit."

Draga joined her boyfriend, and they exited the restaurant, with Tina and I following shortly after.

"Do you want to stop by your uncle's place now?" Tina asked. "My friend texted the address."

As much as I was enjoying my day out, I hadn't forgotten my main objective for coming to Orakia. "Yes, please, that would be great."

Tina asked some of the locals for directions to Lipica Street. Uncle Petar's home, a red brick two-story row house in a subdivision on the outskirts, stood on a nicely maintained small lot. Tina said she would go for a walk around the neighborhood to give me some private time to visit my uncle. The uncle I had never met and who wasn't expecting me.

A plump middle-aged woman answered the door.

"Is Petar home?" I asked, to which she replied that he was expected shortly. When I told her who I was, she invited me in.

"I'm Eva, Petar's wife. Petar didn't tell me he has a niece," she said. "Janko has three sons, but I never heard anything about his sister's family."

I felt like a secret love child that nobody had been told about for some reason.

Eva showed me to the living room and asked what I wanted to drink.

"Oh, nothing, thank you." I inquired about her family, and she told me they had two children, a boy, and a girl, in their twenties. Two more cousins. All this family I had never known about. We waited rather uncomfortably, trying to make conversation.

Petar's car pulling into the driveway brought Eva to her feet. She met him at the door. "There's a woman here who says she's your niece from Canada. Svjetlana."

When Petar entered the living room, he loomed in the doorway, surveying me on his living room sofa. "So, you're Mimica's girl." Like Janko, he had a vague resemblance to Mom. I nodded and said it was nice to meet him. "And what are you doing here, in Croatia?"

When I told him, his response was, "Humph, you're wasting your time coming here. Your parents left this life behind a long time ago. There's nothing of them left here."

I flinched, holding back tears. His coldness shot like an arrow through my heart. "I was hoping you could tell me about my mother, when she was young."

"Mimica was a good girl, a nice girl. She was always happy, playing with her friends, helping Mama at home, even when she was little. She liked animals, she liked to be outside."

"What about my dad? When did she meet him?" Surely the brother closer to her age would know something about his sister's boyfriend.

"Your dad was nothing but trouble." His expression hardened as he spoke about Dad. "He took Mimica from her home, from her family."

"So you didn't like him?" Almost no one knew him, and the few who did had nothing good to say about him. Why was that?

"He was bad news. I didn't know him well personally, but I'd seen him around and heard people talk about him. Mimica didn't dare bring him home to the family. When we heard rumors that she was dating him, our dad forbade her to see him ever again."

I had a hard time believing the man he was describing could be my dad. It sounded so unlike him. There had to be a mistake. "But he and my mom left the country together. Was that because she wasn't allowed to be with him, so she ran off?" This seemed like the story of two star-crossed lovers. Romeo and Juliet.

"She went out to a dance one night and never came back. We didn't know what happened to her for a long time, then one day she contacted our mother and told her she was in Canada with your father and had a baby girl, and that she was happy."

"Yes, she was happy. They were happy, until the accident." The tears spilled again. "We were happy."

"I'm so sorry, Svjetlana. Sorry you've lost your mom and dad." Petar sat down next to me. "My sister fell in love with the wrong man, but she couldn't see that."

"He wasn't the wrong man. They loved each other," I said, standing up for my parents.

"Love is blind, that's what they say. But she should have told us the truth."

"The truth?"

"That she was planning to run away with your father. That she was going to Canada. That she got there safely. If she had done that, maybe my father would still be alive."

"I don't understand. What happened to your father?" My grandfather. Grandma's husband. Mom's dad.

"Your mother killed him."

It was a good thing I was sitting down. My jaw dropped. "My mother... killed her father?"

"After she disappeared, we had no news about whether she was alive or dead. Dad had a heart attack a few months after she left without a trace. Janko and I were left to take care of our mom, who was grieving for her daughter and her husband." The bitterness, now clearly etched into Petar's face, showed he had never forgiven my mother for leaving. "People's actions have consequences," Petar said with sadness in his eyes. "Your mother was selfish, leaving her family behind. Still, I hope there's more of her in you than there is of your father." His words dripped with disdain. "You should go now. Go back to where you belong."

He stood and walked to the door, giving me no choice but to leave.

I left my uncle's house enlightened by some knowledge of my parent's past, but with a heavy heart, knowing their love had caused such pain, and that I had inflicted that same pain on them when I ran away with Jim.

Chapter Twenty-Two

I didn't talk much on the way home. Tina made some attempt at conversation and asked if I was okay, but I told her fatigue from sightseeing had settled in as I lay my head against the headrest.

Grandma sat in front of the television when I walked through the door. "Did you have a good time?" she asked. I told her about my visit with Petar. She nodded, then sat quietly, without a word, for the longest time. "So, now you know."

"Mama ran away because you didn't approve of my dad?"

"Yes." She didn't offer any more information.

"But she loved him. Why didn't you let them be together?" Petar blamed Mom for his father's heart attack, but I blamed my grandparents for forcing my parents to run away.

"He was wrong for her. Came from a bad family. But that's all in the past. It's time to move on."

I wasn't ready to move on. The next morning, I set out again on a walk through the village, telling Grandma I needed fresh air and might stop by Tina's place to see if she wanted to hang out. Tina was eating breakfast when I knocked on her door. "Want to go for a walk?" I asked. "Show me all the exciting places in Molono?"

Tina laughed. "Okay, that will take about two minutes." She wolfed down her food, grabbed a sweater, and we headed out.

"I want to see if I can find anyone who knew my dad," I said. "So people who are around 45 or 50, maybe their parents. He lived on the back road off the other main street. I know it was a long time ago, but I'm hoping to find someone who still lives here and remembers him."

We set off past the public school, toward the highway, then turned right at the church. "I've been to a lot of the houses already, asking about my dad, but I want to check out every single one. If I can find some of his friends, maybe I can learn more about his childhood." Just because his family moved, it didn't mean everyone he grew up with moved, too.

Although the village didn't have a large population, it was spread out enough that it made for slow going, getting around to every house. Sometimes, the homes were spaced apart with barns, sheds, yards, and empty lots in between. Many of the homes contained only one inhabitant, usually an older widow. Some places had clearly been abandoned. Things would have been a lot different when my parents lived there.

None of the people who answered their door remembered Dad.

"No, no Janez Babic."

"Marija Babic lives on the next street."

"No, I don't remember any Babic on this street."

"Marija and Ivan Babic had a couple of boys, but no Janez."

"Maybe you have the wrong village?"

"So, what are you hoping to find?" Tina asked as we went from house to house.

"I want to learn more about my parents' past. To feel closer to them. To know them better. When your parents are alive, you think you know everything you need to know. But when they're gone, you realize you'll never learn anything more about them. I thought if I came here, I'd get an idea of what their childhood was like, what it was like when they were teenagers, and when they met." I didn't add that I also wanted to find out about the mystery man whose birth certificate my parents kept, and whether their past had anything to do with their deaths.

"What about your mom?"

"What do you mean? I've already found her family."

"Your grandma's been here for a long time, so probably lots of people remember your mom. If your dad's family moved away a long time ago, maybe people have forgotten him. Why don't you ask about your mom, and maybe they'll remember her boyfriend. Wouldn't her friends have some memory of him?"

That made perfect sense. I needed to ask people around the age of 50 if they remembered Mimica Babic and her boyfriend, not if they knew Janez Babic.

I tried a new line of questioning. "Do you remember Mimica Babic? Marija's daughter? She moved away 30 years ago. I'm her daughter."

I got a reaction this time. There was a sense of curiosity among some of the old people, who said they hadn't heard anything about Mimica over the years and thought maybe she was dead. Others said she ran away never to be heard of again. Some people said they vaguely remembered her.

But the people around my parents' age seemed absolutely shocked. Expressions of horror and disbelief stared back at me. And yet, it wasn't their reaction to Mimica Babic that made me certain the village was keeping a secret. When I pulled out a photo of Dad, they stared at me like I'd risen from the dead—and not as a friendly ghost.

"Do you remember him, Mimica's boyfriend? He's my dad."

People gasped. They put their arms protectively around themselves. Their eyes searched up and down the street. Doors closed in my face and locks clicked. Everyone seemed to be terrified of me. No wonder Grandma had been selective in introducing me to the neighbors.

"What was that about?" I asked Tina. Molono wasn't turning out to be the friendly little village I had expected it to be. "I don't understand. My dad was well liked back home in Canada." Despite his strict manner and traditional values, he had a sense of humor and drew people to him. "Why is everyone acting this way?"

Tina shook her head and shrugged.

On the road where Dad's old house stood tucked away at the end of the asphalt next to the woods, we stood silhouetted against the bushes. I knocked on one of the houses I had tried a couple of days ago. When this door opened, disbelief and horror flooded through *me*, rather than the occupants of the house.

A trio of zombies stood in the doorway. Ragged, bloodstained clothes, ashen faces, blood dripping from their foreheads and mouths, hair flying in all directions, heads lolling to the side, arms outstretched, mouths gaping open with yellowed teeth. "Aarghhh, hissss, raauughh..."

Tina and I screamed, rooted to our spots in sheer terror, until the zombies laughed hysterically, slapping their hands on their knees.

"Haha! Gotcha! Tina, it's just me," one of them said between guffaws. "We're trying out our costumes for the party."

"You moron! You scared the shit out of us! What the hell do you think you're doing answering the door like that?" Tina narrowed her eyes, then slapped his arm and joined in the laughter. "My boyfriend and his idiot friends," she said, turning to me.

"And who do we have here?" asked one of the other zombies, eying me like I was his next meal.

Tina introduced me to her friends. "Vlado, my boyfriend. And this is Darijo and Filip. This is Darijo's place."

Darijo invited us in. "My parents are at church and then visiting my aunt and uncle." He gave me another hungry look and asked if I was coming to the party.

"What party?" I asked.

"The Halloween party next weekend. Friday night. You can come if you want. It'll be fun. We're having it in a haunted house this year."

Tina asked, "What haunted house?"

Vlado put his arm around Tina. "Don't worry. I'll protect you from the ghosts."

Tina asked again about the location of the party. "I thought it was going to be at your place this year," she said to Darijo. "You're going to decorate it as a haunted house?"

"No. A change of venue. It's going to be at that abandoned house on the end of the road," Darijo answered.

Vlado explained they were going to use a crowbar to break in.

"You're what? Grow up! Breaking into an old house for a party? What are you guys, thirteen?" Tina shook her head, placing a hand on her hip.

"Aw, come on, Tina. Don't be such an old nag. It's going to be great!

Nobody's going to care. No one's been around there in decades."

"Yeah, and this year could be our last chance to have a blast, before everybody moves out of Molono," added Darijo, still in character, flailing about and moaning.

"Or, has a kid and gets married," Filip nudged Vlado, whose face reddened under his makeup.

I asked what house they were talking about, and sure enough, it was Dad's old house. "Who used to live there?"

And they told me a story I couldn't believe. About ghosts.

Chapter Twenty-Three

"It's the murder house." Darijo began as we settled into his living room. "I heard my parents talking about it last night. They didn't know I was listening; they thought I was asleep."

Ice cubes ran down my spine as a chill swept through the room. Someone was murdered in Dad's house. Someone in his family? Who? His parents?

"The murder house? Who got murdered?" Tina asked, turning to me in alarm. She didn't mention it was my dad's house. "When was this?"

Darijo continued his story. "A long time ago, when our parents were young. There was a party. My parents were there, and a lot of their friends. I heard Mom and Dad say four people went missing that night. The police found a body in the woods beside the house. The other three were never found. Everyone thought they had been dragged down to the river and their bodies dumped." He paused for effect. "The police never solved the case."

"Who was murdered?" I asked, trembling with both fear and anticipation.

"My parents didn't mention any names. But, they said someone was going door to door, asking questions about the house the other day."

That would be me. I didn't tell them that, though. "Did they say anything else?"

"No, but it made me think it would be a great place for a Halloween party. Who knows? Maybe the ghosts of the murdered teenagers will show up. It'll be a blast. So, you coming?"

"Yes, I'd like that." I'd been seeing Dad's ghost in other places. Maybe he'd show up here, where he grew up. I looked to Tina for support.

She agreed that I should come. "We always dress up for Halloween. The guys will take care of the music, and everyone brings food and booze."

"There's no power at the house. But that'll make it even more fun," Darijo said, waving his arms as he spoke. "I've got a battery-operated boombox and a small generator. I'll get everyone to bring lanterns and flashlights. And I thought making it an overnight campout would make it more exciting."

"But there's no bathroom there," Tina interjected.

"There's the bush," Darijo laughed. "And there's an old outhouse. We'll rough it. Like in the old days. I'll make sure there's plenty of soap and water, don't worry."

"And toilet paper."

Filip added, "Everyone can bring sleeping bags and blankets."

I hadn't been at a party for so long I didn't know what to expect. A bunch of twenty-somethings getting together at an abandoned house for an overnight party at Halloween? "What kind of party is it?" I hoped my social ineptitude didn't show.

"Usually we dance, listen to music, people get together, hang out. But you know what would be really neat this year?" Darijo suggested. "What if we told ghost stories? We can ask people if they've got some good tales to tell. And games."

"Games? We're not twelve." Tina punched Darijo playfully.

The guys discussed ways of making the party memorable. I had no intention of missing out. Finally, someone had given me a lead to finding out about my parents' past. I suspected more than my grandparents' disapproval of their relationship caused Mom and Dad to skip town—all the way across the ocean.

As Tina and I returned home for lunch, I said, "You know, when I first met you, I thought you were really quiet and reserved. But I'm finding out there's a lot more to you."

She laughed and said she was sometimes a bit shy with strangers. "It's funny because I was thinking the same thing about you. But we're not strangers anymore. I'm glad we've become friends and that you confided in me. I hope you find what you came here for."

I told Grandma there was a Halloween party Friday night, and I wanted to go along with Tina. "It's a costume party. I don't know what to wear, though."

Grandma looked a bit concerned. I thought it was about my lack of costume, but she had something else on her mind. "I thought you'd be heading home before then. Back to work, back to your home."

I assured her work could wait.

"What about the house? And the business?"

"There are people who can take care of things for me. I wouldn't mind spending some more time here, if you don't mind."

"No, of course not. I'd be happy to have you stay." She said the words, but they didn't seem heartfelt.

Was I being a nuisance? She was used to living alone. I didn't think I was causing much trouble, but maybe I was a burden, with the cost of an extra person in the house. I offered to pay room and board.

"What? My own granddaughter, pay to live under my roof? I won't hear of it!"

After lunch, I stopped by the cottage-like house where Grandma said the busybody lived. An orange cat looked out from the window ledge. A black cat wandered out as the hunched-over little old lady dressed in dark clothing and a kerchief on her head answered the door. "Who are you? I've seen you wandering around the village, looking for trouble. I know you're staying with Marija. What's your business here?"

I honestly thought people would have been friendlier in a small village. Politer. "I'm her granddaughter."

She stared at me with hawk-like eyes. "No, you're not. I know her granddaughter. You're not her."

When I explained I was Mimica's daughter, she put her hand to her chest, made the sign of the cross, and backed away as though I'd crawled out of a grave. "My Dear Lord! I thought Mimica was dead."

I told her about the car accident. "Mom and Dad are gone now." Once again I explained why I had come to Croatia. "I've reunited with Mom's family, but I can't find anyone from Dad's family. Not even his friends."

"Your dad had no friends. That is, if he's the same guy who was hanging around with your mom before she left town."

Did that mean he was an introvert, like me? He always seemed to have lots of friends, or lots of acquaintances, at least. People liked him. "Why not?" Maybe he was different as a kid, as a teenager.

"He brought a curse upon this village." I thought she had to be joking, but little about her expression indicated she found it humorous. "From the day he set foot here, I knew we were all doomed."

As the blood drained from my cheeks, she asked if I needed a drink of water, and told me to come in and sit down. "It's not your fault," she said. "But your father was a bad man." She handed me a glass of water and pulled out a kitchen chair. Two cats lounged on the counter. Another purred around my legs. "I know that's not something you want to hear. And I'm sorry you've lost your parents." She spoke in a gentler tone, less like a witchy old woman who believed in curses.

"What did he do?" My question came out as barely a whisper. I didn't think I really wanted to know. Wild thoughts went through my head. Did he kill someone? Was he the murderer from the murder house?

"He was a troublemaker around town. Up to no good. People were afraid of him and his family. But that's all in the past. Remember him the way you knew him. As your father. I never knew him personally. I just heard the stories. Forget I said anything. I'm just a crazy old cat lady."

She showed me to the door before I could question her further.

A couple of guys walked down the street in my direction. "Hey, Svjetlana!" one of them called. I had no idea who they were. I stood still, not answering, still in shock from what I had just learned about my father.

"What's wrong? You look like you've seen a ghost," he continued.

"Are you okay?" the other one asked.

I recognized the voices. Darijo and Vlado. They were a lot more attractive without the zombie getup.

"Yes, sorry, I didn't recognize you. When I met you, you were zombies."

They roared with laughter.

"I was looking for you," Darijo said. "Your grandma said you went out for a walk. Do you want to go down to the river?"

"The river? How far is it?"

"About twenty minutes, across the highway, through the bush."

I hesitated. I didn't know him. For all I knew, he could be a serial killer. He must have read my mind because he chuckled and assured me he wasn't going to murder me and dispose of my body in the river. Vlado vouched for him, then waved goodbye as he continued to Tina's house. And I found myself wandering through the woods of the Slavonian region of Croatia alone with a young man I didn't know.

A well-worn path led to the river. "How long are you staying here?" Darijo asked as we approached.

"I don't know. We'll see."

"Do you have a boyfriend back home?"

"Sort of."

"Sort of?" he asked, arching his eyebrows. "I'll bet your sort-of boyfriend misses you. I would, if I were him."

I felt the red creep up my neck as Jim's image flashed into my mind. I hadn't forgotten I was a happily married woman, but the attention I'd been getting from both Matija and Darijo *was* flattering. "What about you? Do you have a girlfriend?"

"No, I'm completely free. I don't get to meet many girls in Molono. There's work, but everybody there is already taken." Darijo brushed back his dirty blond bangs, sweeping them onto the top of his head only to have them fall forward again.

The river came into view through the dense forest, stretching wide, the other side equally wooded. At first glimpse, the Danube appeared gray with the shadows of trees, but the water took on a blue hue, sparkling like diamonds as the sun's rays bounced off it. Along the edge, evidence of people coming there regularly met my eyes. A few boats sailed on the water, and some people fished farther along the river. The remains of a campfire blackened a spot close to the shore.

"People come out here to party sometimes," Darijo said, seeing me glance in that direction. "There's not much to do here, but we make our own fun."

"Are there a lot of young people in the village? I haven't met many."

"No, about a dozen teenagers. Another dozen or so young kids. And a few people like me, who still live at home. Everyone moves out as soon as they can afford it, unless they need to stay behind to look after their parents or grandparents. Mostly, it's old people. There are a few other villages not far away. The little kids get a ride to the school here. The older kids take the bus to the high school in a bigger town."

"Do you like living here?"

"It's okay. I can't wait to move to the city and have my own place, but it's less expensive at home."

Tina had said the same thing. Molono didn't hold much appeal for the youth.

I asked Darijo about the haunted house and the murders. "Is it true? Did they really find a body there?"

"It sure sounded like it. My mom said she didn't like to be reminded about it, the body found just down the road from us. Dad said it was a long time ago, when they were just kids, and it didn't have anything to do with them. They just happened to be at the party. Mom said she always wondered whether they'd find the bodies of the other three kids who went missing that night at the bottom of the river."

"And your parents are okay with you having a party there?" I found that rather incredulous. "Won't it bring back bad memories for them?"

"Yeah, well, I didn't exactly tell them yet," he grinned. "But once they find out, it'll be too late for them to stop it. And besides, Mom won't need to worry about the house getting messy. So I'm doing her a favor."

I gazed over the blue-gray river, wondering whether weighted-down bodies lay rotting at the muddy bottom. Dragging bodies from the house to the river would have taken a lot of strength and time. The murderer couldn't have done it on his own. "I doubt the bodies are in the river."

"Where do you think they are, then?"

I shrugged. "You're the one who lives here. What do you think?"

"I think we should ask the ghosts Friday night," he said with a wink.

Darijo walked me home and said he'd see me soon. A vehicle sat parked in front of Grandma's house.

"Svjetlana, sit down," Grandma ordered as I entered. Janko and Petar glared at me from the living room sofa. "We want to talk to you." This looked like an intervention, except I wasn't an addict, just a curious daughter, searching for answers.

"It's time for you to pack your stuff and go home," Janko said, getting right to the point. I didn't know what I'd done to outstay my welcome. Turning to Grandma for answers, my mouth opened, but before anything came out, Janko added, "You've been going around asking questions, opening up old wounds. People don't want to be reminded of what happened all those years ago."

"What do my parents have to do with anyone else here? Why is it their business? I'm not here to upset anyone," I insisted.

"You're your father's daughter—causing trouble."

I turned to Petar for support, but from the look on his face, I knew he wouldn't be on my side. "Go home, Svjetlana. Your mother left with your father, against her own father's wishes. Our family went through a horrible time, and Dad died. People around here stick together. They don't want you back, reminding our mom of what happened. End of story."

"I'm sorry, Svjetlana. It's not you. It's the memories that you've brought back with you. Bad memories," Grandma added.

"What exactly did Dad do? Why do you hate him so much?" What had happened to turn the villagers, even Mom's family, against him?

The three of them exchanged a look, and for a moment, I thought I might actually get the truth. But then Janko spoke for them all. "We've already told you everything you need to know. Your mother left her home for a man her parents didn't approve of. There's nothing else. It's time for you to leave."

I went to my room to pack. "You don't need to put up with me any longer," I shouted as I slammed the door. Shame immediately flowed through me for treating my grandma this way, like a spoiled teenager.

The kitchen phone rang, startling me.

"It's your boyfriend," Grandma shouted through the closed door. I almost asked which one, just to rattle her, but decided against it.

"Hello!" I bellowed into the receiver, realizing too late I shouldn't be taking my frustration out on my husband.

Jim asked if everything was okay. "You sound angry, honey. Has something happened? Your phone's off again."

"I'm just peachy." My voice oozed sarcasm. "I've been meeting my family and making new friends."

Jim, sounding concerned, wondered if I was ready to come home.

"No, I'm fine. Don't worry. I'm not ready to come back yet. I'll let you know." Hearing his voice calmed me down. "A little longer. How are Brent and Jamie?" I lowered my voice so they wouldn't hear me in the living room, in case my uncles understood some English. We talked about the kids for several minutes, and I told him I'd call tomorrow. "Love you, too."

I went back to Mom's room to grab my bags and said goodbye to my new-found family.

"Svjetlana, you can't leave like this. Wait a day or two," Grandma coaxed.

"I'm not leaving, Baba. I'm going to stay at a hotel."

Grandma's mouth opened slightly as her eyes moved back and forth between my luggage and my face. "You'll do no such thing! Put your bags back in your room." She held up her hand to quiet Janko as he was about to protest. "You can stay for a while. But you need to go back to your real life sooner rather than later. I'm sorry, Svjetlana, but this isn't where you belong. Nothing good can come from digging into the past. Let the dead lie in peace. Move forward with your life."

Janko and Petar shook their heads, then stood and wished me a safe trip home. Petar said he was sorry they hadn't been more welcoming. My uncles walked out of my life as though my existence held no significance in their own lives.

Late at night, when she thought I was asleep, I overheard Grandma on the phone. "You're going to have to come and get her. She's been asking questions and I'm afraid she's going to find out the truth. Mimi would never have wanted her to know."

Chapter Twenty-Four

I needed to work quickly. They were conspiring to send me home just as the truth was unraveling. The villagers were keeping a secret that concerned Dad. No one would talk about him. No one would admit to having known him. His family had moved away. The house he grew up in sat abandoned, except for the ghost of the murdered person. Or persons.

The next morning, I snuck out early, beating Grandma out of bed, which was quite a feat. I couldn't have her stop me from snooping around town. I planned to move fast and cover every single house in town, including the ones out on the highway, by the end of the morning. In the time it took me to walk to the outskirts of town, stopping to chat with anyone outside, I assumed most people would be awake, as was the norm in Molono. Whether they wanted to have their Sunday morning intruded upon, I didn't particularly care. I, Svjetlana Babic, belonged here in my parents' homeland, and I was on a mission.

The crisp morning air, the sun rising over the hillside, invigorated my soul. Walking up the street, a sense of peace enveloped me, the history seeping into my bones, and I wondered what terrible things had happened years ago, things the locals wouldn't talk about.

On the highway, a few cars passed the village. Hugging the edge of the two-lane thoroughfare, I faced oncoming traffic, until I reached the last house before the countryside took over. Rock jutted out of the hillside, bordering the highway; straggly vegetation grew on top of the hill. I strode back toward the village on the other side of the highway where the houses sat fairly close together, with an expanse of trees behind their back yards, and the rest of the village beyond. A body had been found in those woods three decades ago. Surely someone would have heard about it.

People admitted to knowing Mimica Babic. They respected her mom—my grandma. So that was a good place to start my questioning. Whatever the people in Molono thought they knew about my father, it was a lie. Not only did I need to know the truth about what happened to my parents before I was born and whether that related to their deaths, I also needed to set the record straight and clear Dad's name. That was my top priority. Second to that, I had to find Luka Nikolov, although that didn't seem to matter as much anymore.

Without regard for courtesy, I knocked on each of the doors, asking whether anyone knew Mimica Babic and her boyfriend, and what they could tell me about the body found in the woods behind their house. Someone must have warned the residents on the outskirts. Doors closed rudely before I could finish my questions. By the time I covered the twenty or so houses bordering the highway, fatigue took over, and the villagers left me none the wiser.

I started down the second turnoff into town and stopped again to talk to anyone outside, but apart from a greeting, no one seemed eager to carry on a conversation. I had the distinct feeling that Grandma and my uncles got to them. What were they hiding?

The only thing anyone admitted to and agreed on was that Mimica was Marija's daughter, and she didn't live there anymore. They had no idea what had happened to her.

I wondered whether Crazy Old Cat Lady would talk to me again. As I approached her house, I remembered that I hadn't checked out the house where Grandma said the troublemakers lived. It couldn't hurt to try there. Molono's residents considered me a troublemaker, my dad was a known troublemaker, so maybe I would get lucky with these people. We had something in common.

The man answering the door looked to be in his late forties, in the process of having breakfast, bread in one hand, while his wife took the opportunity to usher two kids (or grandkids?) outside to play. Pulling out Dad's photo, I introduced myself.

"No, sorry. I can't talk to you." He began to close the door in my face.

"Wait, please." I stood my ground, running shoe jammed in the door. "I just have some questions. Did you know my mom and dad?"

"I knew your mother. That's all I can say."

"I want to know more about her, what she was like growing up and as a teenager. My parents were killed in a car accident, and I've been having a hard time dealing with it." I let the tears fall. They were genuine, but the thought ran through my mind that if I could garner some sympathy, he'd talk to me. "I thought if I came here, I'd feel closer to them. But no one wants to talk about Dad, even my own grandma." I sobbed freely. "I have no family. I'm all alone now." The sobs turned into heaves and convulsions as I lied to his face.

"The poor woman. Janez, let her in."

Janez? I stopped crying with a suddenness that startled all of us. His wife sat me down at the kitchen table with a cup of coffee and some home-baked pastries. "Janez? Did you know Mom's boyfriend, my dad?"

"I'm Janez Peric. And this is my wife, Minka. And no, I didn't know your mom's boyfriend. Not well, anyway. We didn't hang with the same crowd."

"But you knew my mom?"

"Yes, very well." He sighed and sat back in his chair.

"You should tell her. She has a right to know," his wife said. I liked her immediately. She was pretty and younger than him. "No one else is going to say anything. It's not fair to keep it from her, even if the truth hurts."

"I don't want to be blamed for being the one to bring the curse back on the town. It's taken years for all that to die down," he countered.

"I already know people think my dad was a bad man. I know about the murder. I'm going to find out the rest one way or another," I argued. "If you tell me, I can stop pestering everyone else in town."

His wife nodded. "Tell her."

"Okay. Your grandma isn't going to be happy," he said. "But they were your parents, so you should know. Then go home before you bring more trouble to town."

I didn't see how my being there was going to bring trouble, but...

"Tell me what you know, please, and I'll be able to go home."

"Mimica and I grew up together. We were the same age, lived a few houses away from each other, went to school together. So naturally, we became good friends and spent a lot of time playing as kids. When we were teenagers, we talked about getting married someday. Our parents thought we made a good match. She was my best friend, and I had a really big crush on her." Janez' wife put a hand over her husband's, linking their fingers. "But things changed when she met your father. Suddenly, she didn't have time for me. We were still friends, but she told me she was in love with someone else." He paused and seemed to consider whether he should say any more. "She said she didn't love me in that way, and I should look for someone who could love me in the way I deserved." He looked his wife in the eyes and smiled. "And it worked out perfectly for me in the end. But not for your mom."

I was about to protest. It worked out for Mom, too. She married the man she loved. Except... she died too young.

"I knew she had been seeing him for several months before she went missing the night of the party. We had parties all the time—at different houses. The young ones still do. There's not much to do around here. Back then, there was even less. When he started hanging around with Mimi, people tolerated him, out of respect for her, but mostly because they were scared of him. Him and his brother."

Dad has a brother? Why did no one mention him before? Was he murdered that night?

"So, it was okay for a while. But then that night, at the house, all hell broke loose."

"What house?"

"At the party. The house where they found the body."

"What happened that night?"

"It started out like most Saturday nights. Dancing, talking, eating, drinking, having a good time. Music booming through the house and down the street. Teenagers letting off some steam. And a fight started, not unusual with a bunch of young bucks. It was just too much having them in the same house—two guys from the local Croatian mob and two out-of-town mobsters from across the Serbian border. Adversaries at the best of times. But the fight involved a woman, and it got ugly quickly. They continued the fight outside and we all believed it was resolved."

I didn't understand what this had to do with Mom and Dad, but I asked what happened next.

"Four people went missing at that party. One turned up dead in the woods beside the house. The other three were never found. If your mother hadn't invited him to the party, none of it would have happened."

"What did Dad have to do with it?"

"He was a dangerous young man, not one you wanted to cross. But he messed with a man who was equally dangerous. When police discovered the body in the early hours of the morning, we all came to a unanimous decision. We were just kids—terrified—but not of the police."

"What were you afraid of?"

"We knew they'd want revenge for the murder. Revenge on the families of the people involved. So we made a pact to keep quiet, to protect our neighbors and friends. But they took it out on the entire village. Molono became a target, the center of a Mafia war. Our parents blamed your father. They blamed your mother, too, for bringing him into our midst."

A pounding on the door startled me. Minka opened it, and Grandma burst in, her face red and sweaty. "There you are. I've been looking all over town for you. What were you thinking, running off without telling me?" Then she turned to Janez, her eyes venomous. "And what lies have you been telling the poor innocent girl?"

Chapter Twenty-Five

J ust when the truth was within my reach and the puzzle pieces were forming a picture, Grandma put a stop to it. But not before I started to clue in.

Wow, the apple really doesn't *fall far from the tree. Mom and I had a lot in common.*

My seventeen-year-old mother must have gotten pregnant with the Serbian criminal she was in love with. Dad? Was that possible? I guess you never really know your parents and the secrets they keep. Until they're dead and their lies are laid bare.

But it didn't make sense. Dad was a good man. He certainly wasn't a mobster, and there was no way he was involved in a murder. So who was he? Where did Mom meet him? When did she meet him? And why would no one admit to knowing him?

And what about Luka Nikolov, the man whose birth certificate my parents kept? Whatever happened to him? Was it his body found in the woods?

When Grandma dragged me back home, she said that whatever Janez told me, I shouldn't believe half of it. "He was so jealous when your mom met your dad. He had such a big crush on her, obsessive, really. When she started seeing your dad, he made up crazy stories trying to get her back. But Mimica never saw him as more than a friend. He couldn't face reality. If he hadn't met Minka, he'd still be pining away after your mom."

I didn't expose to Grandma what Janez had told me. "He said he used to be good friends with Mom. And he didn't know what had happened to her. I think he was happy to hear she'd had a good life and wanted to know all about it."

Grandma narrowed her eyes. "You should stay away from him. Now let's have lunch, and then you need to pack. We're going on a trip for a few days."

I suspected this was my uncles' and Grandma's way of getting me out of Molono, and keeping me from finding out exactly what happened to cause my parents to go on the run.

"I called Zora last night. She suggested that before you go home, you should see the Dalmatian coast," she said. "Especially since you're not likely to come back to Croatia again. You shouldn't miss seeing it on your one and only visit." If I had any notion of return visits to my mom's family, she squelched that thought with her comment. "Zora booked tickets for us to fly out of Orakia later today. Kata's coming along, and Zora's flying in from Canada. She's going to meet us in Dubrovnik tomorrow."

"We'll be back by Friday, won't we?" I wanted to be back for the party, even if it turned out not to be Dad's house.

"We'll be back," Grandma promised. "I know you're looking forward to the party. And you *should* spend more time with people your age, not wandering door to door, sticking your nose into things that don't concern you."

I thought of Jim. He'd be worried if he tried calling Grandma's number and no one answered for days. "I should call Jim tonight. Tell him where we're going. So he doesn't worry in case he can't reach me."

After packing, I called Tina as well.

Grandma suggested, "Maybe the two of you can write to each other when you get back home. Stay in touch. It's good to make new friends. And stop worrying about your mom and dad's past. That won't bring them back."

Tina, Vlado, and Darijo came over to wish me a good trip. They thought I was lucky to be going to the coast. I said it would be a lot more fun if they could come along. And I meant it. I enjoyed having friends to hang out with. I'd been missing Jim and the kids, and it had never bothered me before, having my life revolve around them, but spending time with Haley and Garrett, and now Tina and her friends, reminded me that I had no friends back in Lake Kipling. Only acquaintances and colleagues.

"Make sure you get home in time for the party," Darijo yelled when we pulled away from Kata's driveway. I shouted back that I'd make it even if I had to hitchhike.

Chapter Twenty-Six

T he short flight from Orakia brought us to Dubrovnik airport in less than an hour. From there, a bus continued to the walled city on the Adriatic Sea, the highway carving its way through rock, mountains looming in the distance. Before long, the sea was visible, blue water on one side and rock walls on the other. We approached the medieval town, marveling at the natural beauty of the coastline.

"Fall is never as busy as summer. Still nice and warm, though." Kata provided me with a brief history of Dubrovnik, including the destruction resulting from the War of Independence.

As we approached the city, I understood this journey of mine was not only taking me back to my past and my own roots, but also to the past in general. And that was a good thing. How could you move forward if you didn't know where you came from? Wasn't it important for us all to learn from history—as individuals and as entire civilizations?

Past coastal villages and palm trees, stone walls, and cliffs, the bus wound its way toward the portal to the past. "The town of Dubrovnik is well over a thousand years old. The walls go back about 800 years. It was part of Venice at one time." Kata continued her tour commentary.

A city bus took us the rest of the way, stopping at the old town's gate. "No cars inside the walls," Kata explained as we passed our luggage to the porter who greeted us. "We walk to our hotel."

Grandma told me that Zora had made the plans for our excursion. "She said since you were interested in the past, she wanted to share this experience with you."

I did have an interest in the past, but it was my immediate past, not ancient history that I was searching for. Regardless, as we walked through the gate and crossed the drawbridge, the medieval feel of it mesmerized me, a living, vibrant town enclosed within the ancient walls, different from Ravina's archaic ruins. Blue water, dotted with white sailboats, the archways, old stone buildings and red clay roofs, transported me to a time in the distant past, a time long before my parents and I existed.

"We'll leave our bags at the hotel," Kata said, "and get some lunch. Then we can explore the town."

I hadn't been to many hotels in my life. Jim and I had taken a couple of overnight getaways on our own and a few family weekend vacations, but I'd never been out of the country. During those trips, the four of us crammed into a small budget-friendly room. The hotel Zora had chosen was nothing like the motels I had stayed in. A baroque palace, the three-story limestone building with its red tile roof and shuttered windows, stood close to the old port. The beamed ceilings, wrought iron railings, marble steps, wood floors, stone archways, and antique furnishings blended with the modern amenities of a five-star hotel.

I randomly picked up a travel brochure that showed people walking along the top of the wall surrounding the town.

"Tomorrow, when Zora is here, we'll go there together," Kata said, assuming I had an interest. "There's a lot of walking and climbing to do here."

I asked Grandma if she was up to it, climbing all those stairs, and she said she'd take it slow, but she'd like to overlook the town from the top of the wall. I had hoped to use her as an excuse to get out of going, vertigo already setting in at the thought.

We strolled along the coast, next to boats moored by the stone pier, looking across the shimmering water of a curving shoreline and beyond to the hilly backdrop. Calm cobalt water gently lapped against boats, while white capped waves splashed against rocks, showcasing both the beauty and force of the Adriatic.

On the main street, paved with limestone, we brushed against other tourists, enjoying the architecture. The warm, partly cloudy day made for comfortable walking along the bright, wide open main street with its monuments and historic buildings, which contrasted sharply with the narrow corridors, alleyways, and stairs that dominated the town.

A good night's sleep beckoned after supper and drinks in the open air by the sea. Kata and Grandma shared a room, while I slept in the room, I would be sharing with Zora when she arrived the next day.

I dozed off on feather pillows, under a luxurious duvet, floating away on the peaceful Adriatic to a place where my parents waited for me.

Chapter Twenty-Seven

When Zora arrived early the next morning, she hugged Kata and they held onto each other for the longest time. I hadn't even realized Zora and Kata knew each other, but it made sense—Zora grew up in Molono. Then she hugged Grandma, telling her how sorry she was about what happened to my mom. For the first time in thirty years, she was with old friends; it had been only a matter of days since she'd seen me.

"Svjetlana, I'm so glad you're okay," she said, choking back her sobs. "Why did you leave like that, without telling me? I had to hear it from Jim. He's worried about you, you know." Zora knew better than to mention my marriage and the kids. She'd vowed to keep my new identity a secret 11 years ago.

I explained that I needed to get away, and I thought the best place for me was in my parents' homeland. "I'm so glad I came, Zora. Getting away was the right thing to do. I feel like I belong here."

"I'm glad you're enjoying your vacation, but you should get back to work soon."

I rolled my eyes. Who did she think she was, telling me what to do?

"You must be really tired after your flight," Kata said. "Do you want to rest in your room for a while?"

"It's okay. I slept for most of the flight. I'm too excited to sleep. And we only have a couple of days. It's so good to see you." And she went back to hugging Kata. They must have had a strong friendship all those years ago. I supposed if I didn't see Haley for three decades, I'd be hugging her like my life depended on it, too.

Over breakfast, the three women talked about what Zora had been doing for the last thirty years of her life, and they caught her up on what had been happening in Molono. They were aware I was with them, but didn't make much of an attempt to include me in the conversation. Frankly, I didn't really understand what they were talking about most of the time, and it wasn't the language that confused me. The three of them shared a secret of some sort. Which shouldn't have been surprising—they were from Molono, after all.

"So, is everybody up for a walk on the wall this morning?" Kata asked. "Marija, what do you think? Can you handle all those stairs?"

"I think so, as long as you don't mind waiting for me. I might be a bit slow. But I've heard people say it's one thing you don't want to miss if you get the chance to come here."

The stone walls and walkway of the city walls transported me back to another time, when defending your territory was crucial to survival. Canons stood at juts in the fortress wall, facing the sea. We had an excellent view in all directions—of the old walled town, the sea, the islands, and the mountains. I tried to capture all of it on my Canon. If I never returned to Croatia, the photos would whisk me back, each memory frozen in brilliant color.

Zora walked with Kata, and I helped Grandma by linking our arms when we climbed the stairs. "It would be so romantic to live here," I commented, picturing myself as a princess and Jim as my prince, the two of us overlooking our kingdom.

"I'm sure the locals get tired of tourists, especially during the busy times," Grandma replied. "No, I'd rather stay in Molono, where it's nice and quiet. Most of the time, anyway." She glanced at me as if to indicate I was the reason life wasn't as peaceful as usual.

Although wide vantage spots offered excellent views, in many areas the narrowness of the wall barely allowed room for the two of us to pass comfortably. Grandma stayed on the inside, holding onto the railing, and onto me. I tried not to look over the wall into the bluest of waters as waves rippled and crashed against rocks. The last thing I needed was a panic attack, but I didn't want to miss out on the fabulous view. Focusing my eyes far off to sea, on the boats and the islands, seemed to help. Besides, my concern for Grandma overtook my own fears, even though she seemed more than able to get around on her own. I hoped I'd be that fit at the age of seventy.

I couldn't hear what Zora and Kata were talking about as they strolled along ahead of us, completely absorbed in conversation.

"Were Zora and Kata good friends? Kata is quite a bit older than her, isn't she?" I asked Grandma. Of course, an age gap separated Zora and me, too, but I considered her a good friend. And I enjoyed the time I had spent with Matija, also older than me by more than a decade. I supposed that being the same age wasn't a prerequisite for a good relationship.

"Yes, you could say that. They were best friends."

"I thought Mom was her best friend."

"Oh, she was. Zora and your mom were always together. But Kata was very important in her life, too. They've missed each other."

Clothes flapped on the clotheslines of homes as we walked by, windows facing us. People's lives, their souls, open to the world passing by. What a great place this would be to live as a writer, I thought, not able to resist the temptation to peer inside. What secrets did the people of Dubrovnik keep? What mysteries lay buried in the old town, within the fortress walls concealed for centuries? It made me feel inconsequential in the big scheme of things, with my own secrets, and the skeletons in my parents' closet.

It took a couple of hours for us to get all the way around, back to our starting point. "Well, was it worth it?" Zora asked Grandma and me. We both agreed it was—for Grandma, worth the effort, and for me, worth dealing with my fear of heights.

"Have you been here before?" I asked Zora.

"No. I've wanted to come for years, but never returned to my homeland. I thought it would be a good chance for the four of us to visit the sea together since you were already here. I don't think we'll get the opportunity to spend time like this again." Zora looked wistful, as though she had looked forward to this trip, but regretted it would be the first and last time.

Kata hugged Zora again and thanked her for bringing us all together on such a special journey. "I'll always remember this." Tears welled in both their eyes.

The rest of the afternoon passed quickly, with the four of us strolling along roads and paths that many civilizations trod before us. At one point, I got Zora alone. "You and Kata seem to be very close friends."

Zora took my hands in hers, gazed in my eyes, and said, "There's something I need to tell you. You're going to find out once we get back to Molono. I'm sure everyone will be shocked to see me back."

"Why will they be shocked?"

"A lot of people thought I was dead. They thought your parents were dead, too. But that's a story for another time." I couldn't get her to say more, although the wheels in my head spun with questions. But she did add something that took me by surprise, although, in retrospect, it shouldn't have.

"I lived in the house next to your mother. She and I grew up as best friends. And Kata—she's my mother."

Chapter Twenty-Eight

T he next afternoon, a sign in front of a stone building, advertising a night tour of the old town, caught my eye as we walked down a narrow alleyway. I picked up a pamphlet from the rack inside and showed it to Zora.

The Dark Side of Dubrovnik. Join us for a guided candlelight tour of the old town. Hear stories about murders, ghosts, curses, and the dark side of this medieval seaside town, as you stroll through the most haunted places of Dubrovnik.

"Can we go?" I asked the other three women. Two of them immediately indicated they weren't interested in stumbling along the uneven cobblestones and steps in the dark, listening to nonsense.

Zora added, "I don't think it's something we're interested in, Sunce."

"Well then, I'll just go myself." The thought of wandering around town in the dark with strangers and listening to ghost stories terrified me, but I wasn't going to miss the opportunity. It sounded like a lot of fun, especially since it was only days from Halloween.

Zora saw I was determined to go. She exhaled loudly. "Okay, the two of us will go," she relented, heading inside to purchase tickets. "It starts at ten o'clock and goes on till midnight," she said, handing me the stubs.

After supper, we relaxed on a patio beside the sea, watching people and boats go by. Zora and I sat side by side. "Do you believe in ghosts?" I asked.

She opened her mouth and drew her eyebrows together. "Of course not.

Why would you ask that?"

Not wanting to tell her that I'd been seeing ghosts, I said, "I wonder if any of it's true."

"What's true?"

"The stories they're going to tell us during the tour tonight. Do you think this place is actually haunted?" The murder house back in Molono occupied my thoughts, but I didn't want to ask about that. If she and Grandma knew the venue of Friday night's party, I knew they wouldn't approve of me going.

"I don't think places are haunted, no." Her glazed-over eyes told a different story. "But…"

"But what?"

"I believe people are haunted. By their past, things they've done, things that have happened. Maybe people believe in ghosts and hauntings because it's a way for them to believe anything's possible, like going back and fixing their mistakes." She paused to stare into space. "But nothing good ever comes of going back to the past, looking for our ghosts; it only brings the darkness into the present." Her answer seemed rather philosophical for Zora. Usually, she was more pragmatic.

At 9:40, Zora and I said good night to her mom and my grandma, and started off for the meeting spot to begin the night tour. "Why didn't anyone tell me Kata was your mother?" I asked as we walked along the cobbled street. "Why was it some big secret?"

"I guess they thought that was up to me. I haven't seen her for thirty years, although I've stayed in touch. But when your parents and I left Molono, we put our old lives behind us to start anew. So that part of our lives was over, as far as we were concerned. We moved on. Just like you should be doing." She hesitated before adding, "Continue to move on, as you've been doing for the last 11 years."

We arrived at the clock tower and handed our tickets to the woman holding a lantern. She wore a hooded white cloak, a ghostly apparition herself. An idea struck me. That would be me at the party Friday night—a ghost. Only a handful of other people stood waiting for the tour to begin. By ten o'clock, eleven of us, counting our tour guide, embarked on a ghost hunt.

"Good evening, I'm Ljubica, your guide for this haunted evening," said our raven-haired leader. "Tonight, we'll be visiting creepy places and hearing eerie stories of the past. Some may think they're just legends or myths, but the locals will tell you this place resonates with history, not all of it pleasant." Ljubica waved her cloaked arms as she twirled, indicating the old homes and historic buildings. Then she handed out antique candle holders to each of us and carefully lit the wicks. "If anyone here frightens easily, there's still time for you to back out, full refund, no questions asked."

I rolled my eyes at her dramatic introduction. A little over the top, in my opinion. We were just going for a walk in the dark, and it's not like anyone would be alone. There's courage in numbers.

We began our tour down a narrow, dark back alley, passing closed doors and shuttered windows. Candlelight cast shadows along the cobbles and on buildings, many of which Ljublica indicated had been rebuilt since the War of Independence. I could have sworn there were more than eleven of us, with dark shapes looming around, appearing to follow.

In an open courtyard, our guide told the story of the 1667 earthquake that destroyed most of the city, except for the palace that stood in that spot. "The souls of thousands of people still wander the streets, searching for their homes. Half the members of the nobility were killed." I felt them in the night air, watching us intrude upon their town.

As we continued to the very edge of the pier, Ljubica pointed out to sea. "Over there is the cursed island of Lokrum." She told us about the monks who were forced to leave their monastery on the island. "Donning hooded cloaks, they walked around dripping wax on the land and cursing the island, saying anyone who used it for their pleasure would be damned." Then she went on to recount the inexplicable deaths, shipwrecks, and other disasters that befell those who tried to live on the island. "According to legend, demons cut off heads of lovers, people went insane, others committed suicide. A whole family disappeared there in the 1930s." She stopped before adding, "If you decide to visit the island, make sure you don't miss the last boat back to town. You don't want to be trapped there overnight."

I shivered as a breeze came in from the sea.

We walked through to the other end of the town, toward the west gate. "Do you believe in curses?" I asked Zora.

"They're just stories, Sunce. Made up to scare people. They only work if you believe them. People cause their own misfortunes."

Slipping in and out of narrow alleyways, up and down stone stairs, our guide stopped now and then to recount the history of some of the buildings, and tell tales of spirits still roaming freely. Every so often, yowling and screeching echoed through the alleys. Sometimes, a cat would cross our path, and one even joined us for part of the walk.

At the ornate stone fountain, built in the fifteenth century to bring water into town, Ljubica explained it had been decreed that anyone caught stealing water would have their hands cut off. Then she invited us to take a drink. Most of us declined the offer and some protectively crossed their arms, hiding their hands.

We stopped at one of the churches, and were told it dated back to the sixteenth century. "Legend has it that the ghosts of the aristocratic women who helped build the church can still be seen walking through the doors, carrying building materials," said our guide. Everyone looked around, expecting to see the women appear at any moment.

At the arch of the west gate, Ljubica told us that during medieval times the gates used to be drawn up and closed during the night to keep out invaders. "Of course, it doesn't confine the ghosts. And now, we will leave the safety of the walls of the old town to make the fifteen-minute trek to the cemetery."

We walked at a brisk pace, slowing down to gaze at the stars where the road curved alongside the black sea, then crossed the moonlit street and continued till we came upon the arched stone gate surrounding the cemetery.

The cemetery itself wasn't totally dark, as I expected it would be. Flowers bloomed throughout, covering the raised graves and markers. Candles illuminated the fronts of gravestones. Stone crosses, statues, and monuments, as well as trees, cast long shadows across concrete slabs. In the distance, silhouetted against the lights of the city, the outline of hills beyond the stone walls enclosing us hovered like dark clouds. More than a little spooky, not a place I'd want to be alone in the daytime, much less at night, especially days before Halloween. It gave me the creeps, and Ljubica's commentary didn't make it any less scary.

"This ground where the dead lie was once the site of summer homes for the nobility, but many of those houses burned down during a battle in the early 1800s," Ljubica explained. "A thousand dead souls repose here." She went on to point out specific graves and tombs of well-known families from the area.

I watched as she drew everyone into her stories of supernatural activities in the cemetery. Out of the corner of my eye, to the right, a shadow flashed. When I turned, a figure stood between the trees by the wooden fence, observing us. Curiosity, greater than fear, took charge. Why was someone out here on their own, keeping an eye on the tour? Were they following *me*? Leaving the safety of the group, I approached the trees, but no movement caught my eye. It must have been my imagination. Still, I trod carefully along the narrow paths between the rows of graves to get a closer look.

Although the darkness amongst the trees obliterated the sliver of moonlight, my candle created enough of a glow to keep me from bumping into trunks or branches. Hearing a rustle to my left, I stopped to listen and watch for signs of the person I thought I had seen.

Thought. Who would be out here in the middle of the night? Except for people wanting the thrill of seeking out ghosts, that is.

Keeping close to the wall, I worked my way along the stone, behind the trees, where I would be hidden myself. If someone lurked there, I didn't want them to be aware that I was following them. I could still hear Ljubica's voice, but it had grown distant, eerie. As I peered through the trees, a dark silhouette stood among the graves, unmoving.

Dad?

I clamped my lips together to stop from screaming.

Not wanting to scare him off, I snuffed out my candle, slipped quietly from my cover of evergreens, and crept toward him. I should have been more careful. Something tripped me, and I stumbled forward with a gasp, then righted myself and looked down. The edge of an uneven stone caused my near fall. Undeterred, I continued to slink toward the silhouette. It appeared to have moved farther back, but as I approached, it remained rooted in its spot, as though I might pass if it didn't make its presence known.

When I finally reached it, disappointment swept over me, then embarrassment for being so foolish, taken in by tales of ghosts. Dad didn't haunt this cemetery. It didn't even look remotely like him. A statue perched above one of the graves—its profile displayed above the cross clutched to its chest, lit by a candle below. Why had I thought it was Dad?

Suddenly, I felt exposed in the darkness, surrounded by hundreds of graves, hundreds of bodies buried below, hundreds of ghosts of restless spirits. My eyes scanned the near darkness for my group of living bodies, but none could be seen.

"Zora! Zora!" I waited for an answer, but none came.

I tried again. "Zora! Where are you? Zora!" Silence greeted me, along with the sensation of someone watching. Waiting. I lit my candle using the flame from one burning in front of a tombstone. As I walked along the path, I continued to call for Zora. The chapel stood not far off. Thinking the group must be on the other side where I couldn't see them, I strode as quickly as was safely possible in that direction. As I rounded the corner of the chapel, the distinct sound of footsteps startled me. My scream cut through the darkness as an arm reached around my waist from behind.

Chapter Twenty-Nine

"Shush, Svjetlana. Stop your yelling. You'll raise the dead."

I turned around, my mouth open, to face Zora. How did she end up behind me?

"Where did you wander off to?" Zora let go of my waist and placed a hand on her hip.

"I…I…guess I just got lost."

"We'd better get back to the group before Ljubica sends a search party. This isn't the kind of place you want to explore by yourself at night."

No, it wasn't. Thankfully, she had found me. "I thought I heard something, and when I went to look, I lost sight of everyone. Sorry if I worried you."

"It's okay. We would have found you sooner or later. Ljubica says people sometimes do wander off, but always get found. Still, you need to be more careful. You never know what could happen, especially in a strange place." She was sounding like my mother again. Still, having her beside me settled my nerves.

We hurried to the back of the chapel, where candles flickered beyond.

"Ah, there you are!" Ljubica exclaimed, the candlelight picking up the amusement in her eyes. "Did you run into any ghosts while you were off on your own?"

Later, as we returned to the old town, I confessed to Zora. "I thought I saw Tata in the cemetery. But when I got closer, it was a statue."

"The cemetery can play tricks on you, especially when you're foolish enough to wander around alone in the dark."

"But it's not just one time. I've been seeing him in other places. Someone's following me, and he looks like Tata." I asked Zora for the second time, "Do you believe in ghosts?"

"Ghosts aren't real," she said when she finally spoke. "We make them real. People stay with us, but not the way you're thinking. Not as a physical entity that you can see."

"But I saw him. Several times. I was sure it was him. Am I going crazy?"

"No, you're just grieving. It's wishful thinking. But I can assure you that whoever you think you saw, it was not your dad or your dad's ghost."

"When will I stop seeing him?"

"When you accept that he's gone."

We strode the rest of the way in silence. Back at the hotel, I called Jim to tell him about my tour of Dubrovnik. "I wish you were here."

Silence. I thought we lost our connection. Then he spoke in a near whisper. "Yeah, so do I." Quiet again. "But you didn't ask me to come."

Guilt washed over me once again as I thought of how I'd hurt my husband. Not intentionally. But because of my selfishness. "I'm sorry. You know I wouldn't be here if it wasn't important to me. We'll go to Croatia together next time, the four of us."

Exhausted at the end of the tour, Zora and I fell asleep quickly, Zora first. There was no point in talking to her anymore about Dad anyway. She didn't believe me.

In a few days, though, I hoped to see Dad's ghost again. Maybe he would be at the Halloween party in the house Grandma claimed he once lived.

The next morning, we strolled by the sea, along the pier, and to the beach area. I removed my shoes and dipped my toes in, then waded ankle-deep along the shore, my feet squishing into the sand of shallow turquoise waters, and asked Zora to take my picture. More photos for my record of this incredible journey. There must be hundreds of them. And now there would be one of me in the Adriatic, the fortress walls in the background.

Melancholy at the thought of leaving the beauty and history of Dubrovik mixed with the excitement of getting back to Molono, to the new friends I had made, and inside the old house Dad inhabited.

A short bus ride and plane trip later, we settled ourselves onto the couch back at Grandmas' house. Zora was next door, staying with Kata, her mother.

"Did you have a good trip?" Grandma asked. "You seemed to be enjoying yourself." I confirmed it was an amazing trip, and I hoped to be able to stay longer to enjoy more such trips. That didn't seem to be what she wanted to hear. She pursed her lips, and replied, "I think we've had enough excitement to last for a while. Time for us all to get back to our routines soon."

When she switched on the television for me to watch the news while she made a light supper, an idea occurred to me. I should have thought of it before, being a journalist. When bad things happen, the media reports it. A bad thing had happened in Molono years ago, from what some people were saying, and most were covering up. Wouldn't there be a news report about it? That is, if it really happened. And if the police found out about it. And if the media followed up on it.

There had to be a newspaper for local news, obviously not in the small village of Molono, but in another town nearby. I needed to check out articles from 30 years ago. Would there be something online? If Molono weren't still in the dark ages of no internet, that might be an option. Then it hit me. Surely, there had to be a library nearby, with or without internet. Maybe they would have archives of old newspapers. Sneaking out the door, I jogged over to Tina's place.

"Hi, how was your trip?" Tina asked when I knocked on her door. "I'll bet it was amazing. Wish I could have gone."

"It was. I'll tell you about it in a minute, but first, I wondered if you could help me with something. Is there a library close by?"

She said there was a small branch fifteen minutes away, but the main library was in Orakia.

"Thanks, that's perfect. I'd better get back before Grandma wanders all over town searching for me."

Later that evening, after Grandma went to bed, I picked up the phone and dialed Matija's number. "Hi, it's Lana."

He paused before answering. "Hello. I wasn't expecting to hear from you again."

"Well, I'm still in Croatia, and I was hoping we could spend more time together." I waited for his response.

"Okay, Lana, what would you like to do?"

"For starters, I'd like to go to Orakia tomorrow. Maybe do some sightseeing, have lunch, window shop." I didn't tell him I'd already been there and done that with Tina. I also didn't mention I wanted to check out the library and needed a ride from someone who wouldn't ask questions about why I wanted to look through archives of old newspapers. "And I wondered if you wanted to come with me to a Halloween party Friday night."

Chapter Thirty

I woke early with the intention of canvassing the village one last time, looking for answers about my parents. Only this time, I decided I wouldn't ask about Janez or Mimica Babic. I'd try Luka Nikolov. Even if he wasn't from here, maybe someone remembered him and knew his connection to my parents.

As I made my rounds, I received the same sort of reception I had been given on my previous attempts at getting to know the neighbors. People glared at me like I'd lost my mind, many slammed the door upon seeing my face. When I uttered the name Luka Nikolov, it was clear the people of Molono weren't fans of his.

Even the crazy old cat lady told me to pack my bags and go home. The troublemakers, Janez and Minka Peric, said I should mind my own business. "Don't mention that name again. To anyone," Janez warned as he escorted me out of his house.

Discouraged, I went back to Grandma's. Zora, Kata, and Grandma greeted me in front of the shed in the garden. "Where have you been? Making more trouble?" Grandma asked. "As if we don't have enough."

Zora shook her head, saying this was all her fault. Kata gave me a sympathetic look, then turned to her daughter, putting an arm around her. "It's not your fault, or Svjetlana's. You're innocent victims, both of you."

"What happened?" I asked.

"The chickens," Grandma informed me. "They're dead. Someone has wrung their necks. Mine and Kata's."

"We found them this morning," Kata added.

How horrific! Murdered chickens? Who on earth would kill the chickens? I loved animals. Grandma depended on them for eggs and meat, but I thought of them as pets, especially the baby chicks, even though I knew chicken had been served for supper on more than one occasion. I suppose I convinced myself they had come from the supermarket, prepackaged, already dead.

"And that's not all. I didn't want to put the blame on you, but I've been getting phone calls from the neighbors since you arrived." Grandma directed this at me, arms crossed, disapproval in her eyes. "People's farm machinery has been breaking down. Cars aren't starting in the morning. Gardens are uprooted. In the fields, crops are destroyed."

Kata added, "Things have been stolen. Windows smashed."

"Everyone wants you to stop going around asking questions, bringing up the past. They say you've brought the curse back to the village," Grandma concluded.

Kata corrected her. "There is no such thing as a curse, Marija. Only bad people. While people sleep, thieves and vandals have been sneaking into town. Everyone is too afraid to confront them. Now they're starting to kill."

Curses? Vandals and thieves? Murderers?

"I don't understand. I didn't know this was happening. What does it have to do with me?" I looked from one to the other, searching for a logical explanation.

Zora placed her arm around me. "It's not your fault, Svjetlana. People thought your father was a plague on the village. But they tolerated him. Because they were afraid of him."

"What?" Unbelievable. "*My* dad?"

"The important thing, Svjetlana, isn't what people think or what they say. You knew your dad better than anyone. He loved you. He loved your mother. He was a good man, no matter what you may hear from others. He did what he thought was necessary. He did it to protect us—your mama, me, and you."

"Did what?" I couldn't imagine what my father had done that angered people and caused them to hate him.

"You may hear things about him. Remember they're rumors. People like to talk, make up stories. That's all they are—stories."

I needed more answers than Zora was willing to give me, but I wouldn't get them if they sent me home. "I won't believe anything bad about Tata. I know he was a good man. I just wanted to know more about him, but no one would tell me."

"They don't want to talk about him. It brings back bad memories for them," Grandma reiterated. "No one liked him."

"Did you?"

Grandma looked away and didn't answer. When she turned back, she met my eyes. "I'm sorry, Svjetlana. I didn't. I don't. I never did. But that's not important. What's important is your Mama loved him, enough to run off with him and leave her family behind. I can't blame a woman for following her heart. And he did make your Mama happy, I'll give him that. And he gave her you, so I can hardly hate the man."

"Why did everyone dislike him?" I asked Zora. "They won't even admit to knowing him. It's like no one's ever heard of Janez Babic, as though he never existed. And when I started to ask about Luka Nikolov, people slammed the door in my face. Who is *he*?"

"Where did you hear that name?" Grandma grabbed hold of the corner of the shed to steady herself.

"His birth certificate was in my parents' lock box. I couldn't figure out why they would have kept some other man's birth certificate unless it was really important. And now I'm wondering if… I'm confused… Is it possible… he was my biological father? And Tata married Mama and adopted me?"

Kata grabbed Zora's arm. "Just leave it," she begged her daughter. "Don't make it worse for her."

But Zora said, "No, she has the right to know about her father. And she's not going to stop asking questions until she finds out the truth." Then she faced me. "Your father was Luka Nikolov."

So I was right. Janez Babic was *not* my biological father.

"Then who is Janez Babic? How did Mama meet him? When did she meet him? What happened to Luka Nikolov? Is he dead?"

"Luka was a bad man. Janez was a good man. Your Mama loved them both."

"She loved two men? What happened to Luka? Why didn't she marry him?"

"That's enough!" Grandma shouted. I'd never heard her yell before. "Janez was your father, the man who raised you. He loved you. He loved your mother. That's all you need to know."

I was certain at this point that I had it all figured out anyway. Luka Nikolov, Serbian mobster, hated by everyone in the village, was my biological father. Mom had fallen in love with him and became pregnant. For some reason, he didn't marry her. Was that because he was killed? Mom met Dad, they got married, and I was born. I wasn't sure when she met Dad and how exactly he fit into the picture. Did they fall in love after they were married? After I was born? It didn't matter—he was still my father. Nothing was going to change that.

"I'm going into the city to get a few things for my costume for tomorrow night." I understood the topic of Dad was off the table, and I had other ideas about how to find the truth myself.

"Do you want me to come with you?" Zora offered. "I can drive."

"No, thanks, I'm going with a friend."

"Oh, what friend?"

"Just a guy I met here. He's coming to the party and needs a costume, too." I thought I'd have less chance of being caught in a lie if I told a partial truth. Matija *was* coming to the party, and he *did* need a costume. Besides, no one was being totally honest with me. And I had a right to know the truth about my own parents.

Zora seemed skeptical. "What's his name?"

"I don't think you know him, but it's Darijo." And I *had* met a guy by that name who was coming to the party. "I'd better get going. He'll be waiting." With that, I jogged down the road, waving to the three women, who stared after me.

Matija was supposed to meet me on the highway at eleven o'clock, and it was only nine-thirty, but I thought I'd be better off hanging around the variety store for a while than answering more of Zora's questions. My stock of half-truths was running low.

Having some time to put in, I walked up the highway, in the opposite direction Matija would be coming, past the houses where I had already knocked on doors. I waved to anyone outside, but they ignored me as though I were invisible. Although I normally followed safety rules and faced oncoming traffic, there wasn't much room to walk on the cliff side of the highway. I discovered that during my last excursion. Besides, I wanted to be on the populated side, ready to catch anyone heading out for the day.

When cars approached from behind, I moved to the far edge of the gravel shoulder. But I didn't hear the bicyclist who clipped me as he sped past.

He shouted over his shoulder. "Sorry!"

Continuing on, as though unaware he had knocked me into the ditch, he didn't stop to see if I was unharmed. Nothing seemed to be broken, as far as I could tell, standing up and brushing myself off. Some dirt on the knees of my jeans and a few scrapes on my hands and probably on my legs.

Turning around, I shuffled back toward the variety store to put in some time where it would be safer. I wondered whether someone intentionally knocked me down. Someone who didn't want me going around town asking questions.

Inside the store, I walked up and down the aisles, surveying the products, trying to look like a customer. The clerk at the counter eyed me suspiciously. "Are you looking for something in particular?" she asked. "You're not from *here*, are you?" People in Molono were direct, if not friendly.

"Yes, bandages," I said, thinking quickly. "And do you have a washroom?"

Her eyes scanned me from top to bottom, then she pointed toward the back. I used the facilities and washed my hands and dirty knees as well as I could. When I came out, she had a package of bandages on the counter. "Anything else?"

I indicated a bottle of fruit drink. After paying for my purchases, I waited for Matija on the concrete steps. Taking half a dozen bandages out of the package, rolling up my jeans as far as they'd go, I attended to my wounds, then counted cars as they passed. Lucky for me, Matija was early by about ten minutes.

He got out of the car and hurried toward me. "What happened?" His eyes went from my wet knees to my bandaged palms.

I told him about my run-in with the bike. Matija shook his head. "Some people don't watch what they're doing. You're lucky he wasn't driving a car."

And that seemed to be the start of another lucky streak. Bad luck, of course.

As we drove to Orakia, Matija asked what I had been doing the last week, and I told him about my trip to Dubrovnik and that Zora had joined us. "And I've made some new friends. That's how I got invited to this Halloween party tomorrow night."

"Zora? That's your parents' friend from Canada?"

"Yes, she surprised me in Dubrovnik, and now she's staying in Molono, with her mother. She hasn't been back in thirty years."

"That's a long time to be away from your family. I wonder why she hasn't been back to visit before now."

I wondered that, too. She seemed very close to her mother, and she was happy to see her brother and her nieces.

"I don't really know. But we had a nice trip. And I'm looking forward to the party. It's going to be a costume party, and it's a haunted house theme." I didn't mention that my dad grew up in the haunted house, or that there had been a murder there. No sense in scaring Matija off.

When I invited him on the phone yesterday, he hesitated and said he wasn't really into parties. It had taken some convincing to get him to agree to accompany me.

"I don't know, Lana. I think I'm too old to be going to this party. It sounds like it's for younger people," he said last night.

"Well, if you think you're too much of an old man...." I teased. "You're right, you're no fun. You'll probably be in bed asleep by nine o'clock on a Friday night."

He laughed. "Well, ten at the latest."

"If you want to miss out, that's your loss. But it sounds like it's going to be a fun night."

He didn't respond, so I added, "People are bringing sleeping bags and

161

staying over. I'm an outsider. I won't know hardly anyone there, but if you don't want to come, it's okay. I'll just fend for myself."

And he finally agreed. "No need for that. I'll come and keep you company. And *I'll* show you who's an old man."

As we approached Orakia, he asked what I was dressing up as.

"A ghost."

"A ghost? That's interesting. What should I wear?"

"I think you'd make a really handsome Dracula. We'll have to see what we can find in the stores."

Matija navigated his way through the city to a department store. "They should have some costumes here," he said. "Let's see what we can find."

To our disappointment, the selection of Halloween costumes had been picked through. "I guess I won't be going," Matija said. "Too bad." He didn't sound upset at the prospect of missing the party.

"There must be some other place in the city that sells costumes," I suggested. I found a store clerk and asked where else we might find a selection of Halloween wear. She said we should have shopped earlier and better be quick to pick something before it was all gone. We took another look through the skimpy selection.

"Svjetlana! It's you!" A friendly voice came out of the blue, then turned icy. "What the hell are *you* doing here? You need to leave. Now." Draga's words took on an accusing tone, with a hint of a threat. What had I done to anger her?

I turned around to find Draga with her boyfriend, staring at Matija as though she'd like to kill him. "Is something wrong?" I asked, my eyes going back and forth between Draga and Matija. Matija focused on her, but his eyes flitted to her boyfriend. "Matija?"

"It's okay, Lana," Matija drawled. "Draga and I know each other. She's just surprised to see you with me."

Why was it Draga's business who I spent time with?

Draga grabbed me by the arm and took me aside. "I need to talk to you in private for a minute." She escorted me to the next aisle, leaving Matija and Rok alone, scowling at each other.

"You need to choose your friends more carefully," she said. "Matija is bad news." That sounded a lot like what people said about my father.

"He's been nothing but nice to me. Why don't you like him?"

"That doesn't matter. Trust me when I tell you to stay away from him." I considered whether I should listen to her. Maybe Matija's charm and good looks didn't reflect his true character. And yet, hadn't he saved me more than once? And been there for me when I needed him? "He's from Serbia."

"I know that." Was Draga as judgmental about people as my parents were? "I don't see why it matters where he's from."

"Where he's from is a bad family," she added. "You don't want to mess with them."

Matija materialized from around the corner. "Are you bad mouthing me, Draga?"

She glared at him. "Leave her alone. It has nothing to do with her."

"I know that. I have no intention of hurting her."

I spoke up to remind them I was still there. "What's this about?"

"Nothing. She's just jealous. We used to date, but things didn't work out. I had no idea she was still carrying a torch for me."

Draga shot daggers at him with her eyes. "If anything happens to her…" she began, but Matija put his hand up to stop her.

"It won't. I'll take good care of her. I promise." He steered me away from Draga, and we left the store.

"What was that about?" I asked.

"Nothing. We had a bad breakup. It was neither her fault nor mine. It was just the circumstances. Now let's see if we can find another store that sells costumes."

Matija asked a few people in the parking lot about costume stores, and they directed us to a place in the downtown area. We got lucky and found exactly what we were looking for.

"Now that we've got that out of the way, how about some lunch?" Matija asked. "There's a restaurant I've heard is good, on the river. Actually, on a boat on the river."

I agreed that sounded good. "There's something I'd like to do first, though.

Do you like to read? I want to check something out, find some information at the library."

We drove to the large, older three-story red brick building in the university district. Inside, rows upon rows of wooden shelves, filled with hardcover editions, filled me with wonder. But, my purpose for this library visit didn't include book browsing. Matija made himself comfortable in the lounge area with a magazine while the librarian got me settled at a carrel to go through the archives.

"What is it you're looking for?" Matija asked before leaving me to it.

"Just want to learn a bit more about the history of the area," I said. "I want to check out some articles about past events and festivals, things like that."

I began to search the Orakia newspapers for murders and missing people from the first half of 1978.

I found it with ease. There hadn't been many murders in the local area. In the April 17 city paper, a photo of the old house and the bush beside it stared back at me. I had attended Croatian language school Saturday mornings for a couple of years as a kid, so I was able to make sense of the words.

The caption read: *On Sunday morning, the body of a young male was found in a wooded area beside this home in Molono, where a party was held Saturday night. Foul play is suspected. Police are investigating.*

Chapter Thirty-One

I flipped through to the next day's paper and found an article. The gist of it was: *The body found in the woods at a house party Sunday morning has been identified as nineteen-year-old Vuk Savic. Robbery is being considered as a possible motive for the shooting. Police are looking for three other missing teens. They were last seen at the house party in the village of Molono on Saturday evening.*

I flipped through the papers and found something a couple of weeks later. *Police are still investigating the murder of a young man at a house in Molono two weeks ago. They have interviewed several people who attended the party, including the victim's brother. According to him, the victim and another man had an argument over a woman. The man and woman were unknown to him. When he went to look for his brother, he found his body in the woods and called the police. No one else was able to provide details helpful to the case.*

Matija, immersed in his reading, looked up when I tapped him on the shoulder. "So, did you find what you were searching for?" he asked, raising his eyebrows.

"Somewhat," I answered. "But there's a lot more I'd like to know. I think I'm going to have to stay in Croatia a while longer."

We walked in silence down two flights of stairs to the main floor, the top floors open and visible from the lobby, a metal railing lining the edge.

Someone shouted from above, "Look out!"

My head tilted upwards to the top floor. Matija grabbed me by the waist and yanked me away as several hardcover books flew over the edge of the railing directly above me and landed nearby with a thud.

"Sorry!" A voice shouted from above, but I saw no one.

"Are you okay?" Matija asked, releasing me.

I told him I was fine, but a little shaken.

"You seem to be very accident-prone. It's a good thing I'm around to save you. I guess I'm your guardian angel, little girl." He tried to make a joke out of it, but his eyes conveyed his concern for my safety.

When we arrived at the restaurant, he secured his arm around me as we walked up the gangplank to board the boat. I think he was afraid I might topple over into the river, in spite of the railings bordering both sides.

From our table, we had a lovely view of the river and the far shore. I ordered chicken *rižoto* while Matija opted for veal. During our meal, I asked about Draga again. "How long have you known her? When did you date?"

"It was a long time ago. We met at university. Our families didn't approve of our relationship, and we broke up. That's all there is to it." He indicated that part of the conversation was over, too. "What about you? Your 'sort of' boyfriend?"

I told him Jim, and I had been dating for a few months, and changed the topic to tourist attractions in the area.

When the waiter came to check on us, Matija asked for suggestions on sightseeing in the city.

"Oh, there is so much to see! The walkways and bridges along the river, of course. We have museums, and the cathedral is beautiful. And the catacombs and the fort...."

"Catacombs?" I interrupted. "There are catacombs here?"

The waiter told us their location and a bit of their history. Matija poured me a second glass of wine and raised his eyebrows. "I'm guessing you'd like to go there."

"Yes, it sounds interesting." I told him how much I had enjoyed Ravina and Dubrovnik. "All the history here in Croatia—it's fascinating."

"We'll go after lunch, then."

After I finished my meal and downed my second glass of wine, I excused myself to go to the washroom. On my way back to our table, I slipped outside onto the side deck for a view of the river, and stood at the low railing watching boats pass under the bridge. The wine and the sensation of floating caused me to be a bit unsteady, so I held onto the railing. As I let go and turned around to go back in, a man approached me.

"I think you dropped something." He pointed into the water. I didn't see anything. "Right there, over by the side of the boat." I leaned over the railing for a closer look. The water sloshed, making my stomach queasy. Something floated on the surface, and I strained to see what it was. My hands skimmed the railing as I moved closer to the object, but the railing ended abruptly, replaced by a chain. My hands slipped down, and I lost my balance. The man's arms reached out in an attempt to steady me, but it was too late.

I screamed as I hit the frigid water.

The man scanned the area, grabbed a life preserver from the side of the boat, and tossed it next to me. I managed to strap my arms around it, but not being a strong swimmer, I struggled against the current as it dragged me farther from the boat. On the deck, there was no sign of the man who had tried to save me.

"Help! Help!" I shouted, kicking my legs and keeping my head above water.

Matija ran onto the deck and jumped in without hesitation. He swam up to me in several smooth, steady strokes and tugged the life preserver up to the hull. A couple crew members, having heard the commotion, ran out and threw a rope ladder over the edge. Matija climbed behind me, keeping me from toppling back in.

Our drenched clothing dripped onto the boat's deck as I wrapped my arms around my waist, teeth chattering. The crew brought towels, and we dried ourselves off, then they wrapped blankets around us and apologized profusely as though it was their fault I tumbled overboard.

"You are a lot of trouble, little girl." Matija shook his head, water pooling around his feet. He thanked the crew members as they directed us inside to dry off and recover from the shock. Heads turned in our direction, and I wished I were invisible as my shoes squished by the diners' tables.

Matija paid the bill and tipped generously. He sat me down at our table and told me to wait while he got our clothes. I wondered what clothes he was talking about. "Don't move," he shook his finger at me. "I'm not jumping in after you again."

In a few minutes, he returned with two familiar-looking shopping bags.

"We're not... are we? What exactly are we changing into?" My eyes flitted to the bags and back to him. Matija raised his eyebrows and shrugged his shoulders. "Over my dead body," I said. "I'm not going to be caught dead walking around town in that."

Matija laughed. "Don't push it, baby girl. You've come close enough more than once."

We entered the washrooms with our soggy street clothes and exited as new personalities—a ghost of a girl, and a handsome dangerous count. People had stared as we walked into the washrooms, but even more so when we came out five minutes later and walked through the center of the restaurant on our way out.

Matija spread his cape and said in English, using his best vampire impression, "Thank you evvveryvone... that concludes our performance. But ve'll be back later for zee dinner show. Be sure to join us for zee eevvening entertainment." Then he took a bow and said, "And now ve must fly." With a flourish, he flapped his cape, put his arm around me, and made a production of leading me out of the restaurant.

As we stumbled off the boat, nearly falling off the gangplank as we laughed ourselves silly, Matija said, "I don't know about you, but I'm never going to show my face in there again."

In between giggles, I said, "You're so funny. I really like you."

"I like you, too, Lana. But no more river dates. When I told you before that I didn't want to have to fish you out of the river, I didn't expect to actually have to do it."

We both whooped and attracted more attention, me with the white hooded cloak over my white gown, and Matija with his black pants and shirt covered by a black cape lined in blood red. I hadn't laughed so hard since... well, since before my parents died.

After he opened the car door and helped me into the passenger seat, Matija slipped on his sunglasses. "And now, on to the catacombs. Try not to get into any more trouble."

Matija drove across the bridge to the caves on the other side of the river. We saw no one, thankfully. I would have hated to run into anyone, dressed in our Halloween gear. It could have given them a heart attack, in that secluded area of the old catacombs. Brush overhanging from above partly covered the stone walls of the passageways, built into the side of hills.

We roamed through the tunnels, the dirt floor under our feet and stone archways surrounding us. I felt once again transported to the past, in the remnants of the eighteenth-century fortress, the spooky atmosphere seeping into my bones. Pulling my hood over my head and stretching my arms out, I whirled around the tunnel and made ghost-like noises. Matija joined me, with his collar up and his arms opening his cape, chanting, "I vant to drink your blood. Oooh, but you don't have any."

As we carried on in this manner, I entered another section of the catacombs through an archway and turned a corner, bumping into someone. "Oh, I'm so sorry." A family of four, the mom and dad and two kids, watched us intently. I remembered them from the restaurant. "I wasn't watching where I was going."

"That's okay," the dad said. "No problem. Go on with your show."

Matija and I gave each other a questioning look, then he continued, hamming it up even more. I followed suit, and we danced our way into the next section of tunnels, the parents clapping as we moved on, playing our roles.

We heard the mom say to the kids, "See. This is better than Disney World."

The dad agreed. "They put on a good show, don't they? I didn't know they took Halloween so seriously here."

"Well, we are in the Balkans, dear. Isn't that where Dracula's castle is?"

By the time we got back to the car, we exploded with laughter. "Thank you," I snorted between guffaws.

"For what?"

"Another great day. The more time I spend with you, Matija… whoever you are, the more fun I have. By the way, what is your last name?" I enjoyed this man's company, but I didn't even know his name.

He said nothing at first, then embarrassed me with his answer. "Does it matter? We have a good time, that's all there is to it. You shouldn't expect anything more to come of this, Lana. I'm not looking for a relationship, nothing serious, just some fun." He slipped on his shades.

My face burned as red crept into my cheeks. Although he must have meant friendship, his use of the word relationship caught me off guard. Perhaps I should have made it clearer that I wasn't available, although he hadn't made any inappropriate moves or suggestions. "Neither am I. But, I appreciate having a friend in a strange country."

We drove the rest of the way home in near silence. Matija made some attempts at conversation, but I ignored him as I pondered why he wanted to spend time with me. He had already told me that he had lots of girlfriends, none of them serious. Did he expect me to become a fling, a bit of fun? Did he have a thing for younger women? Was his term of endearment, 'mala', his way of flirting?

When he dropped me off in front of grandma's house, he asked what time and where we should meet tomorrow. I said on the highway at six.

As I slipped out of the passenger seat, he rolled the window down. "Hey, Lana." He pulled off his shades and waited till I made eye contact. "I'll see you tomorrow night, baby girl." He winked. "At the sleepover."

Baby girl? What *exactly* did Matija want from me?

He rolled up the window, did a U-turn, and hit the gas.

Chapter Thirty-Two

"I see you've found your costume," Grandma remarked as I walked through the door in my ghost outfit. "And Darijo? Did he find his?"

I knew I'd been caught in a lie. Grandma had seen me get out of Matija's car. I had to think fast. "Yes, he has his. And a funny thing happened in Orakia. We just happened to bump into my friend, Matt. So the two of us went out for a drink after my shopping trip with Darijo." Surely, she wouldn't check out my story.

"So, what else did you buy?" Grandma pointed to my bags.

"Some Halloween makeup, a white wig, white fingernails." I showed them to her.

"And what's in the other bag?" Grandma took my bag and scrunched up her nose as she peered inside. "Why are your clothes wet? And why do they smell fishy?"

"I sort of fell into the river. I'm going to shower and change."

"You what? How did you end up in the river?"

"I'm kind of accident-prone. But I'm fine. Someone threw in a life preserver and jumped in to save me." I went to the bathroom to change before she could ask any more questions.

After a shower and fresh clothing, I told Grandma I was going to see Tina.

"Be back in an hour for supper," she said as I walked out the door. "And don't make any more trouble." Under her breath, I heard her mutter, "Just like her mother."

Tina's mom ushered me into the living room, where Tina and Vlado sat in front of the T.V., his arm hooked around her shoulder. "Did you get your costume?" Tina asked. She planned to use last year's witch outfit.

"Yes, and I wanted to tell you I'm bringing my friend, Matija. The guy I told you about."

"You're bringing a date?" Vlado asked. "Darijo isn't going to like that."

"Why not?"

"It's just that…." Vlado stopped.

Tina continued for him. "Darijo likes you. He won't be happy if you bring a date." She gave me an accusing look, and I remembered that she'd been friends with Darijo a lot longer than with me. "But whatever."

Vlado shrugged one shoulder. "Darijo and Filip, and I have been busy getting the place ready. It's going to be really cool. Just a few more things to do tomorrow, and we're all set."

"Yeah, you should see it," Tina added. "They've cleaned it out nicely and got it all decorated for Halloween."

I couldn't wait. Not just because of the party. I thought Dad's old house might hold some clues about him. I left the two of them, saying I was excited and I'd see them tomorrow night. Before going home for supper, I stopped by to see Zora.

Kata answered the door. "Zora's not feeling well."

"What?" I burst in through the kitchen and into Zora's old bedroom to find her curled on the bed, crying. She held a piece of paper in her hands and stared at it, but slid it under her pillow when I entered. Did she just get some bad news? I worried that she'd had a relapse of whatever she had during my parents' funeral. Did she have a serious illness and wanted to spare me from knowing?

"Zora, what's wrong?" I put my arm around her shoulder.

She wiped her tears and told me it was nothing. "I'll be fine. Just not feeling quite myself."

I wondered what the note said and how I was going to get my hands on it.

"I'm going to make you a nice cup of tea," I said, as I returned to the kitchen where Kata stirred the soup pot. I let the tea steep and cool before bringing it to Zora. An area rug on the floor of her room somehow managed to trip me. I held onto the cup, but unfortunately, some of it slopped out and onto

Zora's shirt.

"AAH...!"

"I'm so sorry, oh no, I'm sorry...." I apologized. "Are you okay?"

She sat up and pulled her shirt away from her skin. "It's okay. Don't worry."

Once I set the cup on the table by the bed, I said, "Why don't you take that shirt and rinse it out with cold water before the stain sets in."

Zora picked out another top from her closet, then headed to the bathroom to clean up and change.

While she was gone, I took out the note and read it:

Zlata, time to confess and face the consequences for what you did or else. You've seen what could happen to people you care about.

Gasping, fighting for air, I refolded it, put it exactly where Zora left it just as she came through the door, and pulled myself together as my heart threatened to escape my chest.

"Did you get it out?" When she nodded, I added, "Why don't we go for a walk after you drink your tea? Fresh air might be just what you need." I was hoping she would confide in me.

Instead, Zora said, "No, I'm okay. I'm going to lie down for a while and then have supper. I'll see you tomorrow, Sunce."

And just like that, she dismissed me, leaving me to wonder what on earth she had done that needed confessing, and why the letter was addressed to Zlata, not Zora. Why was someone calling her by a different name? Was anyone who they claimed to be?

Chapter Thirty-Three

I slept in Friday morning. I'd been tossing and turning for a good part of the night thinking about the note and what it meant. Zora obviously didn't want to talk about it.

"You must have had a tough day yesterday, in the river," Grandma commented, hands on hips, once I finally rolled out of bed. "It's almost ten. Do you still want breakfast or an early lunch?"

I said I'd skip breakfast and wait for lunch. She didn't seem to be in the best of moods. "I'm going over to see Zora," I said. "She wasn't feeling well yesterday and I want to check on her."

Zora sat at the kitchen table, staring off into space. Kata said she was still under the weather.

"How about a walk now?" I suggested.

She remained unresponsive. I nudged her and repeated my question. Zora slid off her chair and headed out the door without a word. I followed, and we walked down to the highway.

"Do you want to talk about it?" I asked. She shook her head. "Which way do you want to walk?"

"It doesn't matter." She shrugged.

"Okay, how about down the next street?" There weren't exactly a lot of options. We trod in silence, the autumn breeze kissing our cheeks in the morning air, leaves from walnut and oak trees scurrying past on the paved road. A few people walked along the street or got into their cars; some waved to Zora, but most either stared or simply ignored us. "Let's go down this way," I suggested, pointing to the turn off.

Zora froze. "No, not that way." I wondered whether it had something to do with the murder house. Did she know about what happened there more than thirty years ago? "To the river."

We backtracked, crossed the highway, and I followed Zora on the walking trail toward the Danube. Neither of us spoke until we reached the river's edge. As we looked across the blue-gray water, Zora said, "I used to come down here when I was young."

"You're still young."

"No, I've lived my life." Her voice betrayed a melancholy as she reminisced. I wondered again whether she had some terminal illness and hadn't told me. Zora sat on the cold, grassy ground by the shore, and I joined her. "When I was nearly 14, I met a boy. He wasn't from here. He came from a big town down the river."

I thought it best to keep quiet for now and listen. So, I simply nodded my head and said, "Mmhm," to indicate I was there for her.

"We couldn't be together. Our families wouldn't have approved. So we met in secret. He'd bike here when the weather was good and take the bus when it wasn't. We'd come down to the river or the woods. In the winter we'd huddle together in somebody's barn. The first time I saw him I was shopping at a store in his hometown. We bumped into each other in one of the aisles. I knew from the first moment we met I was going to love him. No one knew about us except your mom and dad. The young people used to get together every Saturday night at a different house. He showed up at one of them with his brother. That was the last time I saw him before moving to Canada."

"What happened to him?"

"I moved away to Canada. He never left his hometown."

"Why did you break up?"

"Circumstances. Life. Fate. I guess it was too much to expect to be that happy forever."

"Did he ever marry? Have kids?" She shook her head. "Why don't you go see him, then? Maybe you can still get together, start fresh," I blurted before remembering Mom had told me Zora's one true love died.

"No, it's too late. You can't relive the past." Zora stopped talking and gazed into the river's depths. Finally, she said, "We talked about spending the rest of our lives together. But, it wasn't meant to be."

"Is that what happened to Mama? She loved Luka? But they couldn't be together? And then she ran away with my dad?"

Zora sighed. "No, Sunce. Your Mama married the one and only man she ever loved. Your father. Luka Nikolov."

My jaw dropped, and I stared at Zora, uncomprehending. "What about my dad, Janez? She didn't love him? They weren't married?" It was absolutely unbelievable. There was no way my parents didn't love each other. And I had seen their marriage certificate.

"Luka and Janez were the same person. Luka changed his identity when he emigrated from Croatia to Canada. He wanted to make a complete break from his family."

Of course!

I was starting to understand. "Because he was a Serbian mobster?"

Now Zora's jaw dropped. "No! Where did you get that idea?"

"From one of the neighbors, Janez Peric."

"I see. Well, you've got it wrong." Zora stood up, brushed herself off and started back toward the path leading into town. "It's time to go home and have lunch."

She wouldn't talk on the way home, even though I tried to pry more information out of her.

As we approached Grandma's house, I said, "I bought my costume for the party. Do you want to see it?"

"The party?" she asked with a startled expression on her face. "I'd forgotten about that. You shouldn't go."

Why, all of a sudden, was she against me going to the party?

"I've been really looking forward to it. Of course, I'm going."

"No, stay home. It's not safe to go out at night. Terrible things have been happening in town lately. I hate to think what might happen, especially with it being Halloween. No, you're not going."

I glared at her in disbelief. What made her think she could tell me what to do? "I'm an adult. *I* decide where I will and won't be going. You have no right to treat me like a child."

"You're right. You're no one's child," she said. She must have seen the hurt on my face because she tried to take back her words. "Oh, Svjetlana, I'm so sorry. I wasn't thinking. But I don't want you at that party. It's too dangerous to go out at night. First, the chickens, and who knows what else. Someone wants to hurt us, and I'm not going to put you in harm's way."

"I'm going to the party."

"No, I won't allow it. I may not have the right to tell you what to do, but your safety comes first. And I'm begging you not to go."

Chapter Thirty-Four

The Party October 31

I called home, mindful of the time difference, to catch the kids before school and wish them a 'Happy Halloween.'

"Have fun tonight. Love you. I miss you so much." I wished I could be there with the three of them, admiring the Halloween decorations, knocking on neighbors' doors, and collecting treats. I hated missing out, especially knowing that before long, Brent would consider himself too old to tag along with his family on Halloween. How many more trick-or-treat nights would the four of us have?

But I'd made a decision I couldn't go back on, and now what should have been a family night out would likely be a drunkfest with a bunch of immature twenty-somethings.

"Hold on," Jim caught me as I was about to end the call. "You wouldn't happen to have been on a boat cruise and to the catacombs?"

"Catacombs? Why?" How did he know where I'd been?

"This morning, as I was flipping through Facebook, I noticed a Halloween video from Croatia, taken by a family on vacation. A vampire and ghost performance. The post says they loved the show on the boat cruise, and were thrilled when they had a replay at the catacombs. The funny thing is, the woman looked a lot like you."

"Huh, isn't that strange? Anyway, I will talk to you again tomorrow. Have fun with the kids tonight. Love you." I hung up before he demanded an explanation.

I should have done the sensible thing and backed out of the party, stayed home with Grandma, and handed out treats to kids. But, I defied Zora's wishes and met Matija at the highway at six o'clock, both of us in full costume and ready to party. As well as my white gown and hooded cloak, and white running shoes, I sported a white wig, long white fingernails, white pancake makeup, heavily lined black kohl eyes, and black lips. When I checked the mirror before leaving, I frightened myself. Matija looked even better. Apart from his black vampire costume, fake fangs, and red lipstick, with blood running down the side of his chin, he had gone to the trouble of slicking back his dark hair, powdering his face, and applying eyeliner. Dark and dangerous. Together, we looked like a bride and groom from a horror movie. The perfect couple.

"It's down the road from the church." I opened the passenger door as soon as he pulled into the variety store parking area, lugging with me the comforter off my bed, a flashlight, and a container of Grandma's apple strudel. Before I left, she reminded me that Zora was against my going, and we'd both have to face her 'I told you so' if it resulted in trouble. "You did bring a sleeping bag, didn't you? And a flashlight?"

"I did. And I brought a couple of bottles of wine."

"And the entrance fee?"

Matija nodded. Darijo had told me they were charging a fee to cover costs. The fifty kuna amounted to about ten dollars per person.

As I indicated Matija should take the turnoff from the church road, he asked, "Your friend lives down this road?" His voice caught in his throat. "Which house is it?"

When I told him it was at the end of the road, before the dead end by the woods, Matija stopped the car in the middle of the road and turned to me. "Your friend lives there?" His makeup disguised his expression somewhat, but a shadow fell over him. His eyes darkened, his face set in stone.

What is his *problem?*

"Well, not exactly. It's an abandoned house and he thought it would be fun to have a haunted house Halloween party there."

"Fun?" Matija turned away from me and resumed driving. He parked down the road from the house. It was just as well no one lived directly next door or across the road. The Halloween music boomed down the street, assaulting our ears as soon as we exited the car. Jack-o-lanterns lit the walkway up to the side door, and a skeleton rattled from the overhang. White sheets hung from surrounding trees and bushes, billowing in the breeze.

Matija's body tensed as we walked arm in arm toward the door. For a cool guy, he spooked easily. "You're not scared, are you?" I teased. "Ghosts are only real if you believe in them."

"It's just morbid. This is a creepy old house. Why would they choose to have the party here?"

"I think that's exactly why. It *is* creepy."

I opened the door and stepped inside Dad's old house. They had done an amazing job of decorating. It had been swept out and washed down, thanks to Darijo and his friends. A muted light from lanterns lining the floor along the walls cast shadows through the living area, which was devoid of furnishings except for the boombox, speakers, and amplifier. A space heater sat in front of the window, cords strung out to a generator in the side yard. About a dozen people stood around chatting, competing with the music. A cotton batting spider web hung from the ceiling, with black crepe paper spiders dangling from it. Strings of small pumpkin lights hung along the tops of the walls. The overall effect was perfect for the occasion. I tried to imagine what it might have looked like when my dad lived there. I took the camera out of my backpack, and took a few photos of the living room.

"Svjetlana?" A voice called out from the other end of the room. Tina, the witch. I shouted back, confirming it was me. Voices and mannerisms were the only way to positively identify anyone. She approached us. "And this is your friend?"

I introduced Matija and Tina to each other.

"Great party. I like the music," Matija commented.

"Yeah, the guys put together a mix with spooky sounds and songs," Tina explained. "They went all out this year."

The zombie trio across the room fixed their eyes on us. One of them headed over. "Hey, you look great." Darijo appraised me, then glared at Matija. "Who's this?" After the introductions were made, Darijo said the food and drinks should go in the kitchen, on the counter. "And sleeping bags and blankets up in one of the bedrooms. Did you bring a flashlight?" He put his arm around my shoulder and steered me toward the stairs.

Tina grabbed the apple strudel from me and told Matija to follow her, while Darijo relieved Matija of his sleeping bag and accompanied me to the upper level. I set our sleeping gear on the floor in one of the rooms, where others had already deposited their makeshift beds. Semidarkness embraced us, except for some light coming through the windows, but the extra glow from our flashlights tempered my anxiety.

"Is he your boyfriend? I thought your sort-of boyfriend was in Canada. So who's this guy?" Darijo asked.

"I met him when he was visiting his family in Canada, and we've gotten together a few times since I've been here."

"I was hoping you and I could spend some time together tonight. I didn't expect you to bring someone."

"He's just a friend. I hope it's okay that I brought him."

Darijo shrugged. "No problem." More people came into the bedroom with their stuff, cutting off our conversation.

We returned to the living area. The mix of Croatian and English music continued booming through the house, including the familiar "Monster Mash," "Highway to Hell," "Witchy Woman," and "Superstition." By six-thirty, about thirty of us crammed ourselves into the living area. Darkness engulfed the outside by that time, save for the artificial lighting and a sliver of a moon.

Darijo shut off the music to make a toast, and the party officially began as he raised a glass and spoke in a spooky voice. "Welcome to the party of the decade. May you all survive. Bwahahaha."

181

Chapter Thirty-Five

The Party April 15, 1978

Mimi looked forward to the party for more than one reason. She was going to see *him* again. That always gave her butterflies in the stomach, in a good way. Even though she'd been warned against him, told he was dangerous, his magnetism pulled her in. The first time she saw him, she couldn't keep her eyes off him. The second time she saw him, she couldn't keep her hands off him. And by the third time, she gave herself to him—mind, body, and soul—and she was lost. No going back.

They first met at the New Year's Eve party at a friend's house. He swaggered in, stood in front of the doorway, with his legs apart, one hand in his pocket, and surveyed the room like a prince overlooking his kingdom. The whispers rippled through the house as soon as he entered. No one dared to stare, except Mimi.

They were seen together at a couple of parties since then, the other guests giving him a wide berth and casting furtive glances as he danced only with Mimi.

But that night, he didn't come alone. His younger brother followed him into the room, a little less cocky, but dangerous nonetheless. Their eyes lazily swept the room, making it clear they could have their pick of the young women, whether or not they were already spoken for.

The cool evening breeze swooped in with them, even though it had been one of the first warm days of spring. Sixteen-year-old Mimica attended the house party with her next-door neighbor, Zlata. The two best friends had fallen for a couple of young guys they had no business talking to, much less loving.

Besides the party, the second thing Mimi looked forward to that night was running away with the man she loved, the man whose baby she carried.

After the party, Mimica's new life awaited her.

Chapter Thirty-Six

The Party October 31

"This year, we have a special event planned. Since we're having our Halloween party at the house where a murder took place thirty years ago, we thought it would be neat to have a murder mystery night." Darijo paused and looked around the dimly lit room, building the suspense.

Some people gasped, and others exclaimed, "Ooooh!" or "That's cool!"

Darijo continued, "By morning, one of the guests here will be dead." Silence enveloped the room.

Vlado stepped next to Darijo to give instructions. "Before we begin, Filip is going to come around and collect your entry fee, half of which will be the prize money. The other half will be compensation for the killer and the victim for playing their roles. The person who correctly identifies the killer will collect the prize money, or in the event of a tie, the money will be split equally. If the winner doesn't last the whole night, he or she forfeits the money. If no one wins, the prize gets split between those who are still here and alive in the morning."

Once Filip collected all the money in a jar, Vlado explained the rules of the game. "Any one of us could be the victim. Keep your eyes and ears open. At some point during the night, someone is going to find the body. It's up to all of us to solve the murder. Anything that happens tonight could be a clue, or it could be a red herring, or it could be completely unconnected to the

184

game. Everyone will receive three cards, each with an instruction that you *must* follow without letting anyone know that you are doing so. If you fail to follow through with any of these instructions or share information with others, you forfeit your chance at the prize money."

"You might also end up being another victim," Darijo added with a chuckle, as he passed around index cards with instructions. "And if no one makes it through the night, I keep all the money."

I received three folded cards with my name printed on the outside. Matija received three unmarked folded cards. They must have accounted for the fact that uninvited guests might pop up. "Remember the rules: Follow the instructions. Keep them to yourself. And..." Darijo croaked, "Watch out for the killer."

Vlado continued, "Notice the clock on the wall. It's set to chime once every half hour and three times on the hour. Keep track of the time. Once the body is discovered, the person who has stumbled upon the body will alert everyone by ringing till we are all gathered." He picked up a large bell from beside the boom box and swung it from side to side, piercing our ears with the sudden clanging. "Everyone will meet here with their accusations of whodunit, and the winner will be awarded their prize. Have fun, and remember—watch out for the killer. You could be the next victim at the murder house."

"Read your instructions and hide them deep in your pockets (or your underwear)," Darijo chortled. He then apologized that the washroom facilities onsite were outdated and limited. "A word of warning, guys. If you're going out the back door to use nature, watch out for thistles. Girls, the outhouse is out the side door and to the left, last door in back of the house, fully stocked with soap, water, paper towels, and toilet paper. There's a small battery operated lantern inside. Remember to bring a flashlight with you. Don't want anyone falling in," he joked. Then he added his place down the road was lit up and wide open all night as well for anything anyone needed. "For the ladies who think they're too good for the outhouse. My mom's idea." He invited us to help ourselves to food and drinks in the back kitchen.

"And let the games begin," Darijo announced, his mouth stretched in a grin.

Darijo turned the music back up, and a line formed at the arched opening to the back kitchen; people heaped up their plates, and circled back to the living area. The quantity and variety of food surprised me—everything from snack foods to salads, fruits and veggies, breads, cheese and cold cuts, to covered hot dishes, kept warm with foil and towels around them, to a complete dessert bar. Along with the counter, a folding table had been set up along one wall to hold all the food and the wide selection of homemade wine and rakija. These people obviously knew how to throw a party. A couple of lanterns provided just enough light, and another space heater warmed the room. Matija and I filled our paper plates, with Darijo behind us.

"You've really gone all out for this party," I said.

"I did it all to impress you," Darijo kidded. "But seriously, this is the way we do things here in Molono. Everyone pitches in. It's a small village, very friendly, one big, happy family."

I hadn't really noticed that in my personal experience, but I kept it to myself. Most of the people in town wouldn't say hello to me, much less invite me into their big, happy family. He and Tina had been nice, though, and Vlado and Filip seemed to tolerate me. Then there was Kata. She made me feel like family.

We sat in groups on the old wooden floor in the living area and the kitchen, chatting and eating. Tina, Vlado, Filip and his girlfriend Maja, Matija, Darijo, and I formed a small circle. Once everyone finished their meal, the guys led some organized activities, obviously meant to be icebreakers, to loosen everyone up. Some were ones I'd played before in high school, but with a bit of a twist. Darijo and his buddies seemed to be caught in a time warp, refusing to give up their teen years. I supposed that, given a chance, most people would love to be transported back to the simplicity of life before adulthood.

They divided us into three teams. Three tin tubs filled with water were set out, and we bobbed for liqueur-infused apples, trying not to ruin our makeup in the process. With our hands behind our backs, we ate wine-dipped doughnuts hanging from broom handles and used oven mitts to unwrap mini liquor bottles. We tossed marshmallows into rakija-filled cups in a version of beer pong, and the rules for Spin the Wine Bottle were to kiss the person it points to, and both of you take a swig of wine. I kissed a couple of guys I'd never met before that night, on the cheek, explaining I had a boyfriend back home. By nine o'clock, we were all well fed and well drunk.

Except Matija. He looked dead sober.

Vlado took over the boombox and acted as disc jockey, saying it was time for everybody to show their moves, commenting on the songs and the couples' dancing as they writhed around and bumped into each other in the living room. He started out with a couple of fast songs, then switched to some soft, romantic music. Matija and I swayed back and forth to the melody, and I lay my head against his shoulder. Imagining Jim there with me, I floated blissfully across the room, almost falling asleep in his arms. After one song, Darijo literally swept me off my feet, away from Matija.

"I thought you said he was just a friend," Darijo teased. "It looks like more than that. Even though he seems older than everybody else here. He's probably old enough to be your dad."

"He's not that old. And he's a lot of fun."

"*I* can be a lot of fun," Darijo said, and he kissed me, his tongue skimming my lips. I was drunk, lost in the moment, but I sobered up enough to remember Jim, the love of my life and father of my children.

"Yep, I bet you can," I replied, pulling away and tripping over his feet. "But I do kind of have a boyfriend, remember?"

"So you said. Why are you hanging out with Matija, then?"

"He's a friend, and I like him." I left out the part about how he seemed to be there whenever I needed rescuing. And how I thought he was good-looking. And funny. *And* I wanted to know more about his connection to my parents.

Matija stood against the wall, eyes on me.

When Vlado upped the tempo on the next song, I excused myself from the dance floor, saying I wasn't sure I could remain upright on my own. I joined Matija along the wall, allowing it to hold me up.

"You shouldn't have any more to drink," Matija said. "I'm glad you're having a good time, but let's get you a soft drink and go out for some fresh air." He steered me to the kitchen and grabbed a cola, telling Darijo he'd bring me back shortly. With his arm around my shoulder, he walked me out the side door and down the street. The cool breeze slapped my face.

"It's cold out here," I complained. Matija took off his black and red cape, put it over my white cloak, made me take a few sips of cola, and supported me as we continued walking. "Where are we going?"

"Just sobering up a bit."

No street lights surrounded the house, but as we moved up the road, lampposts illuminated the more populated area where Darijo's house stood.

"I'm going to use the washroom in Darijo's place," I said. Handing Matija back his cape, I entered the brightly lit front entrance. Darijo's mom directed me to the washroom. On my way down the hall, I met a couple of girls on their way out.

"Feeling better?" one asked the other.

"No, I know what I saw."

"You've just had too much to drink, that's all."

I interrupted them. "What happened? What did you see?"

"What's your name again?" the first one asked.

"Svjetlana, a friend of Tina's and Darijo's." I had no idea who these girls were. It was impossible to remember all the people I'd been introduced to, especially with the costumes.

"Petra thought she saw someone in the woods next to the house a while ago. And with all the weird shit that's been happening in town lately, she got spooked. Petra's always seeing shadows in the dark. She's got a vivid imagination."

"The stories Darijo's been telling about that being the murder house and the murder mystery game are really freaking me out," conceded Petra.

"Maybe it's just part of the game," I suggested. "A clue."

Needing to use the washroom, I excused myself. By the time I got out, they were gone. Matija stood outside.

"Did you see where those two girls went?" I wanted to talk further about what Petra had seen in the woods.

"What girls? I didn't see anyone."

Before I could describe them, someone else headed down the street toward us. I recognized the walk.

Zora hesitated when she saw us, then called out, "Svjetlana? Is that you?"

I thought maybe if I ignored her, she'd figure it wasn't me and go away. But Matija said, "Lana? This woman is talking to you."

Busted. At a party she didn't want me to attend, and drunk, to top it off. Then I remembered I was a grown woman, and she had no business intruding on my life.

"Yes. Zora, what are *you* doing here?" I spoke slowly, trying hard not to slur my words.

"Are you drunk? Never mind, that doesn't matter. What matters is you came to this party when I expressly asked you not to."

I turned the tables on her. "Are you spying on me? Because it's none of your business what I do. You can't order me not to go to a party."

"I care about you Svjetlana, and I came to check that everything was okay," she countered. "Your grandma said you planned on staying over. Are you sure that's wise?"

"Everybody else is staying." My ears caught the whining in my voice.

Matija spoke up and said he'd take care of me.

"And who are *you*?" Zora stood with hands on her hips and moved closer to get a look at Matija. "Do I know you?" She narrowed her eyes as she searched his make-up covered face.

"No. I'm a friend of Lana's. And her friend Tina's here, too."

"I'll be home in the morning. Stop worrying. I just want to have some fun for a change. I want to forget about what happened to Mama and Tata for a while," I said, starting to sober up quickly. "Why can't I just enjoy myself with friends?" I turned around and headed back to the party, leaving Zora and Matija behind. I could hear Matija assuring her I'd be okay, he'd make sure I didn't have any more to drink.

He jogged up from behind and joined me in front of the house.

"I'm sick and tired of her telling me what to do," I said. "She treats me like a kid."

"She's concerned, that's all. Now behave yourself. No more drinking tonight."

"And, who do you think *you* are? My father?"

Matija snorted, "I'm not *that* old, baby girl."

A few others hung around the side yard. My eyes searched for the two girls I had seen in Darijo's house, but I couldn't find any trace of them. Darijo, apparently waiting for my return, asked me to dance as soon as we entered the house. Matija told me to go on and have fun.

On the dance floor, Darijo whispered something in my ear. I wasn't sure I understood correctly, but I thought he said, "Are you sure *he's* not the killer?"

Chapter Thirty-Seven

The Party April 15, 1978

As usual, Zlata's heart fluttered at the sight of him, even though she had just seen him yesterday when they rendezvoused at the river and made love on a blanket in the woods near the water's edge. Despite the coolness in the air, heat filled her body as she lay beneath him. The first time had been on her birthday a few months earlier, the night they secretly spent in her best friend's barn.

When he entered the house party that night, goosebumps stood at attention on her arms, awaiting his touch. She had fallen in love with him the moment she first saw him. They'd been meeting in secret for over a year, since they met at that department store in the nearby town of Vlasilo last December while Christmas shopping, and now they were finally going to be seen in public as a couple. She knew people would talk, and it would get back to her parents, but it didn't matter anymore. At fifteen, she was old enough to make her own decisions. Next year, they planned to get married.

The house, full of young people, resonated with loud music and chatter. The dancing and drinking stopped for a few seconds as the two young men commanded attention, then everyone continued on with their own business, eyes shifting away from the newcomers.

Zlata waited for him to approach and claim her as his. Instead, he stood to the side, eyes scanning the room, watching everyone else. His eyes landed on a few of the other young women, assessing them. Doubt assailed Zlata, and she wondered whether she wasn't the first girl he had won over, if he had a habit of stealing young girls' innocence and breaking hearts.

Zlata waited for him to make a move toward her, but when he kept his distance, she flirted with some of the other young men, hoping to get his attention.

The door flung wide open, ushering in the cool evening air. Everyone froze and stopped talking when two strangers entered the house. All eyes took in the tall, dark, attractive young men, one close to twenty, and the other about Zlata's age. They sauntered over to the table laden with alcoholic drinks. "As you were. Don't let us stop the festivities," the older one said as people gawked.

Slowly, people resumed their dancing, but Zlata felt the whispers around the room, though she couldn't hear them. She wondered who these two guys were. On the other side of the room, the love of her life stood with his brother, both assessing the strangers.

Continuing her way across the room, chatting with young guys she knew from the village, Zlata allowed herself to be escorted to the dance floor by one of her neighbors, Janez. Although Zlata knew he had a huge crush on her best friend, she assumed he was trying to make Mimi jealous. Zlata hoped her dancing with Janez would evoke the same emotion in the boy she loved.

A few minutes later, an arm grabbed her and tore her away from Janez. Expecting to see *him,* her smile faded when she looked into the face of the oldest stranger.

"I like the way you move," he said. "I like the way you look. And I'm wondering whether I'll like the way you taste." He pulled her close and they danced to the slow, seductive beat of a love song. Zlata hoped *he* was watching.

"My name is Vuk. What's yours?"

"Zlata."

"And where are you from, Zlata?"

"Right here, in the village. I grew up here. What about you?"

"Just down the road, across the Serbian border. My brother and I thought we'd check out the Croatian girls. I'm glad we did."

Although flattered, Zlata grew uncomfortable as his hands wandered up and down her body. "No, don't. Stop," she pleaded, unable to pull away from his firm grip.

"Don't tell me you're shy. I saw you flirting with practically every other guy here." Tipping her face up to his, he kissed her roughly, then whispered in her ear, "How about you and I go outside and get to know each other better?"

Zlata didn't get a chance to say no. *He* was suddenly by her side, and Vuk was propelled away from her, a swift punch to his jaw knocking him to the ground.

"Keep your filthy, fucking hands off my girl," Branko roared loud enough to drown out the music. "Or I'll fucking kill you."

Chapter Thirty-Eight

The Party October 31

The devil, who'd been dancing with an angel all night, wrested me from Darijo's arms. "Would you like to dance?" he asked.

"Yes, thank you, I'd be honored. I've always wanted to dance with the devil." One of my instruction cards had prompted me to say yes when the devil asked me to dance.

Darijo didn't look impressed. "Hold on!" he shouted. "You've been flirting with me, and I've been wanting to spend time alone with you. First, I have to compete with gramps over there, now you're cavorting with the devil. And you've got a boyfriend back home. Looks like you go whichever way the wind blows."

"Do you want to take this outside?" the devil asked.

Darijo backed off and I danced with the devil. When the song ended, I slapped his face, as per my instructions, although it was more like a caress, as I couldn't bring myself to smack some stranger for no apparent reason.

That was among the myriad of weird things that happened that night. Matija was dancing with the angel by the time I finished my dance with the devil.

I wondered whether I was sobering up or still drunk. "Do people seem to be acting kind of strangely?" I asked Matija when he joined me again. "And a little on edge?"

"I think it's the game. It's getting to everyone. We're supposed to be confused and not know who to trust."

We watched as people switched dance partners and mingled with others. Some kissed, some argued, some left the building.

"I'm going to talk to Tina and get her take on things."

The witch stood in the corner drinking. I approached her and began, "Tina, are you in on what's going...." I stopped once I realized it wasn't her, just her costume. And I wondered whether people were switching more than just dance partners.

"Great party, isn't it?" Vlado spooked me, coming up from behind.

"Where's Tina?"

"I was wondering the same thing."

As I walked back to where Matija stood against the wall, it crossed my mind that it might not be him, but someone else dressed in his vampire costume. "I need to get some more fresh air," I said.

"Whatever you need, baby girl."

Those were the secret code words that assured me it really was him. As we walked down the street, I asked, "Did you do all the things it said on your cards?"

"I can't tell you that," he laughed. "Rules of the game, remember? But I can tell you your friends are weird. I think we'd have been better off going to the boat restaurant for an evening performance."

"You're not having a good time?"

"Not really, except for the fact that I'm with you."

I thought that was sweet of him to say. We stopped in at Darijo's house to use the washroom, chatted with his parents a bit, then headed back to the party. As we approached the house, music blared from the outside speakers, and when we first heard the screaming, we thought it was the song.

"Aaaahhhhh! Help! Help!" The scream transitioned to a plea, and came from the farm fields next to the abandoned house, down the gravel roadway off to the left.

"Do you think it's part of the game?" I asked.

Matija said we'd better check it out. We raced down the dark graveled lane, lined with trees and shrubs. A dark figure with pointed ears pushed its

195

way through hand harvested gray corn stalks.

"Help! There's someone out here! With a gun!" I recognized Tina's voice as the shadow of a huge black cat on two legs sprang from the field onto the gravel, nearly knocking me over.

"What's going on, Tina?" I grasped her hand to calm her, the tremble transferring to my fingers.

Trying to catch her breath, she panted, "I was supposed to... meet Vlado in the field, but he didn't... show up. I thought I heard him, but when I turned around... I saw some guy, his shadow with... a gun in his hand. When I screamed, he took off."

Arms around her, we escorted a shaky Tina back to the house, unsure of whether she was playing a role in the game or telling the truth. If she was acting, she deserved an Academy Award.

"What happened to you?" Vlado asked Tina. "You were supposed to meet me upstairs half an hour ago. Anyway, I'm glad you made it back just in time."

The clock struck midnight. Vlado shut off the music. "Now the real fun begins."

Chapter Thirty-Nine

The Party After Midnight November 1

Vlado instructed us to form a big circle. "Time for Truth or Dare." We sat down as directed. Some people were missing, but I wasn't sure who or how many. As I scanned the room, looking for Darijo, a pirate barged through the door, yelling, "My sword! It's missing! Has anyone seen it?"

No one admitted to seeing it, and he joined the game. Going around the circle, each person asked whoever they chose, "Truth or Dare?" It began with juvenile questions such as, "If you could kiss anyone here, who would it be?" and "What color underwear are you wearing?" Some of the questions were a bit bolder, such as, "How many people have you slept with?" and "Have you ever done anything illegal?"

The dares were childish and invoked laughter, such as "I dare you to kiss..." and "I dare you to sit on...'s lap" and "I dare you to down a shot of rakija in two seconds." But some dares weren't well received: "I dare you to go out alone to the woods for five minutes" and "I dare you to run up and down Darijo's street howling like a wolf and banging on doors."

Someone asked, "Darijo, Truth or Dare?" He chose the truth option. "Are you capable of murder?"

"Yes. Isn't everyone?" I hadn't even noticed Darijo among us till then. He must have slipped in at some point.

When it was my turn, I asked Matija, "Truth or Dare?" He shrugged and said he had nothing to hide. Sincerely doubting that, I surprised him with a personal question. "Have you ever been in love?"

He didn't respond at first, as though he didn't understand. So I repeated the question.

"Yes."

"Who?" I persisted. "You have to answer the question completely."

"Someone I knew a long time ago."

"No fair. Who?"

"That's all I'm saying."

At Matija's turn, he asked Darijo what his intentions were in regards to me.

"To bite her and make her into a zombie, of course," he answered, straight faced. Darijo crossed the circle and nipped at my neck, making zombie noises. Everyone roared.

The next person dared someone to extinguish the lanterns. At the same time, the pumpkin lights flickered and went out, plunging the room into black. We sat in total darkness for several minutes, Michael Jackson's "Thriller" playing in the background, maniacal howls and ghostly moans of inebriated guests joining the soundtrack.

Darijo pointed a flashlight under his chin, and asked Vlado and Filip to restore illumination upon the haunted realm. As the pumpkin lights flicked back on, and the guys relit the lanterns, Darijo asked if everyone was still alive. Bursts of relieved laughter filled the room, and we continued the game. Someone Truth or Dared me. When I accepted the dare, as prompted by one of my game cards. I was instructed to go up to the attic, alone, look in the trunk, then report what I found.

"In the dark?"

"No, take a lantern," Darijo said, handing one to me. "In the hall. There's a rope hanging. Pull on it and a ladder will come down. Be careful."

They continued the game as I headed up the shadowy stairs. I yanked on the rope and wooden steps appeared from the ceiling. Climbing carefully, the lantern in one hand, my other hand on the safety rail, I ascended to the attic and set the lantern on the floor. Cobwebs greeted me. An ancient, ratty looking trunk sat against the far wall, under a small window. The lantern cast dark shadows around the rafters.

The floor seemed solid enough. I walked over to the antique chest and lifted the lid. Inside, I found a yellowed newsprint. Taking the small flashlight from my pocket, I picked up the paper, dated April 17, 1978. The front page contained the story about the murder that took place at this house, the same words I had read at the library. Darijo and his friends must have found a copy and thought it would be funny. I wasn't about to let it spook me. I already knew the history of this house.

I tucked the paper under my arm to bring downstairs and was about to close the trunk when I noticed an envelope taped to the inside of the lid. Opening it, I found a letter and an old photo. The black and white print showed seven grim-looking people—two parents, a grandparent, and four children. None looked familiar. On the back, a list of names identified the unsmiling family and the year—1978. If this was Dad's house, why did the family photo not include him? Did Grandma lie to me about this being Dad's house? She and Zora had told me enough lies and kept enough from me that anything was possible. Why, though?

Or had this been planted here as a joke for the murder game? Maybe it was fake.

I opened the letter and held my flashlight to it, slowly deciphering the Croatian script:

To whoever is brave enough to enter this house:

Run. Now. This is not a home. The house is cursed. We lived here for over ten years. In that time, we had countless tragedies befall us. Death lives inside these walls. The ghosts refuse to leave. Even Father Lasic couldn't chase them away. The final straw for us was that party. One person dead, three missing. Since that day, the curse has grown stronger and spread throughout the whole village.

The curse is real. Get out while you can. We made it out alive. We pray you do, too.

The letter was supposedly signed by the seven occupants of the house.

Someone was playing a sadistic game. Messing with me.

Or, someone thought they could scare me out of digging into my parents' past.

As I returned the photo and letter into the envelope, a creak caused my head to snap toward the top of the attic steps. From the corner of my eye, the outline of a hooded cloak flashed as it knocked over the lantern and scrambled down the stairs. By the time I reached the opening, the door had slammed closed, leaving me in the dimly lit space, two floors away from everyone else.

As claustrophobia, aggravated by darkness, kicked in full force, I wrestled with the door handle, which seemed to be locked. I pounded on the door, screaming, as the room grew brighter, and I turned to see the spilled lantern oil in flames, licking across the wooden floorboards. When I tried to stamp them out, my cloak caught fire. I flung it off, stamping on it to smother the flames, coughing and gasping for air in the smoky enclosed space.

"Help! Fire! Help!" I hollered, banging on the floorboards as sparks crackled and smoke choked me. I ran over to the window and pounded, hoping someone outside might hear. As the fire flared up again, I thought about the letter.

The curse is real. Get out while you can.

Chapter Forty

I began to pray. That was my only chance of breaking the curse. That and screaming at the top of my lungs and banging away. I kept trying to stamp out the fire at the same time.

The praying must have worked. The door flung open, and a stunned zombie doused the blaze with a tub of water. The flames flared higher.

"There's alcohol in that water, you idiot! Get out of the way!" Dracula pushed aside the zombie and removed his cape, throwing it over the floor to smother the fire.

Darijo grabbed hold of my waist and guided me down the attic stairs, then ran back up to help Matija smother and stamp out the rest of the flames. When my heroes returned from the attic, I hugged them, tears rolling down my cheeks.

"Are you all right?" Darijo asked. "What happened?"

I explained someone knocked over the lantern and locked the door to the attic.

"It wasn't locked, it must have been stuck. But I can't believe any of my friends would do that," he said, shaking his head. "Must be one of the out of towners. Too drunk or just stupid."

I relaxed into Matija's protective arms. "You're always there for me. Thank you."

I turned to Darijo and thanked him as well. "If the two of you hadn't come up when you did, I don't know what I would have done."

"I was wondering what happened to you. You were up there a while, so I thought I'd better check. Halfway up the stairs, I heard you yelling and smelled the smoke," Darijo said.

"I saw Darijo go upstairs and come running back down. When he grabbed one of the metal tubs, I knew something was wrong, so I followed him," Matija explained.

When we reached the main level and joined the rest, Darijo officially declared Truth or Dare over, the fire having put a damper on the fun.

"Everyone outside!" Darijo barked. "And I mean everyone!" He wasn't his usual good-humored self.

Darijo opened windows and doors to air out the smoke while we all gathered in the side yard, around a firepit that Filip and Maja tended. Sheets of plastic lay on the ground, covering the recently mowed weeds to make a seating area for us.

"Before we go any further with this evening's activities, I want to remind everyone to act responsibly. We had a close call upstairs." Darijo explained what happened in the attic. "If someone thought that was a good joke, it wasn't." He lectured everyone about being safe and keeping an eye out for each other. Then he added, "Any more problems tonight and we'll have the cops breathing down our necks." When he was done with his rant, he nodded to Vlado.

"And now, it's time for bedtime stories." Vlado invited anyone with a scary story to tell to come forward.

More than half a dozen people recounted their tales of horror by firelight and jack-o-lanterns — ghost stories, accounts of vampires and werewolves, stories about curses, and serial killers.

The grim reaper joined the storytellers. I couldn't recall any grim reapers being at the party.

He began his tale. "More than thirty years ago, there was another party right here, on these premises. What happened that night brought a curse upon the village. A curse that's been recently awakened."

Chapter Forty-One

The Party April 15, 1978

Branko braced himself.

"Who the fuck are you, boy?" His opponent sprang to his feet and returned the punch.

"I'm her boyfriend, that's who." Branko had been holding back on approaching Zlata. As much as he had wanted to rush over to Zlata's side and take her in his arms, he worried about her reputation. The two of them had agreed they were coming out tonight, exposing their relationship to everyone. But when Branko entered the house, he decided he should take it slow, pretend he didn't know her yet, then ask her to dance. If people knew how close they had been over the last year, how intimate they had become, it wouldn't paint Zlata in a favorable light. Sneaking around in secret with the head of the Croatian mob's son wouldn't be received in a positive manner by the villagers, much less her parents.

But he wasn't about to allow some creep to put his hands all over her. "Do you want to take this outside?" he asked the older, larger guy who had been manhandling the woman he loved.

"I don't think you're man enough, son. How about you back off and leave the whore to me. She's been asking for it."

"I'll show you who's man enough." Branko lost his cool, hearing Zlata insulted, and reached into the back pocket for his gun, then came to his senses. "But not here. Outside." He strode toward the side door, turning to make sure his opponent followed.

The man laughed. "Do you know who you're dealing with, boy? My name's Vuk. Like the wolf that howls at the full moon. Vuk Savic."

Branko now understood exactly who he was tangling with. Oldest son of the Serbian Mafia boss, his own father's rival. But it was too late to back down. Not that he would have done so, given the chance. His love for Zlata overpowered his fear.

Chapter Forty-Two

The grim reaper continued his story. "It was the last party on these premises until tonight. That night a man was shot and killed in the woods next to this house. The police considered it a robbery that got out of hand, and the killer was assumed to be a vagrant. They didn't charge anyone with the shooting, although rumor had it the mob was involved. The villagers knew the true story, but they had taken a vow of silence. The family that lived here soon boarded up the place and disappeared, never to be heard from again. The village had a string of bad luck—theft, vandalism, machinery broken, crops destroyed, animals slaughtered. A curse engulfed the village. People spoke of ghost sightings and things that went bump in the night. After a time, things died down. No one spoke of that night again. Until very recently." The speaker stopped and turned his head, taking in his audience.

"The curse has been awakened. Some people claim it has to do with the three people who went missing from the party the night of the murder, the three who it was rumored were likely at the bottom of the river. They say they've come back from the dead, that they've brought the curse with them."

He paused again for effect.

"But the truth is the three who went missing were the ones responsible for the shooting. They went into hiding, and got away with murder. For thirty years. Until now. And unless all responsible pay for what they've done, the village will remain cursed. When they're all dead, the curse will be lifted, and the village will be left in peace."

One more pause, and he ended his story. "But the ghost of Vuk Savic will

forever haunt these woods."

The grim reaper made a dramatic disappearance into the woods. No one followed. I turned to face Matija, who sat very still throughout the story. Something in his eyes frightened me.

No one said a word for a long time.

Eventually, Darijo stood and announced, "And that concludes storytime. Feel free to head upstairs if you're ready to call it a night. For those who still want to party downstairs, try to keep the noise to a respectable level. For everyone's safety, if you're going outside for the washroom or a smoke, don't go alone. I don't think I need to remind anyone—stay out of the woods. And try to stay alive. Let the murder games continue."

"Are you ready for bed?" I asked Matija as we stood up.

"I think I should just go home," he said, barely audible.

I was seriously considering doing the same thing myself, shivers taking over my senses. But I had one more card to play. And if the grim reaper had more stories to tell about the night of the murder, I planned to be there to hear them. "How about a walk first?"

Matija nodded and followed me down the street, past Darijo's house.

When we were alone, with no danger of being overheard, he said, "It's brought it all back, being here. I was barely 14. Just a boy. He was 19. Too young to have his life snuffed out." Bitterness mixed with sadness as he spoke.

"What are you talking about?" I had a bad feeling the lies of my dead parents were about to be exposed.

Chapter Forty-Three

The Party April 15, 1978

L uka watched as his younger brother, Branko, started a fight. He could hardly blame him. He would have done the same if someone had treated his woman that way. Luka wasn't sure whether Branko understood who he was dealing with, though, and his first reaction was to follow them out and give his brother a hand.

Mimi must have read his mind. "Maybe you should go out, too, see if he needs help."

"I would, but I don't want to embarrass him. People will talk, saying he needs his older brother to take care of him. You know how people are." He glanced at Vuk's brother, who seemed barely more than a kid. "But these guys are trouble. Sons of the Serbian mob leader. Bad news." He was well aware that people said the same thing about him and his brother. "I'll give him a few minutes, then slip out and check on him."

The last thing he needed tonight was a scene. He had everything in place for their getaway. Tonight, instead of going home, he and Mimi planned to leave the country for good, abandoning their families and going off to start their own family. Her parents would never approve of her marrying him, a mobster, a man whose father controlled the Croatian area of Slavonia with his network of gang members who threatened and terrorized the citizens. Neither would his father understand why he chose a simple farmer's daughter from a small village to spend the rest of his life with, especially when he hadn't even reached his nineteenth birthday. When Mimica had told him she was expecting his baby, he immediately made plans for them to leave and start a new life. He told her to pack a small suitcase with a change of clothing, her passport and birth certificate, and a few personal items. He had done the same, but added enough cash to get them through until they were settled. Luka had his sights on Austria, by way of Hungary. By the next morning, they'd be there. And no one could stop them being together.

"Zlata, what are you doing?" Mimi's alarmed cry intruded on his thoughts.

"This is all my fault. I'm going to put a stop to it. Make it clear I'm already taken. That I'm with Branko, and it was all a misunderstanding." With that, Zlata went out the side door into the night.

"I don't like this," Mimi said. "I'm worried. We should go after her."

Luka insisted they give them a chance to sort it out themselves. "It's not the first fight Branko's gotten himself into, believe me." He led Mimi to the dance floor and told her not to worry.

When the music stopped, he said, "I'm going to get another drink. Wait here."

Luka picked up two rakijas at the drink table, and walked over to where Vuk's brother stood alone by the wall, arms crossed, eyes roaming the room. "Is your friend always like this?" Luka handed him a shot glass.

"He's not my friend, he's my brother. You can choose your friends, but you can't choose your brother."

"Tell me about it."

"He's a bit of a hothead. But he usually calms down after a while."

"I hope so, we don't need any trouble here." The two men downed their glasses and Luka gave the boy a pat on the shoulder before walking back to the spot where he had left Mimi. Not seeing her, he assumed she must be in the washroom.

The loud music and people dancing across the wooden floor, enjoying themselves, having seemingly forgotten the fight that started in their midst minutes ago, occupied Luka's attention for a couple of minutes. When Mimi didn't come back, he checked the exterior bathroom, but she was nowhere to be seen. Worried she might have gone after Zlata, he listened for any sign of her. The house lights illuminated the immediate area. Otherwise, darkness closed in.

In the wooded area next to the house, whimpering traveled through the trees. Making his way carefully along a dirt path lit only by the half moon and stars, Luka cut through pines and oak trees, led by the sound of muffled sobbing. The first thing his eyes took in was Mimi with her arms around Zlata, both women softly sobbing into each other's shoulders, as though they knew better than to attract attention.

His brother stood over a prostrate man with bullet holes in his back. In his brother's hand, moonlight glinted off the barrel of a gun.

"What the hell have you done? Do you have any idea who this guy is?" Luka's harsh whisper conveyed his anger.

"Was," Branko corrected, his voice cold. "And yes, I know exactly who he was. And he got *exactly* what he deserved."

"Shit! You know this is going to cause an all out war? I don't believe this! What the hell were you thinking?" Luka ran his fingers through thick, dark hair, turning his head in all directions checking for possible witnesses.

The oldest son of the Serbian mob leader, shot down and killed—by the younger son of the head of the Croatian mob. There was going to be hell to pay.

Luka grabbed the gun from Branko, went through Vuk's pockets and pulled out his wallet and keys. "We need to act fast. I want you to find his vehicle, then take the bags out of my car and put them in his car, leaving the door unlocked and keys under his driver's floormat. Got it?"

"Yes, I've got it." Branko didn't argue with his older brother. They were used to dealing with similar situations.

"Then I want you to drive my car home and tell dad I ran off with a woman. Whatever you do, don't tell anyone what happened tonight. As far as you're concerned, you were never here. Got it? Don't worry, no one will say differently. I'll clean up your mess, you idiot. They'll think it was a robbery."

Luka gave his brother a hug, handed him the keys, and told him to get the hell out of there. Branko didn't have the chance to say goodbye to Zlata, who sat on a log next to Mimica, both women shivering from the shock of what had happened.

"You need to come with me and act like nothing's wrong," Luka told Mimi, easing her off the log. She didn't look like that was going to be possible. "All our lives depend on it. And you…" He touched Zlata's shoulder. "Stay here till I come back for you."

Mimi brushed the tears off her cheeks, still shaking. She straightened out her clothing, smoothed down her hair, wiped her eyes, and staggered along back to the house with Luka. Leaving her standing outside the doorway of the house, with her coat collar up around her face in an attempt to hide her distress, Luka grabbed another shot glass, sauntered over to Vuk's brother, and handed him the drink, his expression neutral.

"The fight's over, buddy. Your brother won. My friend went home with his tail between his legs, and your brother's out with the girl, enjoying his victory."

Luka walked through the room, from group to group, saying goodbye and making sure he had everyone's attention. "Enjoy the rest of the evening. We're heading out early. I'm taking Mimi home. She's not feeling the best."

As he made his rounds, Luka jovially put his arm around several of the guys and leaned in to whisper a threat. "Unless you want to see a Croatian/Serbian turf war in your village, keep your mouths shut about what you saw tonight. If tongues start wagging, they'll be cut out. That's a promise. Spread the word amongst your friends."

Chapter Forty-Four

The Party's Over November 1

Matija stopped underneath a street light. "I was at that party. I should never have come back here." Even with the pancake makeup covering his expression, his paleness came through.

He was at the party? "I'm sorry, I didn't know. I wouldn't have asked you to come tonight if I had known."

"It was a long time ago. I knew Vuk. He stirred up trouble all the time. But he didn't deserve to die. Still, what's past is past. And it's not your fault."

I flinched. Maybe it *was* my fault. I was the one who dragged him back to the house where someone had been killed in his youth. "So, you knew the person who was killed?"

"Yes, I knew him. But I don't want to talk about it. Not now. Not here. It's getting late. We should go back to the house."

"If you want to leave, I'll understand. I'm just going to stick around until the sun comes up." I had more questions, and the house held the answers.

"If you're staying, I'll stay. Who's going to take care of you if I leave?" His words reminded me that someone seemed to have it in for me. Today's fire incident was another near miss in a string of bad luck. Was I cursed? "I just need a bit of time to myself, but I'll be fine. You go in, and I'll be there in a while." He kissed my forehead, startling me with his tenderness. Matija's suffering showed in his eyes, yet he was more concerned about my well-being than his own traumatic memories.

Back at the house, the party continued in full swing. I sat on the floor with my back to the wall and listened to the music, watching bodies sway. I closed my eyes, fatigue setting in, as the motion and sound lulled me.

A scream turned all heads toward the side wall where a black widow stood holding the door open.

Something glinted just outside the entrance to the house. Several people, me included, ventured close. The missing pirate's sword lay in front of us, a trail of blood smeared from the tip to the base. More screams pierced through the night, and some people ran up the stairs.

Vlado and Filip calmed the skittish among us.

"Relax! It's fake blood. Part of the game." Vlado shook his head. "Sheesh. You guys. Come on. Nobody's *actually* getting murdered. But don't touch it!" He removed gloves from his pocket and carefully picked up the sword, placing it 'in evidence' on the kitchen table.

Minutes later, Matija returned inside, and together we climbed the stairs to the bedroom where I had left our sleeping gear. A half dozen or so bodies occupied the floor, trying to sleep in spite of the booming shaking the floorboards.

"Maybe we should sleep under the stars?" I suggested. "I don't think we'll get much rest here."

"I'm not sure it's much quieter out there. Besides, it's freezing."

We grabbed our stuff and peeked into one of the other three bedrooms. "Here?"

Matija agreed, and we spread ourselves out on the opposite side of the room from the other two bodies that had already staked a claim to the room.

I didn't plan on staying long. The clock downstairs chimed the half hour. Soon, I had to fulfill another instruction on my game card. I lay awake bundled into my comforter, with Matija next to me in his sleeping bag, hoping I wouldn't fall asleep before the clock struck three. Matija lay quietly, and I wondered whether he was thinking about what happened that night, the last time he was in this house.

When the clock struck three, I whispered to Matija that I was going to the outhouse.

He whispered back, "I'll come with you."

"Don't be silly. I just need to pee. I don't need an audience. I'll be careful."

"Take your flashlight."

I felt inside my pocket where a map, drawn on the back of my instruction card, indicated exactly which direction and how many steps I was to take to get to the spot marked by an X. The card said to keep looking until I found what I needed to find.

First, I made a pit stop in the outhouse. Might as well kill two birds with one stone. Creeping along the house, I found the door. It creaked as it opened. I pressed the button on the battery-powered light on the floor, and checked for spiders, then did my business quickly, fearing I might get trapped inside the outhouse. I had just endured a traumatic experience locked inside an attic, and that was enough for one night. Claustrophobia is a scary entity.

The woods I was about to enter preyed upon my fear of enclosed spaces and the dark. Not to mention creepy crawly things and wild animals. That was nothing compared to my fear of getting lost in the woods and not being found until morning. However, more than anything, the fear of running into ghosts made me jump with every step I took. By that point, I was absolutely convinced that ghosts did indeed exist, and they waited for me in the deep, dark Slavonian woods, eager to make me one of them.

I shone my flashlight on the map. A simple sketch, along with written directions, led me.

Walk along the forest trail 25 long paces straight ahead till you get to the railing...

I reached twelve when a familiar silhouette ahead stopped me in my tracks. It shifted to the right, into the trees.

A ghost.

Dad?

As tempted as I was to call out, I didn't want to invoke the enraged spirit of the man murdered in those woods if he still roamed in the dark. I tiptoed forward, stopping when I heard voices to my right. Two people spoke in a heated whisper. I shut off my flashlight, and listened.

"I won't do that to her. Not after what she's been through." The hushed voices were hard to identify.

"There's no other way, you know that."

The conversation stopped, and they moved farther away. Was this part of the game?

With my flashlight back on, I continued my trek until I counted to 25, then glanced around and felt for the railing. Over to my left. A bit of cedar rail fencing, with fields on the other side. I checked my map again.

Climb over the rail. Walk through the field ten paces.

Lifting one leg over the low fence, then the other, I advanced ten paces across the freshly mowed hayfield, the flashlight aimed ahead. I wasn't sure what I was supposed to find.

It quickly became obvious. Someone lay on the ground ahead, face up in the field.

I screamed. It was a gut reaction. When I remembered the murder game, my heartbeat steadied, and I moved closer to the unmoving shape. A dead zombie.

Just great. I would *have to be the one to find the body.*

A handkerchief stained with blood sat on his chest. I poked the zombie to make sure it was dead, and Darijo sat up.

"You're supposed to go back and ring the bell, not scream and poke at me." Then he lay down and played dead again, popping up a few seconds later to ask if I'd ever had sex with a dead person before.

"Who killed you, Darijo?"

"Dead men don't tell tales," he said before dying again.

In my relief at finding the dead body alive, I didn't notice them right away, but once I climbed back over the fence, I practically ran into them on the path. They must have heard my scream. The man had his back to me, but Zora's face came into view.

"Zora? What are you doing here?"

"Svjetlana? Shush. Was that you screaming? Are you all right?" Her arms encircled me.

She was distraught, but I was furious. I pulled away.

"Are you spying on me? I don't believe this!" The nerve of her, following me around, like I was a two year old at a toddler's birthday party. "I don't need you to worry about me. I'm with thirty other people, for Pete's sake. What could possibly happen?"

"Keep your voice down. That's not why I'm here," she whispered. "Well, it is… but there's more to it. You don't have all the facts."

"The fact is you're treating me like a kid, and I'm not even *your* kid."

"It's dangerous being out here," she continued, her voice low. "With everything that's been going on lately…."

"So you thought you'd just hang around the woods and babysit me?"

"Not just the woods, but yes, we were keeping an eye out for you. In fact, I've been following you for the last several weeks." These words came from the man in the shadows who accompanied Zora. As he turned, the moonlight caught his silhouette.

I couldn't believe my eyes. In that fraction of a second, the ghost that had been haunting me materialized in flesh and blood. My knees buckled.

Dad.

Chapter Forty-Five

From the field, a loud moan permeated the crisp air. Zora jumped. Dad pointed a gun in the direction of the noise.

"I'm dead over here, remember? Go tell the others. I'm getting tired of lying here. It's not exactly comfortable, and it's frickin' freezing. Hurry up, Lana!" Darijo's voice shot through the darkness.

"It's just a game," I explained, my head spinning. "Put the gun away, Tata. Don't shoot Darijo."

Zora shone her flashlight at Dad. "I'm sorry, Svjetlana. There are some things we've kept from you."

Dad's face wasn't quite his own. Plastic surgery? Not the Tata who had raised me. "Who are you?" I gasped, realizing my father wasn't the man I thought he was.

Zora helped me to my feet and ushered me aside. "There's something you need to know."

"Really?" I suspected there was a lot I needed to know.

"We've been patrolling the area all night, keeping a lookout."

"For what?"

"Years ago, before you were born, a man was killed here."

"I know all about that."

"You don't know everything. You're in danger. Branko has been following you to keep you safe." She said it all in one breath, and I thought I maybe hadn't understood correctly.

"Branko?"

She shone the flashlight back at Dad. "Your father's younger brother. We'll

216

explain everything later. "Right now, you need to go back to the house and not tell anyone you saw us."

This man bore a strong resemblance to my father, but I understood then that it wasn't him. Was this the 'ghost' I had been seeing since the accident?

It explained a lot. I wasn't losing my mind, after all. Anger at Zora, and at the uncle I didn't know I had, flared through me.

"You're my…uncle? And you've been following me? Why?"

"Keep your voice down." The man—Branko?—spoke with a cool authority. "The woods have ears. You're in danger. We all are."

"Danger? From whom?" I whispered, following his demand to be quiet.

"They want revenge. For the murder."

"Who? Who wants revenge?"

"His father. And the family."

Revenge for the murder. His father.

Stefan.

Chapter Forty-Six

I awoke to a clanging bell, with people hovering above me. A funeral service? Mine?

A couple of zombies, an angel, the devil…Was I dead?

"Svjetlana? Are you okay?" Darijo asked.

He was dead, so I must be dead, too. Then I remembered we were playing a game.

"Yes, I'm fine. What happened?" I eased my upper body off the living room floor.

"I started to come back to the house for the solving of the murder. I figured you'd have enough time to get back by then. But, I found you at the end of the path with your friend, Zora, and some guy. She said you'd fainted. Thought you'd seen a ghost. The guy carried you in here and told me to take care of you. What are they doing out there in the woods, anyway?"

His mention of Zora reminded me this was more than a game. There had been a murder and someone wanted to make the guilty person pay. Mom and Dad were dead already. Did that make me the next target?

Why was I in danger? Because Stefan's son had been killed?

Or because Vuk was murdered here in these woods, in Dad's childhood home?

I turned my head around the room, gazing at the thirty or so faces and stopping at Matija, his attention glued to me. Worry creased his brow; concern clouded his eyes.

"Now that you're conscious again, let's get on with it. You were supposed to ring the bell, but I did it for you. Everyone's here. Time to solve the murder," Darijo said.

He lay down in the middle of the room, placing the bloody handkerchief over his chest. "I'm dead. This is how Svjetlana found my body in the hayfield next to the woods." And he fell silent, feigning death.

Vlado took over. He arranged everyone in a circle and gave us a piece of paper and pencil. "On the paper, you need to record who killed Darijo, the zombie, when, and why. Write your name on the back of the paper, and put it into this jar."

I guessed Matija, the vampire. He and Darijo had been at odds all night. He had a motive. He had the opportunity. We were separated for a while after the storytelling, when he said he wanted some time to himself. He had as much chance of stealing the pirate's sword as anyone did, and he was there shortly after it reappeared with blood stains. Darijo also hinted that Matija could be a murderer.

But did he do it?

I considered whether Matija was capable of murder.

Once all the guesses were collected, Filip extracted one at a time from the jar, reading them aloud. A couple of people accused me of the murder. Filip got about halfway through when the zombie came back to life.

"Does anyone smell smoke?" Darijo bolted off the floor.

Out of the corner of my eye, Matija sprang to action and ran up the stairs, Darijo following. "Is there a fire extinguisher?" Matija yelled.

"Fire! Everyone out of the house!" Darijo hollered. I assumed that meant no fire extinguisher. Thirty people ran for the main exit of the house, knocking each other over in their attempt to save themselves. "Back door, too!" Darijo shouted down the stairs. Some turned around and pushed their way through the kitchen.

My eyes searched the stairs for Matija and Darijo. Smoke billowed from the attic trap door, filling the upstairs hallway. "It's too late!" Matija shouted as they hurtled down toward me. "Call the fire department!"

"I need my backpack!" I tried to run past them, up the stairs. Matija put his hands on my arms and stopped me. "My camera's in there!"

I pulled out of his grasp. "I need it! It'll just take a second." I'd been snapping photos of the house during the party, as I'd been doing throughout my trip. I wasn't about to let them go up in flames, my whole journey a heap of ashes.

"I'll get it. You get out. Now!" Matija commanded, arm around my waist, pulling me down the stairs, shoving me toward the side door. "Make sure she's safe. Stay with her," he directed Darijo.

Matija ran back up to the bedroom where we had left our stuff.

Everyone stood out on the road, mesmerized, staring at the house. Darijo and I joined the group, my eyes glued to the side door, waiting for Matija to exit.

Arms folded around me, pulling me away from Darijo. "Oh, thank God! There you are! Are you okay?" Zora's tears streamed down her cheeks, her body convulsing. "I don't know what I'd do if I ever lost you. I love you so much."

"I love you, too, Zora. But my friend—he's still in there." I hadn't expected it to take him more than a minute to get my backpack. "I'm going back in after him."

Branko stepped forward from the shadows and ran in through the side door before I could make a move. "I'll go get him!" he yelled, disappearing inside. "Everyone back away from the house!"

Smoke billowed off the red roof tiles. From the top floor, fire flickered out of the broken glass window in the attic. The bedroom below that was where I had sent Matija. Because of me, he went back up. And my uncle ran into the burning house to save him.

The crisp night air filled with smoke. Orange flames reached out to the black sky.

Zora tensed as she held me, and we stared at the side door, waiting for them to come out.

"I called the fire department," Darijo shouted, joining us. "They're on their way."

"I'm going in." I broke away from Zora and ran for the side door.

Zora caught up, and with Darijo's help, dragged me from the house kicking and screaming. They deposited me next to Darijo's friends.

"Don't let her out of your sight," Zora warned them. "Or else." She ran off and disappeared into the house before I could protest or stop her.

Darijo clutched me in his strong arms. Vlado, Tina, Filip, and Maja enclosed us, preventing me from running back in.

I couldn't bear to lose Zora. She had always been a part of my childhood. I couldn't remember a time when she wasn't around, celebrating the holidays, my birthdays, cheering me on with my accomplishments, helping me work through my problems. She was as much a fixture of our household as my parents. I took her for granted. Now she was risking her life because of a stupid camera and photos of a trip to my parents' past.

"Where are the fire trucks?" I shouted through angry tears.

"It'll take a while. They come from the next town," Darijo answered, his grip firm.

His parents and other neighbors, visible in the glow of the fire, had joined the throng gathered in front of the burning house. Their voices filled the smoky air.

"The curse. I knew something would happen tonight."

"It's this house. It's always been cursed."

"They shouldn't have been in there. They awakened the ghosts."

Where was Matija? Why was it taking so long for him to get my stupid backpack? He'd rescued me so many times, and now he was sacrificing his life for me. I should have been in there saving him. But, the harder I tried to pull away from Darijo, the tighter he held.

"It's only going to make things worse if you go in there," he tried to reason with me. "There's nothing we can do but wait for them to come out."

And then there was the uncle I had just met for all of two seconds. I should never have come. To this party. To this country. To the past. Bad things had happened in Molono since I came to the village. As I watched the house engulfed in flames through teary eyes, I remembered the letter in the attic trunk.

The curse is real. Get out while you can.

It was too late.

Darijo tried to shield me from seeing the flames, but I could still taste the smoke as it formed a fog around us. There was a sudden audible gasp from the crowd, and Darijo let go of me enough to allow my head to turn toward the house. Matija ran across the street to join us, handing Darijo my backpack. He pulled me into his arms, pressing my face against his chest.

"I'm so sorry, Lana, I'm so sorry," he whispered gently against my forehead. "They were right behind me. There was nothing I could do. Zora's gone, and her friend, too. The floor gave way under them, and they fell to the basement. I couldn't get to them. I'm so very sorry." He cradled my head and fell along with me as I slumped onto the cold hard ground. The two of us sat there, with him stroking my hair and my back, telling me I was strong enough to get through this.

But I knew I wasn't.

That was the final straw that broke me.

Chapter Forty-Seven

The rest was a nightmare. I lay curled into a ball, alone, despite being surrounded by dozens of people, hands and arms reaching out to comfort me. My body belonged to someone else.

I heard the wailing and sputtering. "I want to go home, I want to go home, please, let me go home, please, please…." It came from me, but an echo from a faraway place.

An insane image struck me: Me, inside my dad's burning house while being carried off in the middle of a tornado. Spinning around the house were a witch, a black cat, a skeleton, a mummy… If I clicked my heels three times, I would be back in Hamilton, with my parents still alive, the three of us at the dinner table, enjoying Mom's home cooking. If I clicked them once more, I'd be back in our cozy little bungalow in Lake Kipling, Jim's strong arms around me, the two of us encircling our children.

There's no place like home…

Someone scooped me off the ground and whisked me away from the flames, the heat, the smoke. The approaching fire engines cut through the night with their sirens announcing, 'Too late, too late, too late.' I was gently deposited on a soft surface with a cover thrown over me. Was this what it was like to be dying?

The last few weeks flashed through my mind like a slideshow. The subway train screeched to a halt, the roses dropped on the coffins, the plane hit the tarmac in Croatia, the doors slammed in my face, the chest opened, the house engulfed in flames. Bad luck. The village is cursed.

The curse is real. Get out while you can. Too late. Too late. Too late.

"Svjetlana, can you sit up?" Matija's voice, Matija's arms, saving me.

"Is she okay?" Darijo's humorless voice.

"Here, take a sip of water." Darijo's mom? A pill sliding down my throat. A warm compress on my forehead. A hand rubbing my back.

Swimming in the Blue Danube, fighting the current. Floating downstream on blue water, muddied by death, toward the Black Sea. My funeral pyre, burning on the water. Mom, Dad, Zora, Branko floating alongside, flames shooting upwards like fireworks. Sinking into the black depths of turquoise blue water deprived of oxygen. The dead zone.

Chapter Forty-Eight

Reality hit me full force when I awoke. Darijo's mom drove me to Grandma's house and stayed for a while, explaining what had happened, or as much as she herself understood. "They think the fire was started by one of the lanterns," Darijo's mom told Grandma. "Zora died a hero, going in to make sure no one was left behind."

I called Jim to tell him about Zora, but broke down before I could say hello. Grandma gently pried my fingers from the phone and told him in Croatian that I would call back. I heard his voice faltering as he kept asking if everything was okay, but Grandma hung up on him, saying, "Kasnije, kasnije." Jim, not understanding a word of Croatian, would have no idea she was telling him to wait till later.

As the phone rang again, Grandma said, "I will call Tina. She can explain it to Jim."

I nodded, incapable of forming words. My phone went to voicemail, then started ringing again.

When Tina showed up minutes later, she picked up my phone and relayed to Jim what had happened using her best high school English, which was much better than my high school French. "Hallo. I am friend of Lana. Zora, she die in fire. Was accident. Lana is okay. She no can talk now. Very sad. Later she call you. Sorry."

All I could do was stare at the phone and listen to Jim's frantic words. "Lana, Lana! Are you okay? I'm so sorry, Lana, so sorry. Are you there, Lana? Lana? Are you in danger?"

I shook my head in response. Tina assured him I was okay, just sad.

Sad.

It was difficult enough to find the right word in one's own language to describe overwhelming grief; in translation, words lost their meaning.

I spent the rest of the day in a fetal position in bed, trying in vain to sleep. According to Grandma, Kata had received news of her daughter's death in the early morning hours, and was sedated, she and her family cared for by several friends in the neighborhood. Later in the day, I called Jim again to give him some peace of mind. He did most of the talking, doing his best to soothe me from a distance of several thousand miles. I managed to blubber a few words, among them that I loved him and wanted to come home.

They brought Zora's body for viewing to the local church the next day. Another closed casket, just like my parents. Kata was inconsolable, as was to be expected, especially given the fact that she'd just been reunited with her daughter after three decades apart. I couldn't take it, seeing her like that.

The shell of Kata stood bravely by her dead daughter. Her pale face, vacant eyes, and drooping shoulders fed my guilt and my own sorrow. Endless drops streamed down from within, puddling around me. Where the tears came from, I couldn't imagine—I thought they had all been shed, that I'd dried up permanently—but the dam burst, setting free the lake's waters. Zora's brother, Lado, his wife, their two girls, along with another brother and his family, stood with Kata, supporting her, physically keeping her upright, next to Zora's casket as guests offered condolences. I couldn't bear to be in there for more than a few minutes. Grandma said everyone would understand, with the loss I had suffered weeks ago so fresh.

Mom and Dad. Zora. Zora. Mom and Dad.

I. Just. Couldn't.

I wanted to say goodbye to Branko, too. My uncle. Dad's brother. I had barely said hello to him, and now it was goodbye. Life wasn't fair.

I was a murderer.

Like my father before me.

The puzzle was complete. A clear picture had formed in my mind about the events thirty years ago.

I had no idea how to contact Branko's family. When I asked Grandma, I wasn't sure she would tell me. She had lied to me before. Dad didn't *live* in the murder house. He *killed* someone in the murder house.

"I want to pay my respects to Branko's family," I said, between heaving sobs. "He's my uncle, my dad's brother."

Grandma's mouth opened wide, then she nodded. "So you found out the truth? About Luka?"

"I know he was my father. I know he was a criminal. And I know that Mama loved him. He was a good man. He did a bad thing."

Grandma said she understood, and she would find a way for me to attend my uncle's funeral, if that was my wish.

"No, I just want to go to the viewing to say goodbye, for a few minutes, that's all," I said. "I want to be here for you and Kata."

Grandma arranged for Tina's mom to drop me off at the viewing, in front of Branko's father's house, which was Dad's actual old house, in the town of Vlasilo, about twenty minutes away. It was a grand old mansion, but I guess that was to be expected for Dad's dad, the head of the mob. Cars lined several streets, mourners in black exiting them.

Tina's mom waited in the car while I stood in a long line to offer condolences to Branko's family. My dad's family. The closed casket, the burned body inside (why was it always fire that took the people I loved?), drew my eyes toward it as I approached the front where an older man, dressed in black, stood stooped over, supported by a young woman also dressed in black, trying to keep him upright.

Draga? What is she...?

It struck me like a bucket of cold water, waking me from a deep slumber. The resemblance was there now that I knew to look for it. Draga was Dad's sister. I caught her attention and my eyes sought confirmation as my mouth hung open. She understood why I had come and nodded. Draga whispered something in her father's ear. He looked directly at me, searching my face.

When I got to the front of the line, he put his arms out. "Svjetlana." Kissing me on both cheeks, he said, "Finally, we meet."

We stood in an embrace for several minutes, holding up the line. "So, you're Luka's girl." A fresh burst of tears sprang from glistening brown eyes, rolling down his cheeks. "All these years, without my son. And now I've lost another."

Because of me. And a stupid party I just had to attend.

"I only have my daughter left." As though he just realized, he added, "And my granddaughter." He tilted my head to get a closer look at me, then let go.

I embraced Draga, hoping for some explanation. She thanked me for coming, then turned to the next person in line.

I'd found my dad's family, but killed one of them as soon as I met him. There was no reason for me to linger any longer. Who knew what damage I could do if I stayed?

Zora's funeral service took place the next morning, and they laid her to rest in the church cemetery that afternoon. Once she was gone, there was only one thing left to do.

It was time to get the hell out of Molono.

Chapter Forty-Nine

Grandma and Kata agreed it was time for me to go home and get on with my life. My parents were dead, Zora was dead. I still had the catering business and the house. That was all that was left of them. I needed to deal with the legal and financial responsibilities left behind and continue on. Without Zora there to take care of things, it was now up to me to take charge.

But, more than anything, I needed Jim and the kids.

The morning after Zora's funeral, as I packed my luggage for the next day's flight, Matija called to ask how I was doing. I hadn't heard from him since the fire. I lied and said I was okay.

"Would you be able to come out for the day? There's someplace I'd like to take you," he said.

The idea of sightseeing no longer held an appeal, but he did go into the fire instead of letting *me* go back into the house. He saved my life. Again. I owed him.

And, I did need to find out the truth about my dad, to get answers straight from the horse's mouth, so to speak. He was there the night Vuk died. Maybe he had some answers about what happened.

Besides, I thought it might do me good to get out and stop the constant crying. It had to be a strain on Grandma, consoling both me and Kata.

"Okay, where?" I asked.

"You'll see when we get there. I'll pick you up at eight in the morning, in front of your place."

As usual, he didn't get out of the car. And as usual, I thought that was just

229

as well. I didn't want to have to explain to Grandma why I was 'dating' an older man, and I didn't want her to have the opportunity to ask where he was from.

Did the people in the village know him? The few times he'd ventured out of the car no one had been around. I couldn't recall whether anyone in Molono had seen him up close, out of disguise.

We drove in silence most of the way. Matija said he wanted to surprise me with our destination. Fog obscured the view, trapping me in the confines of the vehicle. Not a good day for watching the scenery go by. Warm air poured out of the car heater; the radio station softly played classical music. I closed my eyes and dreamed a fantasy where I could relive my life, omitting the mistakes I had made, having learned from them. A second chance. An opportunity to fix things.

After a couple of hours, I opened my eyes, the entrance to Paruka Park coming into view. "Why are we here?"

"You'll see. Somewhere away from everyone else."

The mountain road wound through thick forest. Matija's hands remained on the wheel, expertly maneuvering the car through the ghostly mist. He pulled over once we reached the summit and parked in a spot hidden by trees and brush.

"What are we doing here?" My voice quavered.

"Finding a private spot. Let's get out and walk a bit."

A jolt of irrational fear shot through me like a lightning bolt. I had allowed myself to be lured to this mountain, in the middle of a vast foggy forest, alone.

"There's something I want you to know," he said as we walked deep into the forest, damp tendrils reaching out to grab me. I sensed he was about to confess something ominous. I stopped walking, turned my head in every direction. Thick, dark trunks surrounded me, dead leaves gathered at my feet, the fine drizzle threatened to drown me. If I ran, I'd be lost to the Slavonian forest, wandering to my death. "It's Savic."

"Wh...what?"

"You wanted to know my last name. It's Savic. I come from a family that doesn't do business in the traditional sense. My dad runs the Serbian mob here. Someday soon I'll be taking over."

That couldn't be true. Not Matija. He was a nice guy. He'd saved me so many times. How could he be a criminal? Was he connected to Stefan?

"My older brother, Vuk, would have been first in line, but he's dead," Matija continued.

Vuk? Savic? Matija's brother?

Matija secured his arm around my shoulder. To stop me from running?

"Vuk brought me with him to the party that night. Said he sometimes hung out on the Croatian side of the border and wondered if I wanted to join him. He had a way with the girls—his way. That night, a girl caught his eye, but she wasn't interested. Apparently, she belonged to some other guy. Her boyfriend started a fight, and they took it outside to finish. Vuk never came back. Neither did the woman or her boyfriend. A friend of his told me he'd lost the fight and Vuk won the woman. When Vuk didn't come back after an hour or so, I went out to look for him." Matija choked back his emotions.

"It took me a while to find him. He was lying on his front, three bullets in his back, the blood pooling around him. Your father shot and killed my brother, Lana. There was no proof he did it. But when my dad heard Luka was one of the people missing that night, he knew it *had* to be him, so he got his people to ask around. No one talked.

"But, my dad can be very persuasive. He cursed Molono and put the fear of God in its citizens, having his crew terrorize the village. The owner of the house where the party took place finally talked, for a price, confirming my dad's suspicions that Luka had been at the party. Then he abandoned the house and moved his family out of the region."

Matija stopped to gauge my response. My rubbery tongue sat in my open mouth, incapable of speech. I could only stare into his dark eyes as the fog swirled around us, confining me.

"No one knew Luka's whereabouts. Not even his family. There was talk around the village that he'd run off with his girlfriend. Some said he sacrificed himself to the river rather than risk my dad's punishment.

"Eventually, my dad put an end to his reign of terror in Molono. But, my family and yours have been at war since my brother's murder more than thirty years ago."

That didn't bode well for me as I assessed my current situation. I stood frozen. Matija must have killed Zora and my uncle in the fire. Branko was his target, because he was Dad's brother. Retribution. That explained why Matija escaped the fire, and they didn't.

"A few months ago," he continued, "someone from our organization was visiting family in Canada. He recognized your parents, though they had changed their identities, and word got back to my dad."

Matija looked out over the forested mountains, his grip still firmly holding me in place. "All this *space*. Yet it's a small world, Lana. You can run and hide, but in the end, the past catches up with you."

I stared into the valley, turned my head to the right and left, scanning the forest, searching for an escape. I wasn't sure I could outrun him. And where would I go? Deeper into the forest? What if I got lost? What if he had a gun?

Matija's voice remained calm and steady. "At first, he tried to draw them out through phone calls, telling them to give themselves up to the Croatian authorities and all would be forgiven. Of course, Dad had no intention of letting the law handle family business, and Luka knew that. So he ignored his request to return to Croatia and face my father on their home turf. Then you showed up in Hamilton, and Dad saw an opportunity to smoke out your parents. Dad threatened what was most precious to Luka—you. It was the perfect way for Dad to get revenge. He had some of his contacts in Hamilton set up little 'accidents', just to show your parents what *could* happen if they didn't come back to pay their dues. And he sent me to Canada to oversee things."

Matija gazed deep into my eyes and sighed. "Then your parents died. I'm so sorry. You poor little orphaned girl." He let go of me and reached into his back pocket.

I had heard enough. Unlike 11 years ago, when I faced another son of a Serbian Mafia boss, I had no weapon to defend myself. There was only one thing I could do.

Run.

Chapter Fifty

Through the haunted forests of Paruka, I slipped and slid, dodging trees and fallen limbs, the fog finding its way into my lungs. It didn't matter where I ended up. As far from Matija as my wobbly legs could take me.

Not far at all. My foot caught on a tree root, and I was propelled toward the forest floor.

An arm reached around my waist, jerking me back up. He wrapped himself around me and held tight, so I couldn't run again. "Whoa, baby girl! Where are you going?"

This was it. The end for me. I was getting what I deserved. Poetic justice.

But my will to survive was strong. "Please don't hurt me. Don't. Let me go. Please... I have..." I pleaded, almost blurting out that I had children who needed me, before his words cut me short.

"*Hurt* you?" He loosened his grip. "You don't need to be afraid of me, Lana. I would never hurt you. Trust me." I didn't believe him. "I care about you. From the first time we met, when you were thrown onto that subway track, I was driven to protect you."

"Protect me? From what?" My eyes widened.

"My father. I followed you around as much as possible without giving away my intentions. That's why I was there whenever you had 'an accident'. I wanted to make sure you were okay. And I want you to understand that I had nothing to do with your parents' deaths. Neither did my father, for that matter."

My muscles unclenched the slightest bit. My initial instincts about him had been right.

"But... the gun... you were going to shoot me...." I stammered.

A rustling of foliage startled us both, and we turned toward the sound. Draga strode toward us. She greeted me with a hug and Matija with a kiss, one that went beyond a friendly peck. Matija enveloped his arms around her, returning her kiss, as though I didn't exist.

"So, now you know about your parents' past. Does that make things better?" Draga asked.

I knew Dad was a murderer. I knew my parents had gone on the run and taken on new identities. That didn't make things better at all. "Why did he do it? Why did my dad kill him?"

"I was a kid, twelve, when it happened. Branko was seventeen. Luka was almost nineteen when he went missing. No one told me why he disappeared. But the murder was in the news at that time, and I wondered if it had anything to do with him. Then the rumors started, people spreading the word that he was probably dead, too."

"So, you didn't know what happened at the party?" All this time, Draga thought her brother was dead. So why did she show up at his funeral last month and not mention that?

"Not until I was older, when I was twenty. Branko told me the truth one day. I think he needed to get it off his chest. He was involved in what happened."

"How?'

"Branko and Zlata, or Zora as you knew her, had been seeing each other in secret for a while. They were planning on making their relationship public the night of the party. Our dad heads up the Croatian mob in the area. Branko knew Zlata's family wouldn't approve of them being together."

Draga stopped talking and gazed up at Matija. He took her face in his hands and kissed her again.

"Go on," I urged, unsure of whether I could trust either of them.

"Branko told me some guy got fresh with Zlata and Branko punched him. The fight continued outside. Zlata went out to try to stop it. Vuk, Matija's brother, knocked Branko unconscious with the butt of his gun."

Draga stopped again to tell Matija she was sorry, she understood how hard it must be for him to have it replayed.

"It's not your fault, Draga. Vuk always got himself into trouble. He took what he wanted. I saw how he treated Zlata, and I should have stopped him before it got out of hand. All I did was stand there and watch. The next thing I knew, they went outside to fight. I should have followed. Maybe none of this would have happened if I'd had the guts to stop him." Matija sighed and stared off across the treed expanse.

"You were just a kid, and you had no idea what was going to happen. Vuk was responsible for all this," Draga said. "I'm sorry, but if there's anyone to blame, it's him."

Matija nodded, his softer side coming through, a hint of a tear puddling in the corner of one eye. "Still, maybe things could have been different."

Draga continued. "After a while, Luka went outside to check on Branko. He found him knocked out, and Vuk on top of Zlata, assaulting her. He wouldn't stop, so Luka shot him. He and Mimica had been planning to run away together that night. Mimica was pregnant, and her family wouldn't approve. But with the shooting, it made it more urgent for them to leave right away. When Branko gained consciousness and found Vuk dead, Luka told him to go home and keep quiet about what happened. Then Luka disappeared, along with Mimica and Zlata. Branko never got over losing Zlata."

At least my dad had a reason for killing Vuk. I wasn't sure if that was the only way he could have handled the situation, but at least I understood his motivation. He needed to protect someone he cared about. At the time, it must have seemed like the only way to do that. Yes, I understood all too well.

Like father, like daughter.

Draga filled in a few more details about how Luka was able to get new identities for the three of them with her father's help. "That night, he drove across the border to Hungary and called Dad, saying he was going to need new identification for the three of them and that he wanted to get as far away as possible. Branko said Dad took care of everything through his connections. That's how your parents and Zlata ended up in Canada and started a new life with you."

It was all coming together, the past and how it affected the present. I still didn't understand who killed my parents. Was it simply an accident? Not connected to their pasts? Or, had my first thought been right? Stefan killed them to get even with me for taking his son.

Before I could ask about the accident, Draga explained her involvement with Matija. "I never saw Luka again until I heard about the accident and went to his funeral. I wanted to be there for you, in some small way, to make sure you were okay. So did Branko, but we worried you would recognize him as Luka's brother. That's why he followed you in secret. But when I saw Matija come through the funeral home doors, I thought he would see Zlata, and the news that she was alive would get back to his father, putting her in danger, too. That's why I took her home that night, and that's why she didn't show up at the funeral. I was protecting her."

"But I wasn't a threat," Matija interjected, his eyes seeking mine.

"I didn't know that at the time," Draga said. "When I met Matija again the day you were looking for costumes, it brought back old memories of when we'd been together in university. I called him that night, and we had a long talk."

"We dated for a couple of years in university without our families knowing," Matija continued. "But Draga broke it off suddenly without explanation."

"When Branko told me Luka killed Matija's brother, I knew then we couldn't be together. The conflict between our families was too much. With his brother's death, there was no way we could continue to see each other." Draga gazed into Matija's eyes, and again they seemed to forget my presence. "But now, we've decided to give it another try and if our dads don't like it, that's too bad. Matija explained to me that, unknown to his father, he was following you to *protect* you from his dad's people. He didn't think it was fair to blame you for something that happened before you were born."

Matija added, "I didn't see how getting retribution by killing you was going to change anything. It wasn't going to bring Vuk back. Now that the three people involved in Vuk's murder are dead, I've convinced my dad to call a truce. The vendetta's over. But, I'm going to make sure it stays that way."

As he reached into his back pocket again, I pleaded, "Please, no. I have children. And my husband... Please don't kill me."

"Children?" Matija's eyes lit up. "Husband? And here I thought you were leading me on." He chuckled, then added, "Well, he's one lucky man, your husband. And I told you, I don't blame you for what happened to Vuk. I would never hurt you. But I did want to give you something."

The barrel of the gun protruded out of his pocket as he pulled out a gold chain. "I found this beside Vuk's body. I've known all along that Branko was there that night, but I kept quiet about it. Maybe it had something to do with this." He placed the locket in my hand.

My fingers felt the engraved message on the back of the heart.

I will always love you.

I undid the clasp, and the faces of two very young lovers, cheek to cheek, wide smiles, looked up at me. I recognized Zora's features right away, but the boy...

Dad?

I examined his face closely. No, not Dad.

Branko. Branko and Zora.

"I knew Vuk must have hurt Zlata. Probably Mimica, too. When the three of them couldn't be found, I figured they went on the run because of what they did to Vuk. And I knew Branko had to be involved in it, even though he stayed behind and claimed he wasn't there that night. Everyone backed up his story, and I never contradicted it. I don't know...maybe I thought he didn't deserve to be brought into it, considering what Vuk did to his girl. I guess I've always been a romantic at heart."

Draga wrapped her arms around his neck and kissed him again. Well, at least someone was going to end up with a happy ending through all this tragedy. It just wasn't going to be me.

Chapter Fifty-One

"The people who were following you, causing 'accidents' as a warning to your parents and Zora won't be bothering you anymore. Zora had agreed to turn herself in, to save *you*, just like your parents planned on doing before the car accident, but now that she's gone, Dad has no one to target. All three people who went missing from the party 30 years ago are dead. I've convinced him you're an innocent victim. You don't need to worry about Dad causing more trouble in Molono. Now that the debt's paid, you won't need me hanging around to save you anymore. But I'm going to miss you, baby girl." Matija gave my nose a playful tweak. "We had a lot of fun, you and I."

I was going to miss him, too. Still, I was glad to hear that my streak of bad luck wasn't the result of destiny, but of human actions. That meant I had some control over my life and could change its course.

No curse.

"But, won't we still see each other?" I asked.

"No," Draga answered for him. "You're going home where you belong. If you stay here any longer or come back, it's going to remind people of what happened in the past. We don't need Matija's dad changing his mind about the truce between our families."

"I want to put an end to this conflict for good," Matija added. "Now that the people responsible for Vuk's death are gone, Draga and I are going to join our families through marriage. As the only surviving children, we're going to carry on the family business together. That doesn't mean our fathers will be happy about it. It just means we're not giving them any choice. Your being here will rock the boat. Not that I wouldn't jump into the water for you, anytime." A corner of Matija's mouth turned up and he gave me a last hug. "But, it's time for you to go home, back to your real life, and forget about us. Besides, it takes a lot of effort to look after you, little girl."

Draga joined in the hug and the three of us stood locked in an embrace, overlooking misty fingers threading through trees along the rolling mountainside. "Just try not to open any more Pandora's boxes," she warned. "Nothing good comes from digging up the past. Let the dead lie."

We stood that way for a long time, knowing we wouldn't be together again. I was losing something important, more than just an aunt and a very good friend. They were family. "I hope the two of you will have a happy life, I really do," I said. "I'm glad that *something* good came out of my coming to Croatia. I just wish...."

I didn't get to finish my sentence because my wish came true as two ghosts emerged from the fog, out of the haunted woodland.

Chapter Fifty-Two

My legs buckled as the ethereal vision of Zora and Branko emerging from the mist, with their arms around each other, took the breath from me. I knew it wasn't real. My mind had once again snapped under the stress of learning the truth.

Zora stepped between us and swept me into her arms, a solid ghost with liquid tears. "Svjetlana, I'm so sorry we put you through this. I didn't want to do it, but we had no choice."

"Zora? I don't understand." I turned to Matija, my tear-filled eyes demanding an answer. He had told me they fell through the floor of the burning house and didn't make it.

"It was a ruse," he explained. "To fool my father into thinking they were dead."

"But how…? There were bodies…and a funeral."

"You'd be surprised what we can do," Branko said, his hand indicating himself, Draga, and Matija. "Matija's dad was intimidating Zora. He wreaked havoc in town and threatened to harm you. The afternoon before the party, Zora called me for help." Branko touched my shoulder. "The two of us were there that night watching out for you. But there was another reason for our presence."

"We'd made a plan, Branko and I," Draga continued. "When news got around that Zora was back in town, and a party was planned at the house, we thought of the perfect way to make everyone believe Zora was dead, so Matija's dad would be satisfied that justice had been done. Branko wanted to be reunited with Zora. He told her about our plan, and convinced her it was the only way. With Matija's help, we planted two bodies in the basement before the party."

"Didn't anyone miss the bodies?" Where did one find spare bodies, anyway?

"Let's just say they were borrowed," Branko answered. "For a price. Like I said, we have ways of making things happen—connections with the right people."

"When I was at the party all those years ago, I'd overheard people talking about a basement tunnel built during the war. It leads out to a drainage ditch along the fields and the woods," Matija added. "I thought that would come in handy for Branko and Zora to make their escape when they went in on the pretext of saving me."

"So you *planned* to set the place on fire? There was a crowd there. Somebody could have been killed!"

Who are these people? What are they capable of?

"We were careful. We had it planned for just the right time, and we had a couple of our people there to make sure everyone got out," Draga defended their actions.

Matija explained how the attic fire was restarted by one of their own people. "If you hadn't sent me inside for your camera, I planned to go back to make sure the house was evacuated. Zora and Branko were supposed to follow me in when I didn't come out right away. I had a key for the padlock on the basement door and got them downstairs. Once I knew they were in the tunnel, I emptied the tubs of alcohol-infused apples on the wooden floor and threw bottles of alcohol into the blaze upstairs."

"You could have been killed! Are you crazy?"

"I *wasn't* killed. I had the situation under control. And the plan worked perfectly. Zora and Branko died in the fire. Their 'bodies' were found in the basement. And they made their way to the boat waiting down by the river, and headed upstream."

"So *you* locked me in the attic and started the fire?"

"No, I would never put you in danger, Lana. That would have been one of my dad's guys, a threat to get Zora to confess. Probably the Grim Reaper."

"What if I hadn't invited you to the party?"

"I would have found a way to invite myself. After all, it *is* my job to keep you safe, baby doll." He ruffled my hair while looking deep into my eyes. "I'm sorry if I frightened you earlier."

His expression hardened. "But you *should* be scared. I want you to fully understand the danger you're in if you don't do as you're told. Zora and Branko need to remain dead. You can never tell anyone, do you understand?"

I understood completely. The hard set of his jaw and the steely glint in those brown eyes warned me that Matija wasn't joking this time. For not the first time that day, he gave me a glimpse of the dangerous man lurking just below the smooth surface.

Chapter Fifty-Three

"Come walk with us," Zora said, taking my hand.

Branko and Zora led me aside, further into the dense forest, away from Matija and Draga, to speak to me in private. After a few minutes, we came upon a fallen tree.

"Sit down," Branko said. The three of us sat on the log, overlooking the mountains and wilderness. The fog had cleared, and the drizzle stopped. Through the clouds, the sun peeked, putting up a strong fight to bring light to the gloom.

"Branko and I are going away together, getting married, under new identities," Zora confided. "You won't be seeing me again." She hugged me so tight it hurt.

"Why can't we still see each other?" I didn't understand. "I'm not going to tell anyone you're alive. I've just lost you in the fire and found you again, and now I'm going to lose you forever?"

Branko set his hand on my shoulder again. "It's the way it has to be, Lana, to make sure everyone is safe. Matija's dad or his people could decide to come after us any time to settle the score. As long as they think we're dead, we're out of danger. That includes you." He added, "And your children. We can't give him any excuse to go back on his promise to leave you alone."

"It's important that you understand this," he continued. "Your father was a good man. He was born into a criminal life, not one he chose. That didn't make him bad. It's just the way it was. The way it *is* for me. For Draga. And for Matija. But it's not that way for you. Your parents didn't want that lifestyle for their daughter."

"Your father gave up his criminal life," Zora said. "When he found out your Mama was expecting you, he changed. Your Tata was the man you knew him to be—a good, kind, caring man. Remember him that way. Forget what you've heard people say about him. You knew him best."

"I know he had a reason for killing Vuk. I know what Vuk did to you."

"He didn't kill him," Branko interrupted. "I did. That night, I was the one who started the fight. When we went outside, Vuk knocked me out, and he…." Branko's voice broke. "He took advantage of Zlata. Against her will."

I put my arm around Zora. "I'm so sorry that happened to you." She shook her head and looked down in shame. There was something I still didn't know; I could tell from her reaction.

Branko continued. "When I came to, I took out my gun and shot him. Luka found me with my gun pointing at Vuk's back. He took the gun, wiped it down, told me to go home, and pretend I'd never been there. He was going to make it look like a robbery."

Dad didn't kill Vuk after all. He covered for his brother. Dad *was* the man I knew him to be. I didn't blame Branko. He did what needed to be done to protect the woman he loved.

Zora filled in. "Mimi and Luka already had plans to run away that night. She was pregnant. They didn't think they could be together if they stayed. But I want you to know the whole truth, all of it."

"No!" Branko warned, rising.

"Yes. She has the right to know exactly what happened that night and why."

Chapter Fifty-Four

The Party 1978

Zlata followed Branko outside. It was her fault. If she hadn't been flirting in the first place…

She didn't want Branko to get hurt because of her stupidity. Zlata checked around the exterior of the house, but saw no one. Through the blackness and menacing trees, smacking and grunting noises cut through the air.

Terrified of the dark forest, Zlata slipped back inside and grabbed a candle from the entrance table, then followed the sound of fists connecting with flesh and men groaning in pain.

She found them not far into the woods, off the slightly trodden dirt path. They weren't equally matched, but Branko was holding his own, in spite of his slighter build. Zlata shouted for them to stop.

She caught their attention, but not with the desired outcome. Branko yelled for her to get back inside. Vuk pulled out a gun.

"Glad you could join the party," Vuk said. "But I'm not really into this type of threesome." He struck Branko's head with the butt of his gun, and grabbed Zlata, knocking the candle out of her hand. With a clatter, the metal holder hit a rock, extinguishing the flame. Vuk set his gun down next to it. "Why don't the two of us have some fun while he's sleeping it off?"

He dragged her to the ground and forced himself on top of her as she fought him off, slapping and biting his hands and arms, spitting and kicking.

"I like feisty women." He backhanded her across the face. "Come on. Is that all you've got?"

Zlata lay limp, hoping the lack of a challenge might deter him. When it didn't, she fought harder, screamed louder, but the booming music drowned out her cries. The glint of the gun in the moonlight caught her eye. She tried to reach for it, but the brute pinned Zlata's arms above her head and undid his belt buckle with his other hand.

When Mimi came to check on Zlata, she found Vuk on top of Zlata, snickering. "Stop your blubbering. Don't pretend you didn't enjoy it." As Mimi tried to pull him off her best friend, Vuk gazed up at her, a wicked grin on his face. "Don't worry, there's plenty of me to go around. Just give me a few minutes, and I'll be ready for another round of wrestling." Rolling off Zlata, he fixed his sights on Mimi and pulled her to the cold ground.

Zlata lay curled up, whimpering, listening to the sound of the monster laughing and smacking her pregnant best friend. Her hand felt for the gun on the rock. She sat up, aimed and pulled the trigger as he brought his arm down again. Vuk groaned as he collapsed onto Mimi.

When the shot roused Branko, Zlata stood, still pointing the gun at Vuk's back, shaking and sobbing. Without a second thought, he eased the gun out of her hand, pulled Vuk's body off Mimi, and shot him once more. Mimi, her arms protectively around her abdomen, sobbed, "My baby…my baby…."

Branko placed the gun in Mimi's hand, pointed it at Vuk, and said, "Go ahead. For the baby." The third shot rang out, muffled by the blare of rock music. Branko pried her fingers from the gun.

When Luka arrived in the woods, he found his brother over the victim, holding the gun. The two women on the ground held tightly to each other, convulsing.

Luka brought his hands to the top of his head. "What the *hell* have you done? Do you have any idea who this guy is?"

Chapter Fifty-Five

When Zora finished her story, I said, "It's okay. You did what you had to do. It was self-defense."

"Mimi was pregnant. I couldn't let him do that to her," she cried. "I didn't think about what I was doing. It just happened."

Branko sat in quiet contemplation before he spoke. "I wish I had killed him before he hurt you. I'm so sorry, Zlata. And I let people blame my brother instead of taking responsibility. Like a coward."

They spent the next few minutes arguing about whose fault it was, neither of them wanting the other to feel guilty. Branko insisted he should have dealt with it differently, and Zora said she shouldn't have been flirting in the first place. They finished their disagreement with a tender kiss, then seemed to remember my presence.

Zora trained her moist eyes on mine. "I'm going to miss you, Sunce. Keep in touch with your grandma and Kata. They'll be our link to each other. And Draga and Matija will be here. But never, ever, let on that we're alive. Not to anyone. After this moment, not a mention of us except in remembrance."

I nodded, the lump in my throat swelling. Unclenching my fist, I pressed the golden locket into Zora's hand. Open-mouthed, she examined it.

"A gift from Matija. He found it that night," I explained.

Branko took the locket from her hand and gazed upon the faces of the two young lovers. "Do you remember when I gave this to you?"

"Yes, of course, I remember." A tear fell from Zora's eye, landing in Branko's hand as he held the golden heart. "You said I was the most precious gold you'd ever laid eyes on, and this locket was a poor imitation, but it was a promise that one day we'd be married."

"My Zlata." Branko caressed her cheek.

Zlata. Croatian for golden.

A second chance for the two of them. Thanks to Matija, the man whose brother they had killed.

A hope arose in me, though I knew it was foolish. I struggled to find my voice. "Matija said his dad didn't have anything to do with Mama and Tata's deaths. Does that mean it was just an accident? Or… are they… are they still alive?"

If they were able to fake Zora and Branko's deaths to protect them from Matija's father, maybe they did the same with my parents. I'd had an intuition that something was off about the accident from the start. Was it possible they weren't dead?

Zora asked Branko, "What do you think? Should we…?"

He brought her hand to his lips. "Whatever you think is best."

"That care basket you got with your favorite things?" Zora slipped her hand away from Branko and took mine in hers. "I didn't send it. Neither did Jim. Who else knows you that well?"

"My mother." Of course. A rush of ice water flushed through my body as it tried to catch up with my mind.

"We couldn't tell you. I'm sorry we put you through that," Branko said. "It had to look real to be believable."

"So they're okay?" My heart leapt out of my chest. Provided I didn't have a heart attack on the spot, everyone would live happily ever after. "Where are they? When can I see them?" I jumped off the log, spinning in all directions, as though they might pop out of the woods. "Can you take me to them?"

Branko's firm hands eased me back onto the log. "No. Your father asked for my help in faking their deaths and keeping you safe. When he discovered Matija's father knew they were alive and was using you as a pawn to force them to turn themselves in, Luka decided the only way he and Mimica could stay alive was to die. But Luka forgot to take out the birth certificates in the safe. When I went to retrieve them, you'd already taken the key. I assumed you'd be curious about your parents' identities, so I made the phone call to warn you to go home."

"That was you?" I interjected, remembering Dad's ghost running down the street, and later, the strange call from Croatia.

"Yes. And the other times you almost caught me watching you. Your mother wanted to take you with them, but Luka insisted he didn't want you and your family living your life on the run. So he asked Draga and me to look out for you until the danger was over. That's why we were following you, protecting you, keeping an eye out for the men Matija's dad sent to force Luka, Mimi, and Zlata to turn themselves in. Later, when Draga discovered Matija was secretly defying his father and watching over you, too, we decided to work together. If all the people connected to Vuk's murder were dead, Matija thought he could force an end to his dad's vendetta, and you'd be safe. Now you can go on to live your life, the life your parents wanted, free from criminal activity and threats. Your parents died in the accident. They're lying in a grave. Never give anyone cause to doubt that, or you'll undo everything we've done to protect you and ourselves."

"But..."

"No. No buts." The tone of his voice reminded me of Dad. No room for argument. Discussion over. "Think of your parents, of us, of your children. Matija's father has lifted the death threat against our family. Don't give him a reason to start a war against Molono and to go after your own family."

If Matija hadn't made himself clear enough, Uncle Branko certainly did. The bulge of a pistol, the butt protruding from his front pocket, brought home the extent of the threat posed by Matija's father and the consequences of raising the dead.

Another gun intruded on my thoughts—the Glock I'd pointed 11 years ago—weighing heavy on my conscience.

Zora held my head against her shoulder and said I'd be receiving postcards or deliveries of little gifts now and then. "We'll let you know we're still out there somewhere. Just like your parents will." As in the gift basket.

"Okay," I whispered, defeated. They gave me no choice. My body heaved, overwhelmed with happiness at knowing my parents were still out there somewhere, and with grief knowing I'd never see them again. I resigned myself to the fact there was nothing more I could say or do. Not if I wanted everyone to stay alive.

"I want a few minutes alone with Svjetlana." Zora's cheek pressed against mine, our teardrops blending into larger ones. I'd been reunited with her just to lose her again.

Arm in arm, we walked deeper into the forest, supporting each other as we forged a path through, golden rays breaking through misty wisps weaving amongst the trees. We reached a small clearing, and our tears glistened in the sun's warmth.

"There's one more thing, and I hope you will forgive me." Zora stood at arm's length and held my eyes.

"Of course, I'll forgive you."

What else could there possibly be? These people faked my parents' deaths, then orchestrated their own. My parents had lied about their true identities. My dad was a mobster. Zora killed a man. The four of them covered up the murder and got away with it. Nothing else she could say would shock me. Nothing. I'd heard it all.

"I got pregnant. I couldn't deal with it. I wasn't sure if... I was fifteen and scared. I didn't know if the baby was Branko's or if it was... his, the man who raped me. I couldn't raise a baby on my own. I couldn't raise a baby that would remind me of what happened every time I looked at it. I wanted to get rid of the baby, get it out of my body."

"I understand. I do." Zora wasn't entirely aware of the situation I got myself into at the age of 18. Pregnant by a Mafia leader's son, I kept my baby. But I certainly wasn't going to judge Zora for making a different choice. "So you...you...had an abortion?"

"No."

"You gave your baby away?"

"Yes. It was for the best."

Zora had a child. Given up for adoption.

"Do you know who adopted it?"

"Yes. But no one else knows about the baby. No one. Not a soul. Not my mother. Not Branko. Only the adoptive parents knew I was the mother.

Only two people know."

I couldn't understand why she was telling *me* if it was such a secret. "Did you stay in contact with your baby? Do you want me to tell him or her that you're still alive?"

"I want you to know how much I love you. How much I've always loved you. Always. And I want you to forgive me. For what I…." She couldn't continue, trying to catch her breath between sobs.

"I love you, too. Forgive you for what?"

"For wanting to get rid of you." Zora broke down, her body crumpling in two as she fell to the forest floor, hands covering her face. "Oh, Svjetlana… please forgive me."

"For wanting… I don't understand. Wanting to get rid of me?" I sat on the ground next to Zora, my arm around her shoulder, both in an attempt to console her and to get her to talk. "It's okay, I'm sure you did whatever you had to do, but I need to know…"

Through tears, she explained my mom had lost her baby shortly after the night they were attacked by Vuk. "It might have been the stress or the physical trauma. My baby was born prematurely, about the time your mother would have given birth. Mimi was told she wouldn't be able to have more children. When I told her I was pregnant, she begged me to go through with the pregnancy and hand you over to her. Your parents raised you. But I gave birth to you."

Chapter Fifty-Six

Later that day, as we took a walk through open fields, far from listening ears, Kata and Grandma confirmed they knew Zora and Mom were alive. The rest of the time, they mourned appropriately to keep up appearances. Masters of deception, my two grandmothers. Not to mention the acting skills of my grandfather, who, along with Branko and Draga, had masterminded the whole scheme to keep his sons and granddaughter safe.

I said goodbye to Tina and Darijo, agreeing to stay in touch, though I knew I wouldn't. Kata drove to the airport where she, Grandma, and I cried as we hugged one final time before I passed through security.

It never occurred to me to worry about boarding the plane alone. I didn't think about my claustrophobia or the height at which I'd soon be traveling. The only thing occupying my mind was overwhelming sadness at leaving my parents' homeland behind, and with it, my newfound family. The only thing pushing me forward was the thought of my own little family, waiting for me to come to terms with my parents' deaths. Jim, the kids, our home in Lake Kipling—soon I'd be back where I belonged.

I made the transfer at Munich without a hitch and prepared myself for the long haul home. There was plenty of time for me to think things through as I sat in my window seat, looking down on the clouds. After my biological mother told me the truth about my birth, I gave her my forgiveness and told her I understood and that I loved her, I always had and always would. Everything clicked into place. Zora explained that she lived with my parents until I was six, as my nanny, then moved to her own place when I started school full-time. She had been there when I was a baby, helping Mom and Dad take care of me. After that, she remained a part of our lives, always there, always looking out for me.

Zora gave me some advice before we hugged and kissed for the last time. "Be happy. Stay safe. Live your life the way you want to live. Always remember your parents and how much they love you, and how much I love you. But move forward, not backwards. It's time to close Pandora's box. Lock it, throw the key to the bottom of the deep blue ocean. Forget what was inside."

That was easier said than done. I'd set the past loose, and there was no way to stuff it back in the box. I wasn't sure I would if I could. A silver lining covered that box — my parents were alive, together, in love with each other. I was still in one piece, although I knew I'd be in pieces for a while.

I had embarked on a search for the truth about my parents, and in the process, found my biological mother. Zora was finally going to be reunited with the love of her life, and they were going to start their new life together. It seemed so unfair that I had to lose her in order to learn the truth about myself.

The identity of my biological father was a piece of the puzzle I would never have. Janez Babic turned out to be Luka Nikolov, two halves of my dad, the man who raised me. My biological father was either Branko, Dad's brother, or...

The alternative was too much to handle. Was Matija my *uncle*? The guy I'd been attracted to? Did he sense a connection between us? Did he see a resemblance? Is that what compelled him to protect me, but maintain a platonic relationship? And did that mean my father was a Serbian mobster, a monster who forced himself on my mother, a man who she killed because of it? The similarity to my own life—Brent's biological father, how he died—stunned me. Deja vu. Bad karma? Fate? Was I destined to repeat my mother's choices? Did my genetic makeup determine who I was?

I closed my eyes and recalled the last time I saw Darko, the man whose blood runs through my son's veins.

Darko had followed me when I ran out of his house after telling him I was pregnant. He stormed into the bar and found me in Jesse's arms, crying into his shoulder. Darko grabbed me by the waist and pulled me away. "We need to talk. Outside." I allowed him to lead me to the back exit, leaving Jesse behind.

Stefan barged through the door and yanked Darko from my side, back handing him across the face. "How dare you come running after her. Everything I do, I do for you. And this is how you repay me? By bringing this shame into our family. This girl is filth! The child's bloodline is tainted. Get rid of it."

Darko touched his hand to his cheek. "Never mind the girl. She means nothing to me. I'll deal with her."

But, when Darko whispered in my ear and told me to meet him behind the bar that night, I agreed, hopeful that he had changed his mind and wanted us to be a family.

In the back alley that evening, Darko took me in his arms and said, "We need to hurry before my dad figures out what I'm doing."

"What are you doing?"

"We're going to run away together. Once the baby is born, we'll come back. I know my dad and how much family means to him. He won't be able to say no to the baby once he sees him."

"Or her?"

"Sure."

"What about your dad's job? I know he's into some bad stuff, Darko. I don't want our child exposed to that."

"You don't need to worry about the business. Just let us do our job and stay out of it. We'll keep you and the baby safe.

"I can't live like that. Leave your dad, and let's start a new life, just the three of us."

"No, I'm all he's got. My mom left because she couldn't deal with it. I won't leave him. He needs me."

"I don't know. I just don't know. He scares me."

"Trust me, he'll come around. In the meantime, we need to leave now." He led me to his car and opened the door. As he did so, his backpack came open just enough for me to glimpse the contents.

"Is that...?" Nestled in the backpack was a Glock 17. I recognized it as the same type I had stolen from his dad's study as they argued about me and the baby earlier that day. "What's that for?"

"Protection."

"From whom?"

He looked me in the eyes and at that moment I knew. I would never really be safe. Even if I dared to trust Darko, I couldn't trust his father. And I would never be safe with the lifestyle they led. Nor would my child.

I reached into my purse and took out his dad's gun, pointing it at Darko.

"What are you doing? Where'd you get the gun?" His eyes widened.

"It's for protection."

"From who?"

As we locked eyes, Darko put his hands on the barrel, and tried to wrest it from my hands . "Careful with that. You might shoot me by accident."

"No, no I won't shoot you by accident," I promised as my finger pulled the trigger.

The plane shook me out of my thoughts, rocking back and forth.

Turbulence. It's normal.

Draga had explained that on the flight over. I should relax and rest my eyes. I thought of her and Matija together. Another couple in love, torn apart by their families and by life's circumstances. Their union signaled the end of a thirty-year vendetta, the end of the curse. They were brave enough to stand up to their fathers and stay. No running for them.

Some good did come from digging into the past. Three couples in love were together. I met an extended family of which I previously had no knowledge. I'd also made new friends and had the adventure of my lifetime.

It certainly wasn't all bad. I'd found my biological mother, and father, narrowed down to two possibilities. But Marica and Janez Babic were my real parents, and I'd forever think of them that way.

I wondered whether Matija's father had any idea that I could possibly be his granddaughter. The little 'accidents' I'd been having were ordered by him. My parents had gone on the run because of him, and so had Zora and Branko. I wondered whether the vendetta was worth it. Did it give him some sense of closure, thinking they were dead?

Darkness blanketed the Atlantic Ocean. I recalled thinking on the flight over that if my body ended up at the bottom of the deep blue ocean, I'd never be reunited with Jim or the kids. They would have no body to bury, no gravesite to visit, and no cemetery to house the remnants of my physical being. It would be like that for me now. When my parents died, I would have no idea where their bodies were buried, nothing physical to mourn.

I had been warned not to tell a single soul the truth, but Jim and I shared one soul. As soon as we were alone, no chance of anyone overhearing, I would tell him everything.

Lost in my thoughts, I almost drifted off to sleep, but as the plane jolted again, my eyes flew open, bringing to view the interior of the metal box that entrapped me. A familiar wave of panic swept through me, chilling my bones. Needing to focus on something else, I took my unfinished novel from my backpack and opened it to the bookmark. As well as the bookmark, I found a birthday card with a photo of a white dove in flight, the sun coming through clouds in the background.

Zora had signed it and included a short note. She wished me a happy 30th birthday and a wonderful future with brighter days, and ended with 'All My Love, Zora'.

Zora, my mother. Tucked inside was a photo of a very young Zora in a hospital gown, cradling a tiny newborn in pink, a look of pure joy on her face.

Mama?

The tears poured from my eyes, dripping off my chin. I cried myself to sleep, mourning the loss of my third parent—the mother who birthed me and cared for me as a child, concealing her true identity.

The plane's motion woke me, tossing every which way. Turbulence again. Only this time, it shook the plane like a salt shaker. I remembered the flight over and how frightened I'd been.

Turbulence is normal. Everything is fine.

A flash of light illuminated the blackness outside my window. My eyes flew back and forth between seats. None of the passengers seemed overly concerned.

I gazed out the glass again, taking deep, slow breaths and releasing them as rain pelted the pane. Some passengers had their overhead reading lights on, others were trying to sleep. The 'Please fasten your seatbelt' sign flashed red. Our flight wasn't scheduled to land for at least three hours.

As the plane bounced up and down, I held onto the armrests, head bent and eyes closed. My eyes sprang open to find the source of loud banging noises. An overhead compartment swung open; a stewardess' cart crashed against armrests; seats clanged and rattled. People's voices carried down and across the aisles, distress now evident in their tone.

I shouted to the people seated in the middle row next to me. "What's going on?" They shrugged and shook their heads, worry lines etched into their faces. As the plane tilted drastically to the right, an announcement came over the sound system.

"Ladies and gentlemen, due to severe weather conditions, our flight is being diverted to St. John's International Airport in Newfoundland, where we will be making an emergency landing. We expect to begin our descent in about ten minutes."

Trying to reassure myself it would be okay, I closed my eyes again and started to count to 40, then extended that to 100. If I concentrated on counting, and if I counted to 100 enough times, we'd soon be on the ground.

Halfway through my second round of counting, the captain made another announcement. "We are experiencing some mechanical issues, but expect a safe landing."

I'm going to die.

Was it possible Matija's father arranged this mechanical issue?

Or was there something supernatural happening here?

The curse is real.

Was it real? And what if the curse wasn't over? What if it was passed onto the offspring of the people responsible for Vuk's murder? I started counting again. As long as I could recite numbers, I was still alive.

Another announcement came on. "Please brace for landing." The captain sounded calm, but fear and tension oozed from the passengers surrounding me. Stewards instructed us to place our heads on our laps and cover them.

CHAPTER FIFTY-SIX

A minute later, the plane nosed down to meet the tarmac.

Curses aren't confined to the old country. I've brought mine home with me.

Chapter Fifty-Seven

"Ladies and gentlemen, welcome to Newfoundland, Canada. We have safely landed at St. John's International. After a brief layover, weather permitting, all passengers will be transferred to a Toronto flight."

What? That's it? I'm alive? No crash?

The plane had landed without incident, in spite of the storm, the hail, whatever mechanical issue they were having, *and* in spite of the curse.

Outside my window, red lights flashed. Fire trucks and emergency vehicles stood by.

This is not a drill. It's real. I just got lucky.

I wobbled down the jetway to a boarding area and collapsed onto a chair. If I ever made it home, I would never get on a plane again. My flying days were over. I was self-grounding for life.

Except for one more flight. Several hours later, I settled into the seat of a smaller plane. Stress and exhaustion got the better of me, and I slipped into slumber. The next thing I knew, we had landed. Following the crowd off the plane, I continued through to the arrivals gate, and spotted him immediately. My mouth fell open, and I stared. It had been so long since I'd last seen him. He took my breath away.

Standing off to the side, watching the doorway, his eyes met mine, and he strode toward me, his mouth slightly upturned. A wavy black lock fell across his forehead, bringing attention to dreamy brown eyes and an angular jaw with a couple day's worth of scruff.

"Hi," he said. "I missed you."

"Hello. I missed you more. I'll show you how much once we're alone." No point in being coy, wasting time. I smiled up at him, my love for him displacing sorrow for what I'd lost.

Pulling me into an embrace, he kissed me tenderly like it was our first time. Then, pulling along my luggage with one hand and clasping my hand in his other, we continued toward the exit doors. The firmness with which he grasped my hand made me feel safe, and the way he ran his thumb along my palm sent tingles throughout my body, just as it had done when we were in Grade 10.

Jesse James Jovanovich. The boy I fell in love with the first time I laid eyes on him, squeezed my hand, and said, "Well then. Let's go home."

He held open the passenger door of the Toyota, and I slid in, the familiar feel of my own vehicle welcoming. As he headed north on the 427, I sat up straighter and said, "Turn around. You're going the wrong way. Hamilton's to the south."

Eyes fixed on the road, he said, "We can't go back to Hamilton, Cheryl. I've entrusted our lives to Haley and Garrett. They're going to finish packing up your parents' belongings and prepare the house for sale, take care of the business."

"What? No! Why? I need a few more days to go through their stuff. I want to keep some of it, take it home with us. The kids will be fine for a couple more days. Turn the car aroun...."

"Stefan's watching the house." Jim's eyes held the road; I couldn't read them.

"He's what?"

"Haley noticed a vehicle hanging around when she stopped in to check things. Garrett sent me a photo of the guy. It's him. He's looking for you."

I should have known he'd hunt me down. After spending ten years wrongfully imprisoned for the manslaughter of his son, he wouldn't let me go scot-free. Not for what I had done. Retribution has a long shelf life.

* * *

Two weeks later, in my office at the *Lake Kipling Gazette*, fingers on my keyboard, I added the finishing touches to my article about mysterious rock formations in the area. Geologists studying boulders along the shores of Lake Kipling were stumped by their composition and placement. An archeological study found they may have been used by indigenous people to communicate with the spiritual world, perhaps as a means of trapping spirits to be used against enemies.

History was fascinating. The past held many mysteries. Whether science would ever unravel all the secrets of ancient civilizations, I had no idea.

During my personal quest, I uncovered my family's past and explored the history of their homeland. In the process, I found myself. Enlightenment. Like the Age of Enlightenment, which replaced superstition with reason and religion with science, my journey made me question what I once knew.

I clicked 'send', emailing the article to my boss before grabbing my purse, waving to my colleagues, and crossing the hall to the large panes of glass that fronted the entrance of the building housing the Gazette offices. On the lawn, brown and yellow leaves swirling in circles, the wind mercilessly whipped the branches of maple trees set against a gray sky.

I turned in the opposite direction to go back to the office for my jacket.

It came without warning.

The crash shattered both the glass and my eardrums. I must have jumped two feet off the ground. When I turned to face the front doors, a black pickup truck with some serious damage to its front end, sat in the foyer, so close I could touch it. Glass lay strewn over the floor, the doors knocked off their hinges.

As a couple of my colleagues steered me to a chair, telling me how lucky I was to be alive, offering tea, and patting my back, others took photos and jotted notes in their spiral books.

The news must go on.

Through the ringing in my ears, a voice penetrated my stupor. "There's no one in the driver's seat. The truck's empty!"

Jim beat the police and ambulance to the scene. He rushed to my side, worry lines etched in his forehead. "Are you okay? You could have been...."

I melted into his arms and held onto Jim as if my life depended on him. "You're here," I said. "I'm so glad you're here," whimpered the little girl in me, lost without him.

"Of course, I'm here. Always. I'm always here for you." He smoothed back my hair, took my face in both hands, and kissed my forehead. "Everything is going to be all right. It was just an accident, that's all. They're looking for the driver now. He must have wandered off." Jim tried to reassure me, but we were both thinking the same thing.

Stefan?

The curse is real. Get out while you can.

Reason or superstition? Science or faith? We all make choices we have to live with. I'd been lost for too long, a victim of my own bad choices, a victim of the past, letting it control my life. Now, I was choosing to move forward, no doubt about it. I had something worth living for—Jim and the kids. But I was going there with both eyes wide open, and one eye fixed behind me.

Because…

What was it Matija said?

You can run, and you can hide. But in the end, the past catches up with you, baby girl.

Acknowledgements

It takes more than one person to create a book. Behind every writer is a whole support network. My thanks to everyone who played a role in getting my debut novel out into the world.

First and foremost, I'd like to acknowledge my husband, Brian, for believing in me. He's the reason this book exists. After retiring from teaching, I wrote a few poems, which I never imagined would amount to anything more than a rekindled hobby. At his insistence that they were good enough, I submitted my work to literary magazines, and published many of my poems and short stories. My success led me to something I had always dreamed of doing – writing a novel. Over the last five years, Brian has read everything I've written, offering his opinion, and making me a stronger writer. He is my alpha reader and biggest supporter. Without him, there would be no book.

Also, I'd like to acknowledge my Mom, who is with me in spirit, for inspiring me to write again, decades after I set aside my writer's pen. The stories she told about her youth in Slovenia and emigrating to Canada are an important part of my memories of Mom and have influenced my writing. The Dead Lie is set in a fictional locale in Croatia, on the other side of the Kupa, the river bordering the village where she was born and raised.

To my family, thank you for putting up with listening to me talk about my writing non-stop. Besides backing me with your support and encouragement, each of you in your own way has provided me with what I needed to keep going: the tools and technology to write, legal advice, reading and critiquing my work, and providing me with fodder for my fiction. Mostly, your words telling me how proud you are and reminding me not to give up, along with your very presence in my life, have made my dreams come true. Nothing is more important than family. Thank you to my son and daughter, Bryant and Brittany, my son-in-law, Eric, and my newest love, baby Rowan, for being there for me. To my brother, Joseph, and sister-in-law, Audrey, thank you for your support of my writing endeavors and following me on my writing path. To my nephews, Evan and Reid, my step-nephew and step-niece, Max and Maia, thanks for being part of my life's journey. Thanks as well to my BFF from childhood, Loretta Dunn, for your support and interest in my writing goals. And my appreciation to my feline emotional support team, T.C. and Scruffy (and Lucky for the short time we were blessed to have him), for being by my side as I write. I love you all.

My love of reading and writing began when I was a child. Although I don't recall the exact moment I first knew I wanted to be a writer, there were teachers and books along the way that set me on that path. In particular, I'd like to acknowledge my Grade 9 English teacher, Ian Atkinson, for finding some merit in my words and encouraging me to pursue a writing career. Although it took me a while to follow that path, here I am. Better late than never.

To all those editors and publishers who deemed my poetry and short stories good enough to publish in their literary magazine, thank you for giving me the confidence to keep writing. A special thanks to Ian Allaby, of Spadina Literary Review, for accepting and publishing my first piece, a poem entitled *Worry*.

Thank you to my beta readers who offered their thoughts about my book. A special shoutout to my fellow authors, critique partners and friends, Emily Hann and Norah Blakedon, for their help in making this book better.

To my agent, Cindy Bullard of Birch Literary, my eternal gratitude for taking a chance on me. Your expertise in preparing my work for submission, and your hard work in finding the right publisher for my books, has made my dream of becoming a published author come true. Thanks for all your support and guidance, your kind words and friendship. I appreciate everything you do. You are amazing!

To my editor at Level Best Books, Shawn Reilly Simmons, I am grateful to you for having a vision for my Blue Water series. Thank you for helping me to perfect *The Dead Lie* and for creating a cover I love. As well, my thanks goes out to Verena Rose, Harriette Sackler, and the entire team at Level Best Books, for publishing my debut novel.

Finally, to my extended family and my friends and neighbors who have shown their support, whether in person or online, thank you for your kind words. To you, my reader, thank you for choosing to read this book. Without readers, there would be no need for writers. I hope you enjoy it!

About the Author

Ivanka Fear is Canadian writer, born in Slovenia. She earned her B.A. and B.Ed. in English and French at Western University. Prior to pursuing writing full time, she enjoyed a long career in education. Her debut novel, The Dead Lie, is the first in her Blue Water Mysteries series. Ivanka is a member of International Thriller Writers and Sisters in Crime. She resides in Ontario, Canada, with her family and the stray cats that wandered in. When not reading and writing, Ivanka enjoys watching mystery series and romance movies, gardening, going for walks, and watching the waves roll in at the lake.

SOCIAL MEDIA HANDLES:
  Facebook: https://www.facebook.com/ivankafearauthor
  Instagram: https://www.instagram.com/ivankawrites/
  Twitter: https://twitter.com/FearIvanka

AUTHOR WEBSITE:
  https://www.ivankafear.com/

Also by Ivanka Fear

Numerous short stories and poems published in dozens of journals in the U.S., Canada, and the U.K.

www.ingramcontent.com/pod-product-compliance
Lightning Source LLC
Chambersburg PA
CBHW050152120726
47903CB00002B/589